The FORBIDDEN BETA

JP SINA

The Forbidden Beta

Author: Jp Sina

To the women who wanted to get railed by an Alpha.

TRIGGER WARNINGS

The Forbidden Beta is book three in The Forbidden Series. This is a DARK Paranormal Romance featuring mature themes and content that may not be suitable for all audiences. Some readers may find content triggering or uncomfortable. It contains sex, violence, sexual assault, physical assault, physical abuse, and emotional abuse. Reader discretion is advised. This book is for 18+ readers only.

CONTENTS

A HAPPY MAN

Ethan

Goddess, I fucking love this woman, and she holds more than just my world in her hands.

These are the words that run through my head as she's on her knees in front of me with her hand wrapped around the base of my cock. My Queen leans forward, her eyes on me, as her tongue darts out and licks up the precum at my slit.

I fight the need to throw my head back and moan. She's got me in a trance, and as she licks up the underside of my cock, I can't take my eyes off of her. I reach down and gather her hair into my hand as she wraps her red lips around my hard cock. I want her hard and fast. I want to fuck her throat like we don't have the rest of our lives together.

I want to dirty her pretty little dress.

Her hand around my cock starts twisting as it slides up and down my length. The sight of her cheeks hollowing as she sucks has my toes curling. She takes her time tasting, licking, jerking, and sucking me. My breathing hollows and my thighs tighten as her hand disappears and she takes me deeper.

My chest rises and falls as I hit the back of her throat. She moans and swallows, as it turns her on as much as it does me. Her eyes never leave me, as she reaches below and fingers my balls. Fuck, she's devious. A smirk pulls at the corner of her lips as she takes all of me. She gags, but doesn't stop.

She's going to be the fucking end of me.

I'd die a happy man.

She slides up and sucks on just the tip. Her tongue flicks up my slit and my balls tighten. She bobs her head down, and her lips wrap around my length tighter than before. My fist in her hair tightens, and I thrust hard into her mouth. I pull out and thrust deeper than before, and I drive my hips forward to fuck her mouth. I moan when she opens her throat up to me for the taking.

"Fuck, Adea," I say through gritted teeth, as I fuck her throat hard and deep. My balls tighten and I pull out of her mouth. She stares up at me with wet lips, fuck me eyes, and glistening cheeks. I reach down and pull her into my arms.

***

Adea

My lips tingle and my throat throbs as I wrap my legs around Ethan. The dress bunches up around my waist as he carries me. Ethan held me in his arms like he was scared to lose me and his kiss smashed against my lips, claiming me as his. His need fuels the fire in my veins and I open my mouth to his assault.

My arms around him feel the muscles in his back as he puts me down on the hard surface of the table. He's all man, all alpha, and all mine. He reaches for the material between us, but I dig my heels into his backside.

"I'm not wearing anything," I whisper.

He groans.

"This whole time?" He asks, his voice husky.

"This whole time," I say with a smile.

"Fuck. I'm glad you didn't tell me earlier. I would have taken you during the ceremony," he says.

I laugh.

"No, you wouldn't have," I said.

His fingers force their way between us and a cocky smirk spreads across his lips. "You're wet for me," he murmurs. He drives two fingers inside of me and I throw my head back.

"I'm always wet for you," I moan.

His cock rubs against my tight entrance and slowly, so slowly he lowers himself into me. I am stretched and filled. He pulls out and thrusts into me, and my body hums with pleasure as he fills me again. I feel good. He feels good. I peek up to look at him and find his eyes staring at where we meet. I follow his gaze and watch as he pulls out of me and slams back into me.

The table is sturdy, but moves back and forth with each thrust of his hips. He dives down, capturing my mouth as he continues to slam into me. He pulls back and loses himself to the pleasure as he thrusts in and out of me.

I pull my lip between my teeth as my body tightens. My orgasm crests and then explodes. I let my orgasm ride out as his thrusts pick up. He gripped my waist as his orgasm ripped from him. He continues thrusting through it. I am sensitive and moan with each thrust. He fills me up and I sigh, happy and content.I lie back and close my eyes, as my chest rises and falls rapidly. Ethan pulls out of me and wipes the hair from my forehead. He presses a kiss to my cheek before he pulls me upright.

"Did I hurt you?" Ethan asks.

My heart lodges in my throat, and my chest fills with a warm feeling I could only call love, as I stare at my mate. I push him back and get to my feet. I push him back so he sits in the chair, and he leans back as he looks up at me.

I climb on top of him, my legs on both sides of his waist. I lean down and kiss him sweetly. Knowing that I am his today, body and soul forever, is enough to make me cry. His hard length nudges at my entrance; he is already ready for me. I sink down on him and stare into his eyes as I take every inch of him.

His hands find my hips, and he moves me back and forth on his length. He hits deep, and I moan as he continues to guide my hips.

"I love you," I gasp.

"I love you," he says as he leans forward and claims my lips.

I WOULD

Gabe

The palm of my hand supports my chin, as I gaze out at the setting sun. My best friend and her big bad alpha had left five minutes ago. I wiggled my eyebrows and winked at Ady as he announced their departure. She blushed and slapped my shoulder before he dragged her away. I knew they were headed back to their room for a night of fun, and I did a little happy dance inside for her.

I haven't moved from my seat. Alpha is by her side, so we don't have to be, and my first official day as her guard was over. I have the rest of the night to myself and watch Leo as he makes his rounds. I knew Odis sat three seats down, but I avoid looking at him all night. Instead, I focused on my drinks and enjoy throwing them back. I feel his gaze, but ignore it, and let my eyes scan the crowd.

Left.

Right.

Middle.

Left.

Right.

Sigh.

I am bored and I don't want to think about the reason I linger here. I pick up my drink and lift it to my lips. I down the rest of it, and look around for the closest waitress. I make eye contact with one of them, and she heads toward me with a platter in hand. She has short brown hair and nice curves. Her cheeks flush at my gaze, and she returns it with lust in her eyes. I ignore it. I'm not dumb; I know I'm hot and I know the effect I have on women. I grab a couple of drinks from her and dismiss her.

The party is still in full swing, and I watch Darci disappear with one of the guests. I don't know her that well, but I know from Ady she could handle herself. The old Gabe would have asked to join, or have taken the blushed waitress into one of the meeting rooms. A laugh rumbles in my chest and bursts past my lips. I shake my head.

"But I'm not the old Gabe," I say. My voice comes out slurred and I am surprised. Maybe I shouldn't have these drinks. The thought crosses my mind and my shoulders shake with a silent laugh. I am tipsy, a little bit. No, I think, maybe a lot. I am very tipsy, and quite possibly drunk. Okay, I am drunk.. I still have a few sensible thoughts left in my head. I reach up and scratch my head, as Isip from one of the glasses.

"I think that might be enough," a voice says from above me. Oh great, the heavens are speaking to me now. I shake my head. This wasn't a good sign and I will not look up. The Goddess has a sad ending for me, and I don't need any more of her attention. I will not look up. I will not. I will.

I will.

I look up and my breath catches in my throat. Dirty blonde hair hangs an inch from my face, tanned skin glows above me, and eyes that hold a challenge stare down at me. I don't know if I'm happy or upset that it isn't the Goddess.

Odis.

Odis stares down at me. This man has my breath picking up, my heart tripping over itself, and tingles shooting up the back of my neck. I should look down, or away, or something. I stare at him for a second longer, my chin lifted, my eyes turned up to him. He's bent at the waist as he looks down at me. I look down and remember what he said. A smile spreads across my lips, as I tip the drink to my lips and take another sip.

Challenge accepted.

One gulp.

Two gulps.

I pull the drink down and giggle. This is the lightest I've felt in a while, and I feel the darkness getting farther and farther with each chug. Suddenly, I feel his shoulders press down on mine and his hand wrap around mine.

Thump.

Th-thump.

Th-th-thump.

Th-thump.

"Shh," I whisper angrily.

Stupid heart.

"He might hear you," I explain.

Odis pulls the drink from my hand and I scrunch up my lip. I glare, but focus on the last drink in my hand. He moves towards it and I tighten my hand around it. "Nope," I say. His hand wraps around mine and we play a game of tug-of-war.

"I'm not giving up this one," I tell him. I turn my head to the left, and he's a lot closer now. I can feel his breath on my cheek, and I turn away. "You took the other one. You should be thoughtful, and let me have this one." It makes perfect sense. Old me would have been drinking the stronger stuff. Old me would be sleeping my way through the waitresses. This me is doing a really good job.

He chuckles and releases my hand before he straightens his back and stands. I lift the drink to my lips and drink happily knowing I've won. One second I'm drinking happily, and the next I'm pulled to my feet. The drink sloshes and some spills on me.

"Hey!" I exclaim as I look down at my suit from Ady. I lift my chin to ask him what he wants, but I'm silenced. Silenced by the look in his eyes. There's a warning there, but tipsy me doesn't care about his warning. Tipsy me takes a step closer and I lift my head a little to hold his gaze. I lift my free hand and press my finger into his chest.

"What do you want, Beta," I slur.

He stares at me for a second before grabbing my hand. He doesn't say a word, as he turns and pulls me along behind him. The world is spinning and I stumble to keep up with him.

Stay upright.

The road is rushing below my feet, and I struggle to keep up.

Stay upright.

EVERYTHING

Adea

After the shower, I run and face-plant into bed. Ethan dries himself off and gets into bed beside me. The warmth of his body radiates beside me. I lie by his side comfortably, temporarily satisfied when I open my eyes.

Looking at the table, my eyes take in the new snacks, crackers, cheese, sausage, and fruits. My mouth waters, but the table is far away. Someone had brought us snacks and he'd come out to let them in. When we aren't making love or fucking, we scarf down food for energy.

I reach over and run my fingers along his chest. At my touch, goosebumps break out along his skin, and his body tenses. I turn to look at him. His eyes are closed and my fingers dip lower. He moans and I am entranced by his reaction as his fingers dig into my skin.

The beast awakens. His strong hands grab me and pull me up. "Adea…" he murmurs. I sigh and am instantly wet when I see the look in his eyes. I'll never tire of this, of him, of us.

I look down at him and am not surprised by his hardened cock. I watch as he directs me onto his length. My pussy wraps around him, tightening as he slides into me. My mate moans as he enters me, enjoying my slick tightness. I sit in his lap and wrap my arms around his neck.

"Fuck me hard," My King demands.

He leans back against the headboard and guides me up and down his hard length with his hands. My head drops back and I rock my hips, as I take him over and over again. I can feel the promise of an orgasm already building as I ride his cock. My body is slick with sweat, and breathy moans escape my lips as he thrusts his hips into me as I ground on him.

His thrusts quicken and I bounce up and down. His lips wrap around the curve of my breast and he sucks my nipple. I feel the pleasurable shock down in my core and buck against him.

"I love seeing you like this," Ethan murmurs, as he switches to the other. He thrusts up into me and my mouth goes slack, as I feel every inch slam into me before pulling out to the tip. He looks into my eyes, as he slams into me and pulls me down on him. My moans fill the room, bounce off the wall, and threaten to carry down the hall.

"You're perfect and all mine." We move together as we get closer to euphoria. I pull up and slam down hard, taking his entire length before pulling up and repeating the movement.

"Ethan," I moan.

Without warning, my orgasm explodes and rips through me. I am wet and slick around his hard cock. My nails dig into his back, as I ride the waves of pleasure that spread throughout my body and have my toes curling.

"You're a fucking Goddess, Adea," he breathes.

Ethan

I roll her onto her back, as she spasms and squeezes around me, her legs still around my waist, and I climb on top of her. I pound into her, taking her, claiming her. I'll never get enough of her, never tire of her. She is a drug, and I am addicted to the taste of her.

My hips work, as I pull out of her and thrust in her. Adrenaline and need drive me in and out of her. I lean down and rest my arms beside her head. I fuck her hard; I'll make her cum again. I need it. Her heels squeeze my ass as I pound her. She is tight and small beneath me.

"Yes, Ethan," Adea moans.

The room fills with her moans, my grunts, and the sounds of our bodies slapping against each other. My cock twitches and she comes around me again. She squeezes me tightly, and I feel my balls tighten, as she pulls me over the edge with her. I come with a groan, filling her as she squirms.

We ride the pure high that washes over us. I feel the sweat trickle down my back and stare at her beautiful hair slick against her skin. We are both satisfied—for now. I pull out and fall beside her, not wanting to crush her. She turns into me and throws her leg over my hip. We are side by side staring at each other. She is insatiable, but I love trying.

Her eyes close, her breathing slows, and I know she's fallen asleep. I watch her as she dozes peacefully. When she first slept in my bed, I remember she woke from night terrors. The shadow of that prick haunted her. I assumed it was him that kept haunting her, but when she'd told me about her nightmare, or vision, I wasn't sure what to think.

Nothing matters more to me than her safety, and her well-being. I haven't taken the time to think about what her vision foretells about me; about my death. It doesn't bother me. What bothers me is knowing I die leaving her vulnerable. What rips me up inside is knowing he most likely captures her after my death.

I don't know if I believe in visions, but I'll take it as a warning. I will protect her. Frustration seeps into my bones, as I think about my failed efforts at catching him. He is irritating and moves like a fucking weasel. He is hard to find, and by the time we get a clue about his whereabouts, he disappears.

My mate makes a sound, and I am pulled from my thoughts. I watch her, her beautiful eyes hidden behind her eyelids, her nose twitches, and I run my fingers up and down her back to soothe her. Her eyebrows relax and her body loosens. My heart warms. She is everything.

THREE

Gabe

My eyes focus on Odis's hand on my arm, and I manage to stay vertical. I've lost my drink somewhere along the way, and drunk me is not happy. This means I lost. This means war. As soon as the world stops spinning, I'll set things into motion.

"Where are we going?"

Odis ignores me and continues pulling me along. He isn't looking at me, and I take this time to admire his physical attributes. His blonde hair is slicked back, and his suit does a terrible job at hiding his muscles. With each step, each swing of his shoulders, I get a glimpse of his muscles working together.

I sigh.

"You're shit-faced," Odis says.

True.

I shrug. "I will neither confirm nor de-"

His chuckle has me forgetting what I am going to say.

At a glance, Odis is eye candy, but up close…up close, Odis is a God. His muscles flex, and the material of his suit jacket gives way. It draws my attention longer than I like. A list of what I'd like starts to fill my mind and my face gets warmer.

"Bad, Gabe," I hiss.

He stops and I almost run into him. He turns his body, and looks at me. He pulls me in, and I stand an inch away from him. I can feel and smell him; he smells of firewood and roasted marshmallows. Odis stares at me with an intensity I'm sure makes women melt into a puddle. He has to have a trail of broken hearts behind him, and I wouldn't be surprised if he'd claimed as many as he'd broken.

Am I jealous?

No.

There is only one woman I've ever been jealous of him having.

I nearly stopped breathing when his eyes locked on mine.

"Let's not bother arguing about whether you're drunk or not. We both already know the answer," he says. He is so close I can feel his warm breath on my cheek.

"So… are you going to tell me where we're going?" I ask. I stand my ground when he doesn't step back. I probably shouldn't. The last thing I need to do is flirt with my mate's ex. I don't flinch at the pain that stabs my chest mercilessly. I welcome it. It reminds me she was real, and it reminds me that I need to play it cool.

I feel him before I see him. A big muscular body presses up behind me, and drunk me is purring before my mind can catch up with me. Bad. Bad me. Go away. I turn to see Leo behind me staring at Odis with a smirk on his face. Leo is practically breathing down my neck, and I am trying to remember why I am behaving.

"What's the rush? The party isn't over yet," Leo said.

Odis stares at him.

"I aaaam the party," I say matter-of-factly. Leo gives me a look that says he knows I've had a few drinks.

"I'm sure you are," Leo laughs. "My shift is officially over. Let's have a few drinks to celebrate a successful first day."

"No thanks," Odis says.

"I wasn't asking you," Leo counters.

Oh-kay.

"I didn't know we were that close," I say. Leo opens his mouth to say something, but closes it. Odis smirks at him, and I am in the middle, trying to translate what their expressions mean.

I wonder if I can sneak back to get a drink without Odis noticing.

"We're going to be spending a lot of time together, so, I figured we might as well get to know each other," Leo says.

Hmm.

"I think that would be a good idea for sober Gabe," I start. "Drunk Gabe needs to go to his room. He can't be trusted to make good decisions."

I move out from between the sandwich of Leo and Odis.

"And you," I say to Odis, "how long do you intend to keep me here."

Odis's eyes dart to where his hand is wrapped around my arm. He quickly lets go and I nod for the hell of it.

"Thank you," I say.

Leo purses his lips and sighs. "I'm so disappointed," Leo says as he runs his hands through his hair. My eyes follow the movement before lowering to his lips and traveling down his body.

A sinful idea dances across my mind and nope.

No.

Nope.

Focus.

I solemnly swear not to eye fuck the man who literally tried to kill me just yesterday. I will not make any stupid moves. All I want to do is sit and sip on something. How did I end up here again? Stupid, stupid Gabe. I shake my head.

I lift my finger in front of my chest like I have an idea. "I'll tell sober Gabe you'd like a word," I tell him nodding. I don't miss the wave of disappointment that spreads across his features, but drunk Gabe doesn't care. Drunk Gabe wants to go to the room now. Without a glance back, I take off away from them. I head back to the packhouse, with my room as my goal. The last thing I need is to bump into Sasha. A shiver runs down my back. She'd take the chance to pounce on me, and I didn't want that.

Right?

Right.

I trip along the way, but catch myself before I land face-first on the ground.

"...Had a little lamb, little lamb," I sing. The song cuts off with a hiccup, and before I open my mouth again to sing, I pick up the sounds of gravel crunching. It'sthe sound of footsteps behind me.

Oh no.

I'm going to be hacked to pieces. I'll be headline news.

Gasp.

I need to protect myself. On the count of three.

One.

I'll turn around and fight him.

Two.

Or run.

I haven't decided yet.

Thr-

The person behind me grips my arm and I yelp "I don't want to die!"

OFF-LIMITS

Gabe

A deep chuckle rumbles behind me, and I realize this person is getting a kick out of my fear. I quickly move from scared to angry. It must be nice to laugh at someone's fear of dying. I'll kick this kidnapper's ass, and I steel my resolve before I whirl around. I'm frozen as I come face to face with a charming dimple, nice white teeth, and a clean smooth face.

Odis.

Beta Odis's shoulders are hunched, his head leaning forward, and his eyes squeezed shut. His laughter melts my anger, and I'm not sure I like that. I am stuck between being happy and knowing full well that I wanted to slap him a second ago. I go with the second option and slap him in the chest, but if he notices he doesn't show it.

Bastard.

"I thought I was going to die!" I hiss. I try to sound angry. I am angry. I should sound angry, but my hiss sounds flirtatious. He bursts into laughter, and it is the first time I'd ever seen it. I'm not sure what to do or what to say. Instead, I am stuck staring at him. Beta Odis is beautiful, and, for a second, I can't breathe.

I shake my head until I've successfully rid the spell his laughter casts. "What do you want, Beta?" I ask. I'm still shocked with the Odis in front of me. He isn't glaring at me and there's no look of disgust in his eyes. It probably isn't the right time, but the memory of his firm hand on me when I struggled to get my shit together for Ady resurfaces. The memory of his smile of approval when I'd eaten the food he bought me, the way he always looks so clean, the need to dirty him, the elevator incident where he grabbed Sasha...

"I normally don't interfere with who you sink your teeth into but this one," he said, his eyes sliding up my body, "is off-limits, Sash."

I swallow.

Drunk Gabe loves this memory. Drunk Gabe welcomes the tingles that tickle the back of my neck. Drunk Gabe enjoys the possessiveness he showed that day. Drunk Gabe needs to stop.

"As I said, he's off-limits and he won't be needing your... services ever again."

Odis's words light a fire in my belly, and I can feel my control start to slip.

"I'm sorry," he laughs as he holds his stomach. "I've never heard something so funny!" He swipes at his eyes. "One minute you were singing Mary had a fucking lamb, to stopping completely. Next minute you're screaming you don't wanna die! And you *squealed*!" Odis bursts into laughter again, and I am ready to punch him. Tipsy Gabe is ready to fight him. "You fucking squealed," he gasps.

"I'm glad you find my pain funny, Beta," I say to him.

He freezes. "Don't do that," he says.

I eye him as he stands up and straightens. The laughing Odis is gone, and his usual cool mask is in its place as he stares at me.

Thump.

Th-thump.

"Do what, Beta?" I ask, as I swirl and continue walking. My heart thumps in my chest and I scold it.

Th-thump.

Shh.

Relax.

"You know what," he says from behind me. I don't dare look back at him. I don't wanna know what look he has on his face now. Maybe I do want to know, but I don't trust myself. What If I see something I like?

Why is he following me?

We walk across the driveway and into the lobby, and I ignore the hopeful drunk thoughts that rush to answer that question. The thoughts only make my heart speed up. My shredded heart wishes he'd grab my hand, or tell me he wants more, but my mind tells me that isn't a good idea. My mind only entertains the idea of *if.*

If... he grabs my hand, it will only hurt.

If... he tells me he wants more, my heart will be happy.

If... he follows me into my room, we'll have fun.

If... we cross the line, it will only end in disaster.

If... my heart opens for him, it will only shatter when he finds his mate.

If... that happens, I don't know if I could handle it.

If... we do that, we'll betray Olivia... won't we?

If... we do, will she hate me?

We stand in front of the elevators, and the noise of him pressing the arrow button slaps me to attention. The more these questions swirl in my mind, the more the hold on my control weakens. These thoughts and questions are too much for drunk Gabe. This is dangerous territory. Sober Gabe would agree. Drunk Gabe needs to wait for Sober Gabe. Sober Gabe will make the right decisions. I nod. Yes. Sober Gabe will make the right choice.

But.

But…

But… what if Drunk Gabe doesn't want the right decision?

What if… this is the only time when Drunk Gabe will have the chance to touch him?

What if… Drunk Gabe is selfish?

What if… Drunk Gabe doesn't want to think about anything else right now?

What if… Drunk Gabe doesn't want to worry about what will happen tomorrow?

What if… What if Drunk Gabe does what Drunk Gabe wants?

My eyes swirl to him beside me and look up his frame, as he leans back against the wall. My eyes trail up his body, and the elevator opens. I turn from him and walk to my door, the first one on the left. We are at my door, and I refuse to look at him, as I unlock it and step in. I walk into my empty, dark, cold room, and the familiar feeling of despair starts to creep into the tips of my fingers. Grief whispers in my ear, promising to wait for sober Gabe.

My feet stop moving and I take a few breaths. Would it be so terrible for me to do what I want? Can I be selfish for one night?

The small voice in my head is telling me to keep walking. It begs me to get away from him. I ignore it and turn to face him.

FRIENDS

Gabe

Odis stares back at me with darkened eyes, and I don't need to ask him to know he feels what I feel. He knows what I am thinking, and his presence means he wants the same. Electricity sparks, threatening to burn everything down, and I make up my mind;, I will giveDrunk Gabe full control over my actions. I will do what I want, and I won't put too much thought into it.

For now.

"Err, what are you doing?" He asks, and for the first time since I've known him,Odis looks nervous. His eyes widen and his brows raise slightly, but I don't miss the movement. His shock only spurs me on. I slip my suit jacket off, and his eyes drop to my chest. I'll give him a few moments to stop me. My fingers lift to my collar, and our eyes stay connected.

One, two, three buttons are unbuttoned, and as I work on the fourth, he sucks in a breath. I sneak a peek at him, as I get the fourth unbuttoned, and his chest rises and falls erratically. I unbutton the last one, and my shirt separates and hangs open., I remove it and throw it to the floor. His eyes drop to my chest, and lingers on the wound. We both have her on our minds.

"I meant what I said," I whisper. "I'd take another knife to the chest, if it would bring her back."

"I know," he says. I find happiness in knowing he knows.

Odis stares at me with an emotion I can't place. My eyes drop to his sharp jawline and I inhale that familiar scent that screams his name. My heart pounds and I know what he's going to do before he does it. He closes the distance between us, and in a second, his hand grips my hair. I can't help the whimper when he tugs it down until my neck is exposed.

Just like that day in the elevator.

His eyes dart to my flesh and stop where the mark used to be. The mark is completely gone, and my skin is clean like a blank canvas. His eyes flare, and I watch as his eyes linger on my flesh.

"Odis," I breathe, and his pupils dilate as I meet his gaze.

He devours the space between us and I experience delicious sin, as his mouth crashes against mine. I want to hand myself over to him: all of me, my body, and what is left of my pitiful heart.

A desperate noise escapes me that wouldn't have made me blush had I been with anyone else. But with the man in front of me, I am as red as a tomato, and that's all it takes for him to yank on my hair. I slam into him at full force, and he yanks down on my hair to tip my chin back. I don't mean to moan, but it escapes against my will, and he swallows it up like it is his favorite flavor of ice cream. His tongue pillages and claims my mouth. It makes my heart thump harder and faster than it has before, as it welcomes the man who's made it beat again.

He releases a rumbling growl filled with nothing but need and crazed frenzy. My chest warms, and my heart threatens to explode, as I reach out to touch him. A feeling I'd not felt in a while spreads through my body: desire. I am entirely lost to him, as carnal desire rams into me. My fingers tremble, as they make their way up to his chest and wrap around his neck.

I thought I'd imagined that day in the elevator, but as he ravages my mouth, I know the desire I'd seen was real. It all ends too soon, and in the blink of an eye, his hand releases my hair and drops to his side. He takes a step back, and my hands fall from him. I stared at him in confusion.

We remain quiet, as we stare at each other breathlessly; staring at each other with a hunger that threatens to drive us mad. A hunger that can only be sated by the other person in the room. It doesn't matter if he tries to cool his features and pretends like he doesn't want this, want me. I had felt the evidence of his arousal when I'd slammed against his chest.

He is such a mystery, and his actions confuse me beyond understanding. My lips tingle, and my cheeks are still warm, as I stare at the man in front of me. The look in his eyes resembles regret, and I feel like I've been stabbed again. He stares at me, and I know he won't let this happen again.

"I'm a man who likes control," Odis says. "I don't give in to impulse, and I don't let my dick lead me. I didn't follow you here for this."

"Then why did you follow me?" I ask. I can't help it; the question comes out before I consider if I should ask it.

"I wanted to make sure you got back… safely," he says. "We're friends, aren't we?"

I stare at him, feeling more confused than I already was, when I remember what I'd said to Leo.

Really?

Is that what this is? He only wanted to make sure I didn't bed Leo? I scoff, and Odis' eyes hold my gaze, as he stares at me. I can't tell if it's guilt or regret staring back at me. I need to keep my distance from Odis. Of course, I already know that, but judging by my actions, my heart doesn't know that. The problem iswas... I don't know if I can stay away from him now. Not now that my heart beats for him.

Friends don't kiss friends, dumb ass.

"What do you want, Odis?" I asked.

I don't know where the question came from, Goddess, I don't know where the courage came from. When it came to Odis, I realize I act irrationally. What I do know is that Odis needs to tell me where he stands.

"Come again?" Odis asked.

"I don't think for a second that you believe we're just friends but if you tell that we're friends, I'll drop this."

"I don't know what you're talking about..." Odis trails off.

For once, he doesn't look like the confident Odis I know. He looks unsure, nervous, and panicked. The thought I'd previously had that day in the elevator screams in my mind. I can't help but laugh.

"Whatever you say," I scoff.

As I make my way to the bed, I loosen my belt and unzip my pants letting them drop to the floor. I hear his breath catch in his throat, and climb into bed, as he lets himself out. I'm disappointed and conflicted but I won't be a fool for him.

PRINCESS

Gabe

My head throbs like a mother. I struggle to open my eyes, and I pray for mercy. Where am I? A chuckle gets stuck in my throat. Seriously though, where am I?

"The question is who is here?" My wolf asks He is on high alert; at least one of us is. I grab my head before sitting up and looking around. My jaw drops, and I can't believe who is in my room. I don't know who I was expecting, but it definitely wasn't him. Leo sits at my dining room table as if he belongs there.

He is wearing black shorts that hang loosely on his hips, and a white sleeveless shirt. His elbow is on the table, his head leans on his open palm, and his eyes are closed. I tried to figure out what I was missing.

Why was he here?

How was he here?

I need to figure out why he is here, and how he got into my room. It doesn't make sense. I grab my phone and check the time.

It is only the day after the Ceremony, meaning there isn't any work today. Ady will be with Alpha Ethan and won't need us to guard her.

My eyes wander back to Leo to find brown eyes staring back at me. He is awake and staring at me. My eyes move to the gash above his eyebrow. The last two days have been eventful. From the tournament to the ceremony, a lot has happened.

"You've slept in," Leo says, his voice husky. "Like a princess."

"I'm not a princess," I say. A lightning bolt flashes through my head and I groan. "Why are you yelling," I groan.

Leo chuckled. "I'm not yelling. You're just hungover," he says, and a frown pulls at the corners of his lips. "I would have walked you home, but someone got in the way."

"Someone…" I start to ask, but everything that happened last night hits me at once. "Oh great," I groan. I made one too many mistakes. At least I was sensible enough to do what I'd normally do… the memory of me shushing my heart has me squeezing my eyes shut tightly.

"Did something happen?" Leo asks. It takes me a minute to understand what he means. He is asking if I'd done something with Odis.

"If something had, wouldn't he be here?" I reply sharply. He doesn't flinch though; he doesn't act like my tone bothers him at all. Instead, he smiles as he takes in the empty spot beside me.

"Are you upset that nothing happened?" He asks, and I can't help but glower at him.

"More importantly, why are you here?" I ask.

He ignores me and gets to his feet. I watch him cautiously as he makes his way over to me. His pretty blonde hair and big muscles don't make me swoon. All I care about right now is finding water and some Tylenol. The bed dips as he sits beside me.

"You're way too comfortable in a stranger's home," I say.

"But you're no stranger, Gabe," he says. He leans in, and I don't move back. It feels like he is threatening me… no… testing me. What the fuck does he want? "We're partners," he says.

"We're off today, Leo," I say.

He freezes, and his eyes linger longer than I like.

"Say it again," he murmurs.

"What? We're off?" I ask.

He shakes his head. "No, my name," he says.

"You're being weird," I say.

He leans in until I have no choice but to lean back. When he doesn't stop, I lean back until I hit my head on the bed frame. Hitting your head when you have a hangover isn't the best feeling in the world.

"Mother fu-," I start, but stop when I realize Leo is close. *Too close*. He is so close I can feel the warmth of his body and his breath.

His hands grip my wrists, and before I know it, they are both on each side of my head. Who the hell does this guy think he is? I open my mouth to protest, but he starts speaking before I can.

"Say it," he said.

Of all the ludicrous things, is he still on that? "Are you serious, right now?" I ask. I fight against his hold on my hands, but am still weak. Ugh. This is so frustrating. I huff and lean back against the headboard.

"Say it," he says again, "please."

My cheeks start to heat with embarrassment. I can't believe

he's making a huge fuss over me saying his name! I almost kick his ass; he's lucky I'm weak right now. Shit, he's lucky I'm hungover, or I'd headbutt the shit out of his head.

Cool it.

Relax.

Breathe in.

Breathe out.

Breat—Gah.

Fine.

I look up into those brown eyes. They stare down at me, but are missing the smugness I'd seen at the tournament. Instead, his eyes look soft and hopeful, as they stare down at me. It makes me want to bite my tongue, and hold back the curses that beg to be let out.

"Leo," I say.

He leaned in until his nose almost touches mine. "Again," he says.

This mother fu… I take a deep breath and exhale. "Leo."

"Yes, Gabe," he says, as his eyes flicker and his breathing deepens.

"We aren't working today," I continue. "I don't see why you would come here."

Leo moves his head to my shoulder and turns his head into my neck. What was he - was he nuzzling me? I move my head away from him and fight against his hold. This time, he lets me go.

"I know we aren't working today, but I figured we could get some training in while Luna is…preoccupied," Leo says.

"And why would we do that?" I ask.

"We haven't trained together, and we were thrown in together as partners. As partners, I think we should become familiar with each other. Training together would be good for us, and our Luna. Don't you think so?" He asks.

I wring my wrists and shoot him a glare. He's got a point. I scratch my head, and avoid his gaze. "Well, I need to get dressed," I say.

His gaze trails down my chest, and lingers on my scar before it continues to where my thigh lays exposed. "Don't stop on my account," he says and holds his hands up.

SURPRISE

Gabe

"You need to move out of the way, so I can get up," I say. There is no sign of him being upset with my response. I'm a blunt person and I'm more than used to people not liking me. So when Leo simply smiles and flashes a dimple at me, I am too stunned to slap him.

He gets to his feet, and I watch him as he makes his way over to the table. I sigh before I throw my legs over the edge of the bed. The question still remains, how did he get in here?

I glance at Leo and watch him as he leans back against the chair. My eyes automatically dip to the muscles that peek out from under his shirt. They are pulled taut, and I didn't miss the fact that Leo is mighty fine.

I'm blunt, not blind.

When I realize I'm drooling, I look up to find him staring at me. Damn it. What could be worse than being caught ogling him after I snapped at him? His eyes dance with laughter, and a slow cocky smirk spreads across his face.

I pull my eyes from Leo, and get to my feet like nothing happened. I strut across the room to my dresser. I hold my head high, despite the fact he'd caught me eye fucking him. He's a handsome guy; it's not like I wouldn't notice. I ignore the fact that I am walking without pants in front of someone I'd only known for two days.

I've done the walk of shame many times, and this isn't any different. Usually, I did the walk of shame while my partner was sleeping, and I didn't have to see him. I gulp. The fact that he was blatantly staring isn't helping, but I won't let him know it bugs me.

I grab some clothes, and turn to find him staring at my ass. My cheeks warm, and I hate myself for being so easily swayed. I have no right to be enjoying this morning's eye candy. I should be mourning my mate, and yet here I am flirting with Leo.

My daily reminder finally hits me and I don't miss the way it fills my chest: guilt. "Can you stop staring?" I ask. I don't bother keeping the anger out of my voice.

Am I being dramatic? Maybe.

Am I going to think before I speak? Definitely not.

Should I? Yes.

"Don't be shy, Gabe," Leo says. He shrugs and caresses his stomach. "We're going to be seeing *a lot* more of each other from now on. You might as well get used to it." I fight the urge to look down at his stomach.

"Yeah well, stop staring at my ass-sets," I murmur, as I got dressed under the watchful eye of my partner. I fight the urge to rush, and force my body to relax.

"Why?" Leo asks. I chance a look at him, and find him pouting. "I really like your ass," Leo starts, "*sets…your assets.*"

I glare at him before I pull the fabric of my shirt over my eyes. "Yeah well, you won't be seeing much of my assets from here on out." I pull my shirt down, and freshen up in the bathroom. As I walked out of the bathroom, Leo jumps to his feet.

"About time!" He exclaims, "For someone who claimed not to be royalty, you get dressed like one."

I ignore him. "I can commit to a couple of hours of training," I grumble.

"A couple? Do you have plans today?" Leo asks. I can feel him getting in my space, but I don't say anything. I want to eat, but don't want to suffer through cooking something while Leo watches. I'd have to offer him something to eat too, and I don't want to make him a meal. Call me petty.

"This one hasn't heard of a personal bubble," my wolf says.

"Tell me about it," I say. I pulled my socks on, and head to the hallway.

"What?" Leo asks.

"It doesn't matter if I have plans for today or not. I can offer you a couple of hours. A couple. I'm a busy man, so take it or leave it," I say.

Leo remains silent, as I pick out a pair of shoes for training. I head for the door, and ignore the towering dark shadow on my heel. I am so ready to get out of here. Being surrounded by four walls, and being alone with Leo isn't good for my mental health.

I turn the doorknob and throw it open. I rush out of my room so fast I don't see the person on the other side of the door. I walk headfirst into a broad chest. A bag of something warm got squashed against my chest, and the smell of Asiago bagels hits my nose.

"What the act—," I lift my head to look at who is standing in front of my door. I am more than ready to rip this dude a new one, but the words get caught in my throat. I gulp. The person in front of my door has blonde hair and sun-kissed skin. He is wearing dark gray sweatpants and a white shirt. His muscles, and something else, bulge against the fabric, and I want to slap myself. I am like a female in heat. He is tall, so freaking tall, and stares down at me with a hint of a smile on his lips.

My eyes widen as I realize he came to my room early in the morning. Even after everything that happened last night. What shocks me even more than him being here, is the fact that he brought food. Beta freaking Odis stands in front of me, looking amazing in his not-so-usual attire.

He opens his mouth, and is about to speak, when his eyes darken. A hand drapes around my shoulders, and panic sets into my stomach. Odis' eyes settle on Leo's arm as Leo leans into me.

"Good morning, Beta," Leo greets. "Surprise seeing you here."

MAD

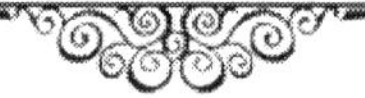

Gabe

Well fuck.

This is the most awkward situation I've been in, and I don't even know why. I can sense the tension between the two, as Leo's words hang in the air between the three of us. Goddess, you can cut the tension with a knife.

The silence is stretching out and filling the hallway. As I stare at Odis, a blanket of guilt covers me and starts to make its way down to my center. I try to shake off the feeling; I have no reason to feel guilty. Odis is glaring at Leo, and Leo is glaring right back.

"I had to wake you up the other day. I wouldn't have pegged you for an early bird," Odis says. I hold back the urge to laugh, when Leo mumbles 'rude' under his breath.

"I didn't know we knew each other that well," I say. Am I being a little mean? Yes, but I am feeling a little bratty this morning. I want out of this situation.

"What's going on here?" Odis asks as he nods towards Leo

beside me. His question comes before I can sidestep him.

I shake my head, having no idea how to answer him. My eyes automatically skim down the length of his body before snapping back up to meet his gaze. I know what this looks like, but the brat in me doesn't want to explain. I want him to misunderstand, and I want him to wonder.

His gaze slides over me in a way that makes my body heat up, and that only makes me get even more frustrated. I'm supposed to be mad right now, not want to jump his bones. Maybe I should be happy that he wants to be friends; a relationship between the two of us would only be complicated.

I sigh loudly, and they both stare at me for a second before Leo speaks.

"We don't have to explain anything to you… or is that an order, Beta?" Leo asks. The tension is only thickening between these two. I don't even know where this is coming from, but I feel like a bucket of cold water is emptied over my head. The heat I was feeling a second ago is washed away.

Poking the beast is not the way to go, and I glare at Leo before elbowing him in the side. I move out from under his arm, and gave Odis a smile that he doesn't return.

Well, fuck me.

Odis coughs, and he slowly lowers the bag in his hands. "Where are you guys headed?" He asks. I'm about to answer, when Leo beats me to it.

"Oh, you know," Leo teased. "Out."

He's definitely picked up on Odis' demeanor and is enjoying this way more than he should. The words get stuck in my throat when I look up at Odis and find sadness etched in his features.

"We're going to get some training in while we can," I say. Odis's eyebrows rise before a smile spreads across his face. He opens his mouth to say something, but I ignore it and finally make my way past him. I don't bother looking to see if Leo is following me. This whole thing is his idea; I have no doubts that he will follow.

Whatever tension I was feeling between the three of us isn't something I want. I mean, I like attention, but I don't want that kind of attention, and I certainly don't want it today. I don't have time for it in my life. Okay, I was lying. I do have time for it, but I am upset *someone* pushed me away the night before.

I am upset at myself for being that drunk when something finally went down between us. I know I hadn't imagined what I was feeling from Odis. He kissed me last night, but was sending me mixed signals. I don't know what the hell is going on in his mind.

"Are you mad because I interrupted your early morning bagel with your boyfriend?" Leo asks from behind me. His voice rips through my thoughts and pulls me back into the present.

My footsteps come to a halt, and I turn around to look at Leo. I have to tilt my neck to look up at him. "I'm not mad, and he's not my boyfriend," I hiss. I know hissing proves that I am mad, but I don't care. I don't even want to be out of bed right now, and I don't want to go and workout or train. I want to stay in my bed and be dead to the world.

I do want to know why Odis came by, but I'm not going to admit that out loud. Especially after he kissed me, and then friendzoned me, all in the span of 5 minutes. What I did and who I did it with is none of his business.

I can't believe he thought he had the right to ask what I was doing. I want to be angry, but my heart is sad at the thought of him misunderstanding why Leo was in my room. A small voice in the back of my head whispers that he'd come with bagels, but I ignore it. I turn on my heel and continue to walk.

"So… a guy who was outside of your door… early in the morning on the weekend… who also brought you breakfast… isn't your boyfriend?" Leo asks. He catches up to me and the look on his face when I turn to answer him tells me he doesn't believe me.

"Yes," I say.

He grunts and follows it up with a shrug. "Don't have to tell me twice," he says and continues walking.

Good, because I don't think I could say it again. I may like the thought of something with Odis more than I wanted to admit.

BRING IT

Gabe

The rest of the walk to the field was done in silence. Leo doesn't try to ask any more questions about Odis, and I am relieved. When we get to the open field, Olivia's replacement is running laps. I watch her for a few minutes until I feel Leo's gaze. I shake off the sadness that tries to creep up whenever I think of her; I don't need that now. I do, however, have a few questions for my partner.

"Do you want to explain what that was all about?" I ask as I turn around and face him. He is shocked for a second, but regains his composure.

"I don't know what you're talking about," Leo says. He is lying through his teeth, and I am so close to losing my shit.

"Oh really? You don't know about the tension between you and our Beta back there?" I ask. He shrugs innocently, but he is anything but.

"You didn't see a problem with taunting your Beta?" I ask.

"I wasn't taunting him. All I did was ask if he was ordering us around," Leo says. I stare at him for a second. We've just become the Luna's bodyguards, but Leo is acting like... like... Whatever. I don't want to give Leo the idea that he can start asking questions, or strike up another conversation.

Leo cocks his head, and before I know what I am doing I am checking him out. For a second, I consider playing around with him. He would be fun; he could be a reprieve from what I've been going through. I grab my forehead and close my eyes. I forgot; I don't deserve a break from the pain.

Plus, mixing pleasure and work? Yeah, that is the stupidest idea I've ever had. I want to punch something. I open my eyes and look at Leo again. What better target than a willing punching bag?

"We're sparring," I say.

"Oh yeah?" Leo asks. "I think we should loosen up first, maybe stretch."

"I think I'm already loosened up," I start "I don't want to talk."

"Noted," he says.

"Bring it," I mutter. He smiles and his eyes light up at the challenge. I watch his movements, as he makes his way closer to me. He charges for me, and I slam my fist into the side of his face before I move out of the way in time.

"You should think before you charge at me," I say. He staggers back and bends down low before charging again. He aims low and tackles me to the ground.

"I don't have to think when I fight. I just move," Leo says. "And damn, that punch felt personal." He props himself up on his hands. His legs are on the outside of both of my legs. He stares down at me, and I know he is waiting for an explanation.

I'm not in the mood to talk, so I throw punch after punch into his stomach. My fist meets with hard chiseled abs, and I wonder if I am even hurting him. When I look up and find him smirking, I know it didn't.

"Get off," I growl.

Leo stares down at me, and I can see the gears churning. He is actually weighing his options, but I won't give him the time. I bring my knee up, and when it connects with his junk, I am satisfied with his groan of pain. He lowers himself so we are chest to chest. I take the opportunity to push him off before I roll out from under him and sit up.

"Why don't you tell me what's really going on?" Leo's voice strained. I turn and find him lying on his back. He watches me, and when I don't answer, he pouts. He actually pouts. I almost want to smile, but I'm not going to. There is no reason why I should find a guy built like a tank cute.

He is't cute.

"Mm-hmm," Felix says.

"I'm going to ignore that," I say to my wolf.

"Didn't I say I didn't want to talk?" I repeat my words from earlier.

"I think you might be someone who needs to talk," Leo says.

"Why don't you shut up," I say.

I lunge at him, and this time it is his turn to dodge. He doesn't. I quickly get to my feet, and kick him while he's down.

"Mother fuc—," Leo starts, but I kick him again.

"You could always tap out," I say.

"What…are we wrestling now?" Leo asks as he gets to his feet. To my satisfaction, he is holding his side.

We spend the next two hours sparring. By the time we are done, we are both exhausted and a little bruised. I am laying on my back, and Leo sits beside me. His lip is cut, and his left cheekbone is starting to bruise. The inside of my cheek is bleeding, and my body was aching - and not in a good way.

"You know that sparring is supposed to be where you lightly fight, right?" Leo asks. "We're supposed to minimize injuries, and feel each other out. You know, get comfortable with the other person?"

"This is news to me," I lie.

"Uh-huh," he says. "Why are you so angry? If you talked to me you'd feel a lot better." His words catch me off guard and I look up at the sky.

"I'm not angry." He stares at me for a few minutes.

"Why don't we get to know each other?" He asks again. I stretch before I sit up.

"I told you I didn't want to talk, and I didn't come here to get to know you," I start, "I came here to train with you because SOMEONE showed up in my room early this morning."

"I know you don't want to talk, but that doesn't mean you don't need to. Come on, I could be your friend. Let's go get something for brunch," Leo says.

SHOWER

Gabe

"You want to go to brunch?" I ask. "As in, the two of us?" My fingers twitch, and my palms get clammy. This sounds too much like a date, and I'm not doing dates any time soon. Don't get me wrong, Leo is hot, but emotional baggage prevents me from even thinking of moving on.

"Lies," my wolf murmurs.

"I don't know what you're talking about," I grumble.

"It's not that the emotional baggage is preventing you from moving on," Felix says.

"Then what is it?" I ask.

My wolf smiles and I fight the urge to smile in return. "You're not interested in using Leo to move on or forget. There's only one person you want to tickle your pickle, and he tends to be of the suit-wearing variety."

Felix's words hit too close to home, but I pretend to ignore him, as Leo shrugs his shoulders. "Yeah, just brunch," Leo says.

"I didn't eat anything before I came to get you, and you didn't get to eat any of those bagels this morning from your 'non-boyfriend'." He uses finger quotes around the non-boyfriend. "I'd say you are as hungry as I am." As if on cue, my stomach growls. "See? He agrees with me, and you can get to know me," Leo says in response.

"I don't need friends and I don't need to get to know you," I say.

The silence stretches between us. "Don't be like that," Leo says.

"Be like what?" I ask.

"Like you wouldn't spend time with me if I was the last person on earth. I'm new here, and you are one of the first people I've met outside my old pack that I'd actually like to hang out with. On top of that, we're working together. If we're going to see each other often, shouldn't we get to know each other?" He asks.

And there it was again, that ugly feeling: guilt. I know what it is like to be the new guy. I'd been the new guy here, but I had Ady… and I had… "Fine. Let's get brunch," I agree, "as friends."

He lights up like a puppy, and I get to my feet before I give in to the urge to pet his head. I look down at him, and offer my hand instead. Leo takes it, and I pull him to his feet. He doesn't say anything, and I start to wonder if something is wrong. He is quiet. I lean in and nudge him.

"What's up?" I ask.

"I'm just surprised," he says.

"About?" I ask.

"I fully expected you to say no to brunch," he says.

"But I said yes," I say.

"You said yes," he repeats.

"Yeah, I mean... I'm hungry and I wouldn't mind... some company."

"Sweet, do you know any good breakfast places?" Leo asks as we head off the field.

"Matter of fact, I do," I say. I've been thinking of those waffles I had with Ady.

***

Adea

When I wake up, it is already noon and Ethan isn't in bed. The sound of the shower tells me where he is, and the smell of pancakes leads me to the breakfast on the table. There is a platter of pancakes stacked high, scrambled eggs, bacon, and sausage. My mouth waters, and my eyes trail over the bowl of fruit and jug of orange juice. The food is untouched, and I stretch before getting out of bed.

I don't bother with clothes; I have a hunger, and it isn't for food. Steam billows out from the bathroom, as Iswings the door open and I take a step into the warm room. Ethan stands in the shower, his eyes closed, and the water cascading down his body. I take a moment to look at him: the tattoos that line his biceps and chest, the hard-defined abs that tease me, and the powerful thighs that stand on both sides of one of my favorite parts of him.

His eyes open, as I pull open the glass door and step in. I'm to say good morning, but his mouth finds mine, and he kisses me hungrily, as his arms wrap around my waist, and he pulls me in. I sigh, as the hot water splashes over me. I kiss his chest, and start to trail lower, when he grabs my chin and pulls me up. He wraps my arms around his neck, and pulls me up into his arms. I wrap my legs around his waist and hold onto him tightly.

He lines himself with my entrance, and I feel his tip against my folds. He leans forward and kisses my neck, sucking, licking, biting, as he thrusts into me and impales me on his hard length. I gasp as he fills me, and he groans at the feeling of me clenching around him.

"Ethan," I breathe.

He lifts me slowly, and I feel every inch, as it leaves me, and then he pulls me down so I take it inch by inch again. I moan, and he captures my lips. I hold onto his shoulders, my nails digging into skin, as he lifts me up, and slams me down on his thick cock over and over again. I am intoxicated on the feeling of him stretching me, filling me.

"Fuck," he growls "You were made for me."

His fingers bite into my hips, as I slide up and down his length roughly. I arch my back, as he takes what he wants from me, and gives in return. I clench around him, as his pace quickens. I let him use me for his pleasure, and I moan, as I tighten around him.

I come with his name on my lips, and he groans, as my orgasm pushes him into oblivion. He follows me, grunting my name, as he thrusts into me as he comes. His grip tightens, as he spills into me, and he holds me until I am full of him. He gently places me on the floor. His hands find my cheeks, and he leans down to kiss me.

"Good morning," he says with a laugh after we break apart.

RECOIL

Leo

Gabe has been on my mind since he put me on my ass during the competition. He is a challenge I want to take on. My wolf wants nothing more than to feel him writhing beneath us, and I want the same. He may have gotten on top of me out there, but if I could have him in my bed he would be below me at my mercy.

The two of us won the competition, and I see Gabe as my equal. I gave up on finding my mate a long time ago, and I am used to playing around. I'd never seen someone as my equal before, but here he is. Sitting in front of me willingly. I haven't had a chance to get him all to myself, and when I woke up this morning, I decided today would be the day.

Two things have happened since the competition. Alright that's a lie, a few things have happened, but there are only two things I mark as important. First, Gabe is my equal and he is my partner. This morning, when I watched him sleep, I thought of him as pretty, and I don't know many guys I'd call pretty, but he is.

I sense he is holding back, and I am curious to know what is under the mask he wears. I want to peel it off. I know he has something with Luna by the way she reacted whenever he was hurt during the competition.

The second is when I got him to agree to come out this morning with me. I'm not sure if he really wanted to, but I won't look a gift horse in the mouth. My partner is my type, and I don't mean one you fuck once and forget. I doubt there would be anything I'd want to forget when I get the chance to play with him. He is hot, mysterious, and holds me at a distance.

I can't remember a time when I wanted someone's attention as badly as I want Gabe's. I want to get closer to him, so much closer. He sits across the table from me at this little place called 'The Sweet Note'. The smells of waffles, heated croissants, and other breakfast entrees being cooked waft through the air and have my mouth watering.

I wanted his time and now I have it. I fight the urge to bounce around and blush like a love-sick girl when he orders for me. He tells me to trust him, and the food orgasm will blow my mind. I'mhappy often, but when I am I can't help but show it.

I was thankful when Alpha Ethan announced us both as winners of the competition. I watched him all day yesterday while on duty. I wanted to get to speak with him, but the stupid Beta got in the way. An image of Gabe's reddened cheeks when he was drunk makes me wonder where else I could get him to redden.

When the waitress leaves, Gabe reaches across the table and pokes at my cut lip. I fight the urge to flinch from the pain and stay still.

"Does it hurt?" He asks. He continues staring at me. I am not used to him looking at me, and it makes me shift in my seat.

"Only when assholes poke it," I tease. He runs his fingers along the line of the cut and pokes it again. HE POKES IT AGAIN.

"Ouch, asshole," I mumble.

Gabe pulled his fingers away, and I wish I'd just kept my mouth shut. "This whole thing was your idea," he says defensively. I watch as he turns his head and looks around the cafe.

"I didn't know it would end up with me getting my ass handed to me," I say. That is a lie; he didn't kick my ass. He laughs and something flutters in my stomach. I feel the need to grab him by his throat and pull him in for a bite, but I don't think he'd like that.

"Mm-hmm," he hums. "Well, Ady brought me here last week, so this is only my second time here. I haven't stopped thinking about the waffle I got," he declares.

"Ady?" I ask. Who the fuck is that?

"Sorry, it's my nickname for her," he says. I am getting more confused by the second. Her? I am pretty sure he is into guys. My radar is rarely wrong, but if it is, that would fucking suck.

"Who is Ady?" I ask casually. Maybe I should have asked if he had a girlfriend when he said he didn't have a boyfriend. Damn.

"Our Luna, silly," he says. Thank Goddess, and I can't help but smile at the small bit of personality that slips past his mask. Little by little I'll see what is under it.

"You gave her a nickname?" I ask. "Are you guys close?" Goddess, I hope not.

For the second time today, he smiles at me. "She's my best friend," he says. "She's the reason I'm still here."

"Were you planning on going somewhere?" I ask.

He avoids my eyes and runs his hand through his pretty blonde hair. "Here or there," he says.

"I have a question," I start.

"I might have an answer," Gabe says.

"You were here before I came along. Darci and I are close, and she hasn't made any friends here yet. I am curious about the person who held the Gamma position. Do you know much about him?" I ask.

Gabe visibly recoils before he looks right into my eyes, and I can't look away. Those things flutter in my stomach, and our moment is interrupted when the waitress places our food in front of us. I watch him start to dig in, and I think of Beta outside his door this morning. I am not blind, I know there is something going on between them. I crack my neck and knuckles. That won't stop me though. I don't care if they have something. I want him and I'll have him.

WANT

Gabe

Do I want to keep pressing him? Yes. Am I going to? I don't know yet. He stares at me expectantly, and I try to think of an answer. My mind is distracted by images of what he could possibly want.

"Well?" Odis asks.

"Uh, I-I," I stutter. I stutter, like a second-grader who is cornered on the playground during recess by their crush.

"What did you do with Leo this morning?" Odis asks. He leans down, and his breath on my neck is making my body overheat.

"We...," I start, "trained."

His lips slowly slide down my neck and I swear I can feel him smile. He opens his mouth, and I shutter as his teeth replace his lips. He bites my neck—not just anywhere, but where my mark had been.

"Oh fuck," I groan. He bites me hard on one of my most sensitive areas, so roughly I cry out. His hand leaves the back of my neck and slides down my chest.

“Is that all you did?” Odis asks.

“We went to brunch,” I murmur. I am aching and needy and I look down, as his hand grips my towel, and rips it off roughly.

“Goddess,” I breathe.

Odis takes a step back from me, and I want to protest at the loss of his warmth. I look up, and my words die on my lips. His eyes roam my body hungrily, greedily, and I bite my lip. He is too far away; he needs to be closer.

He reaches out and slides his fingers down my chest. He takes his time, and slowly circles my left nipple. I swallow when he squeezes it with his thumb and index finger. He leans down and takes my right one between his teeth.

It’s been too long, and I know I am not going to last long. I am already ready to blow all over my chest. His tongue flicks across my sensitive flesh, and I arch into him, and my hips buck forward. I look down at him, and he stares up at me with fuck me eyes, as he bites the little nub in his mouth.

“Ah, you asshole,” I hiss.

The corners of his lips curl up in a smile, and I instantly forgive him. His finger slides lower and trails over my abs. I don’t dare move; I don’t want to distract him from what he is doing. His mouth leaves my chest. His fingers trail slowly up my length, as I hold my breath. He slides over the wet slit on my tip, and I can’t help the needy moan that escapes my lips. I watched as a line of pre-come hung from my tip to his fingers.

“You’re ready for this, aren’t you?” Odis asks. He brings up his thumb and index finger, and I die as he rubs my wetness between his fingers. I want to climb under a rock, and get on my knees at the same time. Why is he so fucking hot?

My hard length is pointed up at him, like he is a fucking magnet. Goddess, kill me now. Of course, I am fucking ready for this. I know. He knows. I am turned on, and am more than ready. I am not thinking about anything else. I can't fake it, and I am not going to make an excuse. I am tired of pretending I don't want him.

"I am," I say. "Aren't you?"

Odis opens his mouth and places his fingers in his mouth. He sucks them clean, and I am panting at this point. I am at a loss for words, surprise surprise. He takes his fingers out of his mouth and crashes his mouth to mine. He kisses me like he can't get enough. He kisses me like I am the most precious person in the world. He kisses me like it will hurt him if he doesn't, and I kiss him back.

The kiss ends, and when I open my eyes I find Odis staring back at me. His hands lower, and I know he is going for his pants. *Fuck yes.* He pulls his sweats down. He stills, and I let my eyes drop. He has pulled himself free, and I stare down at his thick length. It's been a while since I've been with a man, but this is definitely bigger than I've had before. His tip is smooth and glistens. It makes my mouth water. His length is long and oh so thick. He is fucking beautiful, and I want it. I want him.

Odis leans into me, and I groan when his length presses against mine. He is hot and I want to feel him. Odis' fingers find my wet slit, and he spreads it down my tip. I sigh and sit back, resting my weight on my hands. He leans down and spits right onto my tip, and I watch as he coats my cock with it, and does the same with his hard length.

"Fuck," I grind out through clenched teeth. "Stop teasing me."

"I'll do whatever I damn well please, Gabriel. You've been teasing me all fucking week. I think you can take a few fucking minutes. Now sit still like a good boy and let me get your dick wet," Odis orders.

And damn, if that doesn't turn me on even more. My dick hardens, and all I want is for him to do something about it. I love it when he says my name, I love the way it sounds coming from his lips. I love his lips.

I groan as he lines up our cocks side by side. "Don't make me punish you," Odis warns. I know that's a threat, but I also want to find out what his punishments entail. "There," he murmurs. I look down to find his hand barely wrapped around our lengths, but he has a good hold on both. He spits on our lengths, and I watch as it spreads over his length and drips onto his fingers. I almost come, as he slowly slides down our lengths.

"Odis," I plead.

SHOW ME

Gabe

Our conversation comes to a standstill after he asks about Olivia. The food arrives, and I shovel the delectable goodness into my mouth. Leo watches me as I eat, but I pretend not to notice. I ask him how his food is, and he says the food orgasm is amazing, and he will definitely be coming back. As soon as we are done, we head back. Thankfully he reads the room, and doesn't ask any more questions. I need space, and a shower, as soon as possible.

I don't miss the way he throws his bottom lip out in a pout when I say goodbye. When we get back to the packhouse, I run upstairs and lock the door behind me. I don't want any more uninvited visitors. I jump into the shower and breathe a sigh of relief when the scalding water burns my skin.

Pain. It is pain that erupts and spreads as my skin cries. It is my friend and will stay by my side long after anything else. I only need to think about it and her. I know what Leo wants, but I also know I don't want to ruin anything with Odis. I can't help but laugh; I don't want to ruin anything with *my friend*, Odis.

Today is my last day off; tomorrow Leo and I will guard Ady again. The water drips from my hair into my eyes and the world becomes blurry. What I did before on a day off was clear but what I would do now on a day off was a mystery. Or is it? I could lay in bed until I fall asleep and maybe when I wake up it will be a new day.

Eventually, I wash and get out of the shower. As I dry myself down, a knock sounds. Thank Goddess, I locked the door. I hear it, I know I hear it, but a part of me doesn't want to open it. I want to stay in my home, alone, and curl up in bed. I sigh and wrap the towel around my hips before I open the bathroom door.

I inhale sharply, as the cold air hits me, and goosebumps break out down my arms and chest. I can feel the water from my hair starting to drip down my neck and back. My breathing comes out slowly as I make my way towards the door. When the person on the other side of the door knocks again, I reach for the handle. I open the door, and I am shocked to find Odis standing on the other side. I don't know why, but I was expecting to see Leo.

"Hello, Beta," I say, keeping it professional. I reach up and hold onto the doorway above my head. He is still dressed in the same clothes he'd been wearing this morning.

"Is he here?" He asks. He doesn't say hi, and he has the nerve to glare at me.

"Who?" I ask, feigning innocence.

"Is he here, Gabriel?" He repeats.

Well.

I shake my head. "No, Beta, he isn't, but I don't see how that's any of your business."

In an instant, he is on me, his hand wraps around and grips the back of my neck. He pushes me back, and I stumble as I try to stay upright. "Don't tease me," Odis warns. "Not today, not after what I saw this morning. You don't even know the feelings and thoughts that have plagued me over the past few hours."

He pushes me until I slam into the table. I can barely breathe, as I stare up at him; he is angry. I'm not sure why, and I'm not sure that I cared. I like seeing him like this. I want to see him so angry he loses control. I want to see what lies behind the mask he always wears. I like knowing that he is losing a grip on it because of me.

"Why don't you show me then?" I ask. My jaw almost drops after the words leave my mouth. What did I just say? I didn't know I was so bold… or did I? Memories of last night play over and over again. I want to know what could have happened; what maybe should have happened.

"What?" He asks. For the first time since I opened the door, I see the hesitation in his eyes.

"Show me what you've been thinking about all morning; show me what you want."

His lips part, his eyes darken, and his hands slide up into my hair. He grips a handful and pulls on it harder, exposing my throat to him. "And what exactly do you think I want to show you?" Odis asks.

I meet his eyes, which are darker than I've ever seen them. "I want you to show me whatever it is you want. I don't want you to lie to me and tell me you want to be my fucking friend. I want you to show me what you want. I want you to show me all of those dirty little thoughts you're hiding."

Time stands still with me sitting on the table, staring up at him tauntingly, and him standing in front of me, glaring down at me. I don't know how long we stay like that, but I hold my breath while I wait for him. He leans in, his thighs press against mine, and I feel a hard bulge press against my stomach.

A very impressive, hard, bulge. I swallow thickly. Okay, Beta is hung. Who am I to downplay him? "You not only wake up early, but you spend your morning with another man, doing goddess knows what?" He asks. The non-caring, mask-wearing Odis I wanted to dirty and rile up is gone. The Odis in front of me is furious, and his possessive tone makes me shiver. "Were you just training, Gabriel?" He asks, as he leans down so he is close, so close. "Or did you do something else that required a shower?" His voice is low and dangerous and all the things I like.

HER

Gabe

"Yes?" Odis asks innocently, but he is far from innocent and he knows it. His fingers are still at the base of our cocks.

"Please," I beg. I am past caring about how pathetic I sound. At this moment, I am needy, and Odis is the only one I see. He slides up and down our lengths, and I am fucking weak. "Fuck," I moan. His hand slides up, and as he slides down, I thrust up. "Oh fuck," I groan.

He slides up and down our lengths slowly. I need more. "Say my name when you come, sweet Gabriel," Odis says. He is breathless, and when I look up at him, his eyes are focused on me. "You hear me?" Odis asks.

"Yes," I moan. Odis watches me, as I moan with each stroke of his hand. My eyes flicks down to where his hand slid up and down our lengths.

"This feels so good," I choke out. "You feel so good."

"Spit," he demands.

I can't do anything, but obey. That's all I want to do. I lean forward and spit right on our tips. His hand speeds up, and I can feel myself getting close. He must be able to tell because the smile that spreads across his features is pure fucking sin. He grips us harder, and I can feel my body tremble.

He slides up and down faster, harder, and I grip his shoulders. I need to touch him, feel him, hold on to him. "I've thought of this moment more than I should," Odis says. His chest rises and falls. His words and the fact that I knew he was feeling good too drives me closer.

He leans forward and spist. It is wet and warm, and I watch as he brings his other hand up to my mouth. "Open your mouth," he orders. I open my mouth, and he pushes two fingers into my mouth. "Spit." His fingers leave my mouth and, "Oh fuck," I moan, as his fingers drive me closer and closer to heaven. His hand reappears and I jerk up as his warm wet fingers caress my sensitive balls.

"Come for me, Gabriel," Odis groans. His words are a command I cannot disobey. It builds up and my balls tingle. I throw my head back, and come and come and come.

"Odis," I moan. I come on my abs and chest. He doesn't stop; he continues sliding up and down our lengths. He leans forward, kissing my neck, and I drop my head down and kiss him. He kisses me back and bites on my bottom lip.

He leans back, and looks down at where he continues to slide up and down my sensitive length. "You're beautiful when you come," he says. I don't know about that, but I am feeling tired and I'm not going to argue with him... right now. "But you made a mess," he says with a smile.

"I did," I laugh. "You didn't come… did you not feel good?" I ask.

"It felt good," Odis says. "You felt good, but I want more."

"More?" I ask.

"Oh, Sweet Gabriel," he says. "Did you think we were done?"

"I mean…"

"No, we're far from done. I've been wanting you, and now I finally have you."

Well. Fuck me.

Before I know what's happening, Odis flips me over onto my belly. I practically twirl in the air before I am pushed down on the table. One of his hands traces a finger along my spine, and goosebumps break out all over my body, but this time it isn't because of the cold. I am messy; I can feel it as I lie face down on the table.

Where did he go?

I look up in time to see him walk into the bathroom. He'staken off his sweats and I bite my lip, as he walks over to me butt naked. I forgive him for the fact that he took his time in there. As he makes his way over, I notice he is holding her coconut oil; the one she used for her skin. I don't want to know how he knew it was there or why.

What I do focus on is the fact he was making his way over to me. One of his hands pushes down on my back, and my eyes dart to the items he drops on the table: coconut oil and condoms. His hand reaches close to face, and grabs one of the condoms. The sound of it ripping is followed by his hand reappearing. I watched as he pumps coconut oil into his hand. I swallow when his hand disappears, and he tenses behind me.

"Brace yourself, Sweet Gabriel," he says from behind me. "I'm not going to prep you, I think you're ready after coming. I'm going to take you, fast and hard."

I gulp.

He presses against me, and my mouth goes dry. He is hard, harder even. He is big, and I try to think of a reason I'd want to say no. Will I stop this? The more I think about it, the more the answer is clear. I won't stop this. Why? Because I want this just as much as he does.

His fingers trail up my back, and touch the area my mark was. It hurts a little from when he bit me earlier. "I know we shouldn't," he says in a whisper. "I know that, but I've never wanted something so badly. You're so fucking beautiful, and watching you come was the highlight of my fucking year."

"I don't want to think right now," I say. "I don't want to think about what we should be doing, or what we shouldn't do." Tears start to well in my eyes, but I ignore them. "I just want to focus on us, right here, right now."

"Fuck," he says. "If this isn't okay, I need you to tell me right now because if we go any further… I won't be able to stop, Gabe, even if you beg me."

TELL ME

Gabe

His fingers hesitate on my neck, and I know he is thinking of her. Not a day goes by that I don't think about her. I know we shouldn't do this, and I know if I said no this would all stop. I close my eyes, as the word forms in my throat, but I swallow it down. I know what I want.

"That's the problem, Odis. I don't want you to stop. This is more than fucking okay. I want you to take me right now. If I beg you to stop, keep fucking going." He groans at my words, and his fingers press against my mouth demanding access. I open my mouth wide, and they make their way in roughly. When they hit the back of my throat, I fight the urge to gag.

I want this.

I want you.

I want you to ruin me for anyone else.

I need it so fucking bad.

"Suck it."

I run my tongue along his fingers and close my mouth as much as I can to follow his command. I am at his mercy, and I revel in it. I want to do what he says I want to know he is happy. I want to see him smile when I do what he wants.

"That's it. You want this, don't you?" Odis asks.

"Yes," I breathe, and his fingers move deeper. I want it so fucking much.

"Be good for me," he growls. His other hand slides down my back, and I tense. He pulls open my cheeks, and I feel exposed, knowing he is staring down at me. "I'm going to make you feel it, Sweet Gabriel. You're going to take every inch of me inside you. I'm going to fuck you so hard, you won't so much as look at another man. Every time you ache tomorrow, you'll think of me."

Oh, yes. I love hearing the possessiveness in his voice. Knowing he wants and desires me does things to me. His hips press against me, and I squeeze my face against the hard surface of the table.

"Fuck, I'm so ready to be inside you," Odis murmurs. The saliva pools in my mouth, and I try to swallow with his fingers lodged deep. "You want this so much, you'll let me do anything I want to you." It isn't a question, but I nod my head anyway.

"Do you want me to fuck you, Gabe?" He asks. I moan, as I feel his tip at my entrance. "Tell me."

"I want you to fuck me, Od-"

Before I can finish my sentence, he shoves his cock deep inside me, making me cry out. His fingers go deeper, and I still at the intrusion. I scream against his fingers. He is thick, and I feel every inch of him that has thrust into me. It hurts, but it feels so fucking good at the same time. Pleasure erupts in my body, and I am coming.

Fuck, fuck, fuck.

"Fuck, you're tight," Odis groans.

Well, it's been a while.

"Wait… did you just come?" Odis growl from behind me.

"I did, I'm sorry, it's been a long time," I murmur, as embarrassment warms my cheeks.

"I didn't say you can come," Odis says. "But I like knowing you came with half of my cock." He is hard and thick inside of me. I pant, as I try to get used to his length, his girth, his hardness, but he doesn't give me a chance. He pushes deeper, and I groan, as he buries himself in me until I feel his hips against my cheeks. He is so deep; I shut my eyes, and my mouth goes slack.

"Look at how your needy little ass took me so fucking well. You were fucking made for me, weren't you, Sweet Gabriel?" He asks, as he pulls out and slams inside me again. My body has no choice, but to stretch for him. He pulls his fingers from my mouth, and places a hand on both of my shoulders.

I cry ou,t as the pain melts into sweet, torturous pleasure. "Yes," I say, my voice coming out breathy.

"Yes, what?" He asks, as he pulls out and thrusts into me again. His grip on my shoulders tighten, as he uses them for leverage. He pulls out and slams into me to the hilt. I cry out, as pleasure changes my groans to moans. His strokes are hard, brutal, and unforgiving. His fingers dig into my shoulders as he fucks me.

"Yes, I was made for you," I moan, as he fills me up over and over again.

The sounds that come out of Odis are more animalistic than human, and I don't think I could come again, but the pleasure is building. My balls are tightening, and my abs are flexing, as I take everything Odis has to give me. He pounds into me, and I feel every thrust in my stomach. I am delirious with pleasure, as he pulls out and thrusts into me hard and fast.

"Odis, oh Goddess, I'm-" I moan and tighten around him.

He fucks me so hard, I don't know where he ends, and where I begin. He drives me closer and closer to my climax. He plunges into me, thrust after thrust, and as his balls slap against me, I buckle and break.

"Oh, Sweet Gabriel, come for me," Odis groans. "Come for me."

"Oh fuck, oh fuck, Odis, yes" I moan.

He thrusts into me, and I come. I come until I am empty and my balls hurt. I come so hard it wrecks me, but he doesn't stop. He pulls out to the tip, and thrusts home, harder, faster, and I can feel him expanding. Odis comes with my name on his lips, and happiness blooms in my chest. He fucks me through his orgasm, and thrusts into me one more time before he collapses.

PLEASE

Gabe

The pleasure is toe-curling. I grip the table, and his hands steady me before he takes a step back. As I look back at him, I flinch as he pulls out of me slowly, inch by inch. He pulls the condom off, and throws it in the trash. I'm ready for a nap. I push myself up with shaky hands, and Odis reaches out to help me.

I don't think about what this could mean, and I don't wonder what comes next. I start for the bed when strong hands gripped my waist, and he turns me to face him. I'm swept up into his arms. He crashes his mouth to mine, and I kiss him back with everything left in me. Instead of releasing me, he sets me on the table.

"Odis, what are you doing?" I ask. I've never been picked up before, and I am not used to the feel of my feet dangling.

"Wrap your legs around me," Odis growls against my lips.

"What? You can't carry me, Beta," I laugh. He looks down at me, clearly amused.

"I don't like having to repeat myself, Gabriel."

I almost say 'Yes, sir,' but the stubbornness in me has me biting down on my lips to stop the words from escaping. I wrap my arms around his shoulders, and my legs around his waist. If he's about to do what I think he is, I'm going to need to hold on tight. My jaw drops, and my brows almost fly off my forehead, when I feel his hard cock bounce against my cheeks. Oh, I think the fuck not. I can't take him again; I'm tired and sore.

I'm lifted into the air, and the words die in my throat. Never in my life have I ever been seen as light, and never has a man picked me up like I was nothing. I mean in fights, yes, but never in the bedroom, but Goddess am I impressed. His strong chest against mine, the firm set of his muscles against mine. My eyes dropped to his lips before meeting his gaze. I stare into his eyes as he slowly carries me to the bed.

"Listening isn't so hard, is it?" Odis taunts.

"I feel something hard, and I don't understand how you're still hard," I grumble.

"I'm hard because we're not done yet," Odis says, as he lays me on the bed. I relax into the bed, and he's on his knees above me. "There are so many things I want to do to you, Sweet Gabriel."

"I think we've done enough today, don't you?" I squeak.

Odis ignores me but his eyes trail down my body. My body is already betraying me, hardening as I watch him watch me. I follow his gaze, my legs are on both sides of his hips, my cock stands between us, and his hands squeeze my thighs.

His cock is slick and glistening. He tears a condom open, and I watch in disbelief, as he pinches the top and slides it over his length. He leans down and grips his hard length and presses his tip against my ass.

Oh shit. This is really happening again.

I said I was done, and I hate how my body trembles in anticipation.

Traitor.

"My Sweet, Gabriel," he murmurs. The heat in his words causes a shiver to run down my back. He leans down, his tongue darts out, and glides slowly up my neck. His arms slide under my arms and up behind me, and his fingers grip my shoulders. My cock is squeezed between us giving me the friction I need.

This time he doesn't slam into me, his tip breeches me. He's hard, and thick, and everything I could ever want. He pushes a few inches into me, and I groan at his girth. He is unbearably huge, and I can't believe I am taking him again. I can't move; I hold still while his fingers pierce flesh.

"Damn it, Odis."

He slides a few more inches into me, and I am panting. He is so big, and I am so full. I just had him, but as he fills me,I feel like he is ripping me open. His mouth wraps around my neck and he sucks roughly before biting into my sensitive area.

Oh, fuck.

Oh fuck.

"Such a good boy," Odis breathes against my neck. I whimper at his words, praise kink unlocked. "You are being so good for me, Gabriel. You're so tight around my cock."

I groan, as he slides the rest of the way in. He spears through me, and I curl into him. I am so full that I try to move left and right. I can't. He is so deep that I can feel him in my stomach. It is too much, he is too much.

"Please," I beg. "Please, I can't, Odis, it's too much," I

whimper. I turned my head to the left, and shut my eyes.

"Open your eyes while I take you," Odis growls.

I open my eyes and turn to face him. I look up at him even though all I want to do is thrash around wildly, like a fish out of water. He must see the desperation in my eyes. "I'll make you feel good in a second, Sweet Gabriel. You want that, don't you?" He asks.

I nod. Odis stares down at me, his eyes darkening as he watches my every move. Being face-to-face with him, being chest to chest, makes this feel like more. A need to make this moment last longer fills me and threatens to explode.

He pulled out a few thick, hard, inches before thrusting into me. I cry out, as he pulls out slowly. I shiver violently, and I shove my hips up, as he thrusts hard into me. My arms wrap around him, and my fingers dig into his back, as he pulls out to the tip. My thighs quiver by his side, and he thrusts into me slowly.

SELFISH

Gabe

"Fuck, your ass feels warm and tight around my cock," he says. I moan, and time disappears, as he fucks me slow and hard. The feeling of his cock claiming me, combined with the pressure of his flesh against my cock feels so fucking good.

"Please, Odis," I beg. "Oh, Goddess, please," I moan.

"I love hearing my name coming from your mouth. What do you want, Sweet, sweet Gabriel?"

"Please," I cry.

"Tell me what you want," Odis says, as he continues his slow torment. *I won't be able to stop even if you beg me.* His words echo in my head. I won't beg him to stop. I'll do the opposite.

"Fuck me, fuck me hard and fast. Please," I groan as he pulls out, and slowly pushes into me. Every slow thrust feels like the first time he pushed into me; opening, stretching, filling. He pulls out of me, and presses back in to the balls. He does this again, and again, while keeping that painfully slow pace.

"I like seeing you like this," Odis murmurs, his breathing ragged, as he forces himself to pull out and pushes in slowly. "Needy, aching, pleading looks good on you." I moan, as he pulls out and slams into me.

He, and time, stand still as he stares down at me. My chest rises with each breath I take. Odis starts moving again, but this time he gives me what I want. The only thing left is him above me. His fingers grip my skin painfully, and he pulls out and slams into me over, and over again. His balls slap against my cheeks, and it only adds to my pleasure. Odis's muscles flex around me, and his cock thickens.

Oh, Goddess, I can't.

"Odis!" I cry, as he slams into me. Each thrust harder than the last. "Oh fuuuck, I'm coming, I'm coming." I come hard and fast for him. He grunts above me, as I squeeze around him; my come spurts out and coats our flesh.

"Yes, fuck, like that, just like that" Odis groans. His thrusts become faster, his cock thickens and his grip tightens. He pumps into me hard and fast, as he empties himself into me. We're a panting jumbled mess of arms and slick bodies.

He leans down and kisses me. It's warm, and soft, and everything I didn't know I needed. Silence settles over us for a moment, as we come down from the high of our orgasms. My body goes slack, and I relax against the bed.

My eyes flutter, and I know if we stay like this, I'm going to knock out. Odis moves first, and my eyes follow him, as he pulls up off of me. I just had sex with - okay no. Odis fucked me, but still. Odis and I just had mind-blowing sex, and I am sure what to say. The bed dips, as he gets off the bed, and I watch as he disappears into the bathroom.

I rest my eyes, and am about to fall asleep, when something warm and wet presses against my ass. My eyes fly open and land on Odis between my legs. Emotion threaten to strangle me, as I realize he is cleaning me up. I want to cry at the tender way he takes care of me. I don't want to think about the last time I'd cared for someone, or had been cared for by someone. I want just a few more moments of this peace, this calm, that Odis gives me. He sits at the edge of the bed, and I make my way over to him. I lean my head against his back.

"I'm sorry," Odis speaks first. "I don't know what came over me. I brought you food this morning because I knew you'd need energy after how drunk you were last night. I was only bringing you food. When Leo came out of your room, the thought of you two together hurt more than it should have."

I listen to his heartbeat as he talks. This is the first time we are having a conversation about the sexual tension, the misunderstanding. We are communicating and it feels good. I want to hear what he is thinking, and I want to know how he feels.

"When I left with the bag of bagels in hand, I think something snapped. Next thing I know, I'm charging into your room, trying to lay claim to you," Odis says.

"Do you regret it?" I ask.

Odis didn't respond.

"You don't have to worry about Leo. We're partners. Friends, even."

"See, that's the thing though. I'm not yours, and you aren't mine. You shouldn't have to explain your relationship to him."

I lift my head from his back, as confusion seeps into me.

"What are you trying to say? I was explaining why you had no reason to apologize for being angry. I know I'm not yours, but... am I nothing to you?" I whisper.

"I'm saying this shouldn't have happened," Odis says firmly. "I'm Beta, and the pack is my responsibility."

"What does the pack have to do with us? Are you pushing me away because of the pack?" I ask.

Odis sighs, and I can hear the faint sound of what remained of my heart cracking. I am not asking for him to be my boyfriend, I am not asking for more, I just... I like being with him. Why can't he just admit that he wants me?

"This is about her, Gabe," Odis says. "I love her, you love her. This? This feels like a betrayal to her."

His words are a slap in the face, and thoughts of her flood my mind, my chest. I can feel the gaping hole in my chest that her death left."It's because of her that this isn't. Our love for her brought us together. This... I feel with you."

"That's selfish," Odis says. He is being cold again, and I don't have to look at him to know his indifferent mask is in place. He gets to his feet, and starts to get dressed. My heart reaches out to him, but I force it back into the gaping hole.

"Can't we be selfish?" I ask, as tears blur my vision. "I've missed her, I've mourned her, and I've hated myself for not being able to help her. She's gone, and she's never coming back!" Odis doesn't look at me; he hasn't since he'd been in me. Instead, he opens the door, and walks out without another word.

LIFE

Adea

We rush back into the room, and his tongue presses against my lips. I moan softly, as I force his pants down. We peel each other's clothes off and kiss fervently. Ethan backs up against the floor-to-ceiling window, and I squeal, as my back presses against the cold glass.

"That's so cold!" I say and push his chest. He is a stone wall, and doesn't budge, but that doesn't stop me. He releases me, but doesn't take a step back. My back is still pressed firmly against the window. Then I feel it: hot skin against my stomach. His hard cock presses against my flesh.

Ethan flips me around, and my peaks harden against the cold glass. He kicks my feet so they are almost touching. I have to stand on the tips of my toes, and I sigh, as his hard tip presses against my wet entrance. He stretches and filled me slowly. He grabs my arms and crosses them behind my back. My mate grips my wrists, as he thrusts home.

A sound between a cry and a moan erupts from my lips. With my legs closed, it feels tighter. He pulls out and thrusts into me hard and fast. Cry after cry falls from my lips, as he buries his cock deep inside me over, and over, again.

"Your pussy squeezing my cock is my favorite thing in the fucking world," Ethan says from behind me. He pulls out of me, and slams his cock back into me. I cry out when he does it again. I am trapped between his hard body and the window.

"Fuck me harder," I demand.

Ethan gives me what I want. He shoves into me brutally. The sounds of my tight pussy clenching around his cock as he pulls out and plunges into me are driving me to the edge. The sound of his skin slapping against mine fills the room, and mixes with my moans.

His pace quickens, as he continues to thrust into me. He fucks me harder than he's ever done before. It is what I need. It is what I want. It is too much. I clench around his cock, and come, as the intensity of my climax rips through me.

"Oh yes, Ethan!" I scream.

He presses deep into me, and grunts, as he erupts inside of me. He releases my hands, and I feel his chest against my back, as he leans against me. I moan, as I feel him empty himself in me.

***

Ethan

"I'm not ready to go back," she whispers.

"I know," I murmur. Goddess do I know. I know it isn't going to be easy for her, but I know she can do it. She is the strongest person I know, and I don't deserve her.

"I've loved the time we've had together the last couple of days," I say. I lift her into my arms and lay her on the bed gently.

She sighs. "If I could, I'd stay inside and roll around in bed with you day after day."

"So would I," I laugh. I get on the bed, on my knees. She watches me with suspicion in her eyes. "We still have the rest of the day; I can make that happen."

It is her turn to laugh, and it is music to my ears. Fuck, do I love this woman. I love everything about her. And now she is mine; I get to keep her forever. I grab her ankles, lift her legs, and place one on each of my shoulders. Her eyes widen, as she looks up at me.

"Ethan," she breathes. "I need to clean myself up, I'm all gross."

"You're not gross," I say. "I'll take care of you after, my queen, I want to fuck you senseless, and roll around in bed."

She smiles as she stares at me; her eyes darken, and I fold her in half. I thrust inside her, and she cries out in pleasure. "I like knowing you're full of my cum." I like feeling it seep out of her. This position lets me take her deeper, and the way she clenches around me has me close to coming right now. The way she takes me is damn near magical.

I slide in and out of her, fucking her as she pants and moans. She is wet and tight, and I fuck her harder.

"Oh, fuck, Ethan," she whimpers. "Ethan, I'm-I'm coming, oh Goddess." She squeezes her thighs together before she comes on my cock. She grips me harder, and I groan at the feeling of her wrapped tightly around me.

I slide my hands down and grip her thighs. She cries out, as I fuck her through her orgasm. My hands slide down further and grip her hips. She cries out, as I drive into her. She is squeezing and pulling my cock. I pound her tight little pussy and she screams out beneath me.

"Yes!" she cries out.

"Who does this pussy belong to?" I growl, as I slam into her. I take her hard and fast; my orgasm is close.

"You, Ethan, it belongs to you," she whimpers. She doesn't even hesitate, and I give it to her harder. She cries out louder, and I grunt as I spill inside of her again.

"Fuck," I groan.

I drop her legs and pulled out. I spend a few minutes holding her until I get out of bed. She needs some aftercare, and I am going to take care of her. After I clean myself, I am back with a couple of warm towels in hand. I spread her legs, and gently wash her. I wipe her body with the other.

I pull her into my arms, my heartbeat against her cheek, and her hair spills across my chest. I lean down and press a kiss to her neck, over her mark. Goosebumps erupt across her skin, and I savor the feeling of having her in my arms.

"I love doing life with you."

"I love you, Ethan," she murmurs as she snuggles closer.

"I love you, too."

INSECT

Shane

The moon sits high in the sky, and I wonder if the Moon Goddess is watching me. Would she smile favorably on me tonight? Does she enjoy it when we suffer? I am not sure if I was blessed or cursed growing up. I am tired of caring; I won't let her, or anyone else, decide how my life will go. From now on, I will take what I want and choose for myself what happens in my life.

I walk through the crowd of men I now call my soldiers. I'd run into a few rogues when I was exiled. I clench my fists by my side as the memory of that day flashes through my mind: my mother's face, Mavy crying, the loss of connection to my pack. I was stripped of my title and thrown out with nothing.

It was after I ripped one of their men to shreds and the others bowed to me that I got the idea to start all this. The two men joined me, and we began hunting rogues. Whenever we found one, they either joined us or died. I needed soldiers, I needed the strength numbers would give me.

A voice fills my ears as I inspect my soldiers. This is the Deltas job, but I built this myself and I want to make sure we are ready. Tonight will be the night, and there is no room for mistakes or failure. Someone is talking, spouting poison for the others to hear. I smirk as I hear the words of an insect. I hate insects. I hate disobedience. I hate being undermined, but I loved finding insects. I love squashing them.

"Why are we starting a war? We're a pack of our own, aren't we? If this doesn't go well, many of us will die," the insect says.

His words bring a smile to my lips. I turn to find one of the Deltas Liam chose to help keep the rogues in line. A line of men are gearing up beside the dumb ass. I love when someone tries to use their brain, and steps out of line. It's so much fun putting them back in their place.

I'm slow and controlled as I walk over to them. I don't want them to sense my anger and tip him off. I roll my head and crack my neck as I get closer to the Delta. He's unaware of the pain I'm about to give him. He's still running his mouth and I can't wait to break it.

"I don't understand why we have to ..."

His words are cut off, as I grip his face with my hand. His eyes widen with fear as my fingers wrap around his head. Blood trickles down his face, as my claws dig deep. He starts to plead, but my hand muffles his mouth. I punch him in the stomach, and his body tries to double over. I hold him still, as I land blow after blow to him. He tries to protect his body with his arms, and bones crack as my knuckles connect with ribs.

He makes a gurgling sound, but I won't show any mercy. Mercy is for the weak, and I will not appear weak. His body falls limp, and I assume he is knocked out from the pain. I throw him to the ground, and his body flies like a rag doll. I walk over to his body, and wipe the spittle on my hand off on his shirt. Disgusting. Traitors are insects, and I will trample on every one of them.

"You don't have to follow my orders, if you don't want to," I say with fake kindness. The soldiers are quiet; all eyes are on me. Good. I've got their attention. "You don't have to understand your orders either," I say with a smile. I press my boot into the back of the insect's head. I cock my head to the side, as I look up at the soldiers around me.

"If you want to stay, instead of fight, tell me now."

I'm met with silence. No one speaks; no one so much as breathes. No one runs to help him, no one defends him. Good. This pleases me. This is the way it should be. My word is law, and they should follow it without thought.

My eyes trail along the line of the boys and men before me. I drop the fake pretenses, my smile disappearing, my eyes threatening, as I hold eye contact before they drop their eyes. I've made myself very clear, and now they all understood.

"Good."

I dig my boot deeper into the back of the asshole's head. "You don't have to understand why you're doing what you're doing. You are soldiers. You don't have to think, you just have to do. There is no need for you to understand my orders. That isn't your job." My eyes trail over my soldiers, as I search for a hint of defiance. "I'm Alpha. I'm king, and you are not. I give the orders. Do as I say quietly, and we won't have issues like this," I say and nod down to the insect.

"Are we clear?" I ask.

"Yes, Alpha!" My soldiers answer.

"Good."

"Next time you think about questioning me, and my authority, first ask yourself if you'd like to live another day. Maybe then, you'll remember your words have consequences; the wrong words are punished."

The insect is squashed, and I remove my foot from his head. Everyone is here; everyone is ready. The taste of The Moon Goddesses' favor is in the air, and I know I will be victorious. The soldiers gather behind me, and Maximus mentally steps forward.

"You have orders to win at any and all cost. The battle will be bloody, but the reward will be worth it. When we've won, I will reclaim my title and my people. Tonight, the Moon Goddess smiles down on us." Cheers and growls filled the night air. "Let's go home."

IT ISN'T YOURS

Odis

As soon as my pants are off, I shift. If I'd stayed any longer, I wouldn't have been able to leave. There was no other choice, but to tell him it was a mistake. My heart throbs in my chest, but I only ran faster. As if I could run fast enough to leave the pain behind.

I'd left without looking at him. I couldn't bring myself to look at his face. I didn't trust what I would do. I don't know what I'd do if I saw the pain I knew I'd put there. I am a coward and I know it.

I don't have the courage to be selfish. If I'd looked him in the eye, I would have crumbled. I would have caved. I am not capable of turning my back on her. I don't have it in me. I just can't. One moment of weakness, and I've done something unforgivable. Being with Gabriel? I can't mentally let myself go back there, if I do, I'll turn around.

Being with Gabriel?

We haven't been that happy since Liv.

Can we not be happy?

I didn't see anything wrong with being with him.

Are we not allowed to hold onto him?

It's not too late to turn back.

My wolf doesn't see it as a betrayal to her or her memory. Love is love; that's what he said. He is right though: for a moment, I was happy with Gabriel. So happy, and I haven't been that happy in a long time.

No, we can't be happy. We don't deserve it after what we've done. It doesn't matter if it's been years since it happened. We did it, we dug our grave, and we're lying in it. We don't get to jump out just because we think we've spent enough time in it.

Our mistake is a life sentence. Forever. We had everything once, and because of one night, we lost it all. We don't get to reach out and grab onto him. It is too late; this shouldn't have happened in the first place.

The piercing wind howls and whips against my cheek. I search the sky for answers, but find none. Instead, the moon taunts me. Tall trees rise up and block my view, as the hooting of an owl announces the arrival to the woods. My ears pick up the crunch of leaves and the snapping of twigs, as my wolf's powerful paws carry me deeper.

The same woods she was taken from.

My wolf shakes his powerful head, and he begs me not to think of that night, or of any night after. I try to shake her from our thoughts. She is replaced with images of Gabe beneath me. If it isn't her, it's him. My stomach is in my throat.

I took what I wanted from him, and left him shattered in an

empty bed. He doesn't deserve the way I treated him. My throat constricts, and my chest tightens with guilt. There had only ever been her. When had he wriggled his way in? When did it start?

Is the guilt because of her or him?

Blonde hair, long enough to make my fingers twitch with the need to run through them. A scar that hurt me in a way I'm not ready to admit. His terrible voice, as it manages to not hit a single note when he sings. The cute way he tried to run from me when he thought I was a murderer.

I like him. I like him a lot.

I retreat into the deepest parts of my mind in hopes of a break. Instead, I'm dragged from the darkness and thrown into the light. The smile on my face feels wrong, as a teenage Olivia stares up at me. Her jaw is clenched, and the look in her eye is off. I'm worried about what she's going to say. Deep down, teenage me knows it isn't going to be good.

"I'm pregnant."

I stare at her, as my brain connects meaning to the words. I blink once, twice. She's pregnant. The fear of what I thought she was going to say is extinguished and happiness blooms in my chest. I feel the excitement I felt that day. I was ecstatic. The thought of marking her and starting a family together was something I hadn't even dared hoped to dream of.

"I don't understand, Liv. Why the long face? This is good news. Did you think I'd be mad?" I laugh. "This makes me happier than you could ever know. I won't leave you. I promised, remember?" I take a step close to her, fully intending to pull her into my arms.

She takes a step back from me, and I falter. Her shoulders

shake, as she continues to stare at me with that same look in her eye. My hands drop to my side and I wait for her to come to me. I won't touch her if she doesn't want me to. I'm not him.

"It isn't yours, O."

The words are a sledgehammer to the chest. I can't breathe; the pain lights a fire in my chest, and it threatens to consume me. I am not expecting that at all ,and thoughts of what he'd done to her are at the forefront of my mind. I want to hide my thoughts from her, but she knows me better than I know myself. I can't hide anything from her.

The only girl I've ever loved stares up at me. Her tears fill to the brim, and curse me for not protecting her, as mascara-stained cheeks lead to the slight quiver in her chin. I want to shake the truth from her.

I want to tell her this doesn't change anything. I want to kill him all over again for taking this from me. The absolute truth is reflected in her eyes, and I'm at a loss for words because this is the truth.

DESPERATE

Odis

A teary-eyed Olivia turns into a swinging door. I hold a bag of hot food, and a heavily pregnant Olivia sits on the couch, as she stares blankly out of the window. She'd been craving lobster, but doesn't bounce up and down like she normally does. She's spiraling, and I can see it.

"I don't want it, O. I don't want it."

"You don't have to eat the lobster if you don't want to. I'm sorry I wasn't faster, I ran as fast as I could."

"I don't want the baby."

Her words steal the breath from my lungs. If I hadn't been holding the bag tight, it would have dropped on the floor. I set the bag on the table and walk over to her. I sit behind her on the couch and pull her into my arms. She doesn't look at me, and I don't speak until I trust myself to.

"You don't mean that, Liv," I whisper. My hands slide around her belly, and I stare at her side profile.

"That's the thing though," Olivia murmurs. She slowly turns her head until gray eyes lock me in their gaze. "I do mean it. I don't want it, I don't even want it in me. I don't feel anything for it. How can I be a mother to it? I don't want to have this child. Maybe the Moon Goddess is punishing me, but I can't do this."

I nuzzle into her neck, and my hands tremble on her belly. I want to make it better, want to make her better. The words wouldn't form. I can't fix her, I can't fix this. Silent tears slide down my cheeks as I hold her.

"I'll take care of it, Liv."

I'm desperate as my surroundings change and she vanishes into a puff of smoke. Beeping fills the room, and I'm filled with nerves. A bundle of pink chunkiness is placed into my arms. Blonde hair, fat cheeks, a wrinkled forehead, and a cute little nose. I'm overwhelmed with a feeling I can't place. I wasn't sure how I was going to feel when she gave birth to a child that wasn't mine. We'd argued about marking each other, and being chosen mates over the last month. She doesn't want to, and it breaks me every time she says it. Life at home has been rocky, but I want her. I want us.

"His name is Paul," she says weakly.

My vision blurs, as I stare down at the baby in my hands. She named him after my father. I am not ready for the warmth that fills my chest, and the tears that flow. Tears slide and drip onto the baby. I quickly wipe away the tears, and pull him close to my face. It doesn't matter if we don't share any blood.

A boy.

He is perfect.

He is mine.

Darkness descends again, but this time there is a star nightlight in the corner. Paul whimpers against my chest as I hold him. He's a toddler; his hair is longer, and his cheeks are chubbier.

I'm exhausted from a day of work, and I'm dozing off. Liv is in the other room; she doesn't come in here. She doesn't hold him. I rock back and forth, back and forth, back and forth. I'm hypnotized by the motion, and I start to sing the song, You Are My Sunshine.

Everything changes again. The sun is coming up, and I'm holding Paul in one hand. He is fussy this morning, but I get him dressed and ready for daycare. He's calm now that I'm carrying him, but it's a struggle getting out the door.

"Liv, can you hold him for a second?" I ask as she steps out of the bathroom. She looks at me and her eyes drop to Paul. There is no spark, no emotion, as she stares at him.

"No."

"Please, Liv? I just need to get a few things in a bag."

She shakes her head.

"I don't want to be around him, O. When was the last time I held him? I don't even want to see him. I can't, I just can't." Pain and sadness fill my chest. I'm tired, and I need her. It's exhausting doing this on my own.

I need a break.

The noise in the bar is loud and the world is spinning. Liv presses into me, and pulls me by the tie. I'm on my feet, and struggling to stay upright, as I follow her into the bathroom. We have a quickie in the bathroom. She pulls up her skirt and brushes her dirty blonde hair.

Wait.

Blonde hair?

I squint through the blur of the world spinning faster and faster. She turns around and looks down at me.

"Thanks, doll," she says before she opens the door and saunters out.

No, no, no.

I'm home and Olivia sits across from me at the dining table. Her eyes are closed and she's crying into her hands.

"I didn't want to lie to you. I'm sorry, it's all my fault."

"It is," she cries. "I can't be with you knowing you've been with someone else. I'm done. We're over."

"I love you," I cry. The world is ending, I'm losing her. I've lost her. "I don't deserve to beg you to stay. I have no right to try and hold onto you. I-I'll talk to Ethan about you getting your own place. I'll keep my promise, Liv. I'll always be here for you." I'm helpless as she cries uncontrollably, her shoulders shaking violently, as the pain of my actions tunnels through her.

I'm ripped to the present as we come to a stop at the packhouse. I shift back into my human form, and put on the sweats I'd discarded by the door. The elevator dings, and as I walk down the hall, I can't help but glance at Gabe's. Shaking my head, I walk on and opened my door.

Paul is curled up on the couch. His head rests on a cushion, his hair frames his face, and his breathing is shallow. He's fallen asleep waiting for me. Seeing him is my undoing. I fall to my knees, and close my eyes as the tears fall.

GAMMA

Adea

The doors close behind us. My nerves are starting to get to me, but Ethan closes in on me. Giggles erupt from me, as he peppers me with kisses. He lifts his head, and levels me with a look that almost has my underwear dropping. I stand on the tips of my toes and kiss him.

I love this man.

I am still trapped in his arms, and the elevator hasn't moved. I nod towards the buttons, and he smiles as he presses the button for the first floor. Finally, we are off. The elevator comes to a stop. He releases me from his hold, but not before he steals another kiss.

The doors open, and I blush when I see some of the pack members. Heads turn as we walk through the lobby. I feel like I am taking a long walk of shame, but I have nothing to be ashamed of.

We are officially Alpha and Luna. I hold my head high and smile at the pack members. I can't screw this up, can I? Murmured greetings pass us by, as we walk towards the dining room. I fight hard not to spiral into my concerns, but I can't help tensing. Sensing my nerves, Ethan grabs my hand, and brings it to his lips.

You have nothing to worry about.

He smiles at me, and his voice in my head soothes me. I nod. He is right; I know he is. Ethan and I had talked this morning. There is a combination of things that are making me nervous.

We're just getting something to eat, My Queen. Relax.

I nod. We're just getting breakfast, it's nothing to stress over. Today is my first official day as Luna. I need to show a strong front even if I am having an anxiety attack on the inside.

The door to the kitchen and dining room area comes into view. Before we get any closer, Ethan steps closer, his arm snaking around my waist in casual possessiveness. His finger pulls my chin up, and our eyes met.

"You good?" He asks.

"Yes, My King," I breathe.

He releases my chin, but keeps his arm around me. "If we didn't have important things to do today, I'd drag you back upstairs and stay in bed with you all day," Ethan says quietly. "I miss you already."

My heart. "That would be amazing," I say. "You're being corny," I tease, "but I miss you already too."

Ethan smiles wide for me. "I'm corny for you."

I laugh out loud. "You're being too much! I don't know what to do with you."

My mate presses a kiss to my neck, and we continue for the door. He opens it wide for me, and I step in first. The workers in the kitchen greet us on our way through. There are a few people at the table.

As we sit at the table, Odis wipes his mouth, and bows his head slightly. "Good morning, Luna. Morning, Alpha." Darci bows and returns to her conversation with the Deltas.

"Morning Beta, how was your weekend?" I ask.

Beta Odis' eyes darken for a second, and I wonder what brought that on. The look is gone as soon as it appears, and is replaced by a smile. "It was pleasant. I had a relaxing weekend."

A plate of buttery goodness is placed in front of us. Jelly toast, scrambled eggs, and breakfast sausages. I thank the worker before she heads back to the kitchen, and I pick up my fork and spear one of the sausages before biting into it.

"Would you like the position of Gamma?" Ethan asks. I stop chewing, and turn to look at Darci. Her conversation with the Deltas stops, and she looks at Ethan.

"Yes, Alpha," Darci says. "I would."

"I've been watching you since the day you arrived here. From what I've seen, you are more than capable of the position. I didn't think I would be able to find someone who could fill those shoes, but I have faith that you can."

Darci swallows hard, and she hesitates for a second before speaking. "Thank you for your trust, Alpha. I won't let you down." I can't help but smile; the imbalance left with Olivia's absence is now fixed.

"Welcome to the team, Gamma," Odis says, his shoulders tense, but the look on his face says he means it. We are all a little tense when it comes to anything that is a reminder of Olivia.

"Thanks, Beta," Darci says. Her smile is radiating. It is the first time I've seen her smile like this.

"I look forward to working with you," I say.

"Thank you, Luna. I look forward to getting to know you better."

"I've got a meeting with Odis after. Please join us, so we can go over your responsibilities and the territories you will be overseeing," Ethan says to her.

"Yes, Alpha."

"We haven't seen any rogues for a few days," Odis says. "It's oddly quiet."

"Let's talk about it in my office."

Odis nods. It's a little awkward, and I wish Gabe was here to lighten the mood. Darci goes back to talking to the Deltas and Odis returns to eating. If I didn't have the training to go to, I would go to the meeting. I make a mental note to ask Ethan to fill me in.

The door swings open, and I turn to find Gabe and Leo walking in. I can't hide the smirk from my face, as I wonder how they came together. Did they meet up beforehand, or were they together all night? Korra's interest is piqued too, and she's at the forefront of my mind.

I'm about to ask him how the two of them coming to breakfast together turned out when I see Gabe's eyes slide over Odis. His gaze lingers on the back of his head before he makes his way over.

Interesting.

"Why, good morning, Gabe. You're late to breakfast; you almost missed it."

BESTIE

Adea

My best friend gives me his signature crooked smile. Before Ethan and Odis have a chance to get up, Leo passes Gabe and drops down opposite me with a taunting grin. I watch his facial features, as he bows his head slightly in greeting. I still am not sure how I feel about him. We will have to get along, but I am still suspicious. Gabe comes to a stop by Ethan's chair.

"Good morning, Alpha," Gabe says in greeting. Ethan gets to his feet, leans down, and kisses me goodbye before facing Gabe.

"Morning, Gabe."

"Leaving so soon?" Gabe asks.

"Yes, I'd stay longer, but work's calling," Ethan says.

"I was wondering if it was me," Gabe teases.

"No," Ethan says, his lips twitching with amusement, "Have to get back to work sooner, or later."

"I hear that," Gabe says.

"I'll see you later," Ethan says to me. He nods to Odis before heading out the door.

Leo's eyes roam over to the kitchen. When his gaze locks on one of the workers in the kitchen, her back straightens, and she grabs a couple of plates. She rushes over with them in hand, and places the food in front of him.

"I think you're forgetting my partner," Leo says. Her eyes widen, and she nods before heading back to the kitchen. A few minutes later she returns and places Gabe's food in front of him.

"Thank you!" Gabe says. He flashes her a smile before she disappears. "Good morning, Luna," Gabe says, as he makes his way to the vacant seat at my side. He gives me a small bow before dropping into the chair. I slap his arm, and he grabs it like I've tried to rip it off. "Ouch!"

"Oh, you're fine. Good morning, Gabe, and don't call me Luna. It's weird," I laugh. Now that we are closer, I notice the dark bags under his eyes. His eyes are a little red. I whistle. "You look like you didn't get a wink of sleep."

"You don't look like you did either," Gabe teases. His eyebrows bounce up and down impressively high on his forehead. I bark a laugh, as his joke catches me off guard. I can't help, but be happy when Gabe is around. Leo is shoveling food into his mouth. He looks up. I don't look away fast enough, and he catches me staring.

"Welcome back to the land of the living," Gabe whispers in my ear. My chest tightens, and I fight the smile that wants to spread across my face. I'm not one to talk about my sexual experiences, but I am tempted to swap stories, if I can figure out who Gabe is seeing. I have a feeling it is Leo by the way he looks at Gabe.

My eyes dart to Odis. I am not counting my Beta out just yet, though. The fact that he hasn't looked at Gabe hasn't gone unnoticed. I'm not totally out of the loop. Gabe hasn't greeted Odis, and I haven't missed that bit, either. Gabe has some explaining to do.

"I'll tell you mine, if you tell me yours," I tease. I watch Odis for a reaction, and when he tenses, my suspicions are confirmed.

Gabe gasps, and his hand flies to his mouth. "I've never seen you so interested in my nightly activities. Actually, if I recall," he says dramatically, "You used to close your ears when I tried to tell you about the fun I've had." He crosses his arms and pouts at me. "Also, I don't know what you mean."

"Mm-hmm," I say. I don't believe that for a second. "And I wouldn't say I'm interested in your nightlife, Gabe. I'm interested in you, and what's going on in your life. So if you need to talk to me about the fun you have at night… I'm listening."

"We didn't have any fun last night," Leo says through a mouthful of food. Gabe rolls his eyes, and I muffle a giggle.

"You aren't the only guy with muscles around here," Gabe says. "And I never said I was sleeping around." Gabe grows quiet, and I want to hug him. Before I can lean in, a big smile spreads across his face. "But maybe it's time I started getting out there." I can almost visibly see Leo's wolf ears perk up in interest, his eyes focus on Gabe, a smile on his mouth.

I run my fingers down my braid where it hangs by my chin, as I stare at my best friend knowingly. I doubt he meant it, but the weight on my shoulders lifts slightly. I know better than to expect him to be over Olivia. I am hopeful that he will find someone that can make him happy. I pray to the Goddess for a chosen mate that can help heal the hole Liv left with her death. The sound of metal against the table brings my attention to Leo.

"So..." Leo throws his arm around Gabe, and leans into him. Gabe doesn't try to get out from under Leo, despite the death glare I feel coming from Odis. "You're saying I have a chance?" Gabe doesn't take it this time, he grabs his arm and tosses it aside.

"I'm saying get in line," Gabe says sensually. My jaw drops at the sight of my bestie flirting. It has been so long since I've seen this side of him. I am shocked, but glad to see him playing around.

"Okay, bestie," I tease. "I see you." I lean back, and gave him a clap off, nodding while smiling at him.

"Well, you know," Gabe says, continuing with the joke.

Odis shoves to his feet with a force that pushes the table back. I get a glance of his face before he turns his back on us. I am expecting jealousy, maybe a little anger, but what I see is pain. I feel a twinge of guilt, as he slightly nods my way.

"Have a good day, Luna." Odis doesn't even turn to look back to look at me. Now that he is standing, my eyes drag down his body. His suit is ruffled and he seems... defeated.

"You too," I say as he headed for the door.

"How long has it been?" Leo's voice brings me back to the table. My best friend is watching Odis; his eyes follow him as he passes the kitchen and disappears. Leo is staring at Gabe, and he clears his throat.

"What?" Gabe asks. He looks confused, as he stares at Leo.

"Are you guys ready for training?" Leo asks. He chooses not to repeat himself ,and I want to scoff at him.

Chicken.

"I am," Gabe says. He pushes himself to his feet with his plate in hand. He walks over to the kitchen, and I smile as he tries to place his dishes into the sink. The kitchen workers rush and try to take it from him, but he just smiles at them. It reminds me of our days in Half Moon.

"Same. Are you ready to get your ass kicked again?"

Leo growls, and I smile at him, as I grab my dishes and head over to the kitchen. The women look like they've seen a ghost when they see me. I put my dishes on top of Gabe's. My best friend gives me a small smile.

ASS

Adea

Gamma Darci is still eating, as we make our way out of the kitchen. Gabe runs by my side, as Leo chases after us. He catches up to us, as we make it through the lobby. Leo glares at me, as Gabe walks between us.

"We're supposed to be protecting her, not chasing her, Leo," Gabe says.

"We were having a little fun, weren't we, Luna?" Leo asks. He leans his upper body forward and holds eye contact.

"We are having fun, but not only am I stronger than you, but I'm also faster." I stick my tongue out at him as I tease him. Serves the big blockhead right.

I leave them standing there while I open the door. Gabe and Leo follows me, as I head away from the packhouse, and toward the training field. My gaze shifts to Leo, as he gives Gabe not-so-subtle glances when he thinks he isn't looking.

I don't know what happened over the weekend, but from what

I saw at breakfast, something did happen. If it was spicy, Gabe would have told me, wouldn't he? I make a mental note to get to the bottom of it. As soon as I can get him alone.

On the way there, we meet a few others from training. I spy Zoe, the only other girl in Tier 1 with me, as she walks with a couple of guys in Tier 2. Her short ,curly hair bounces as she walks. She holds the guys' full attention until she smiles at me, her dimples flashing. The guys with her greet me and continue on.

A lot has happened in the last week: training, the competition, and the Luna Ceremony. I wonder what everyone thinks, now that they know I am their Luna. I hope it doesn't get in the way of training together. I need the experience of fighting against others.

Life has been a whirlwind of events, and I am thankful I had a weekend alone with Ethan. I am thankful for the break, and now I am ready to focus on getting stronger. My dreams remind me of what is coming if we don't stop Shane. I need to be stronger, if I am going to be able to protect anyone.

The field comes into view as we turn in. We arrive early, but there are already a lot of people here. A group of men are stretching on the field, three men are running laps, and a few are sprawled out on the grass.

Gabe and Leo will be training today, but they are still on guard duty. They will be taking turns sparring; one watching me while the other spars. It feels like they are on babysitting duty, and I can't help feeling like a child. I know the thought is silly, but I can't help thinking it.

"I'm going first," Gabe calls over his shoulder, as he heads towards the group of men stretching. Leo nods, and I watch as my best friend starts doing lunges. I look beside me to find Leo pulling his shirt off and throwing it to the ground. He stretches, and his muscles ripple as he interlocks his fingers behind his head. He smirks at me, and I don't fight the need to roll my eyes.

"Like what you see, Luna?" He asks.

"Nope, not at all."

"Could have fooled me," he says nonchalantly, but I can hear the sarcasm. It is there, clear as day. He pushes his chest forward, and I hear a pop, followed by a groan. "Yeah, that felt good."

His hands drop to his side, as his eyes followed Gabe's movements. I follow his gaze, and recognize a guy from Tier 1. He holds down Gabe's feet as he does sit-ups. Every time Gabe sits up, they come nose to nose, and I smile. Leo cracks his neck beside me, and I arch my eyebrows.

Could he be more obvious?

"Do you like Gabe?" I ask.

He cocks his head to the side in thought. He is no longer upset, as he mulls my question around. It isn't difficult to answer. He leans to the right, and his shoulder is close to my left one.

"What not to like?" Leo asks, his eyes are lit with excitement.

"Are you seriously answering my question with a question?"

"I don't know, Tiny, what's it to you?" He asks. I sigh. If this conversation wasn't about Gabe, I'd be over it.

"Do you like my best friend or not?"

Leo stands straight, and runs his fingers down his imaginary beard. I am close to punching him. Would it be considered training even though we haven't started yet? There aren't any rules prohibiting my guards from sparring with me. I smile wickedly at that, but don't make any moves, yet.

"If I answer your question, will you answer one of mine?" Leo asks. This time he is serious as he stares at me. There are no jokes, and I'm not sure how to feel about this serious Leo. Is this the Leo that Gabe gets to know? Is the animosity between the two of us only because of the day he lost to me?

"I don't see why not," I say hesitantly.

"So yes?" Leo press.

"Yes, I think I can answer one of your questions in exchange for answering mine."

"Done," Leo shrugs. "Yes, I like him. He's the first person that's been nice to me since I got here, maybe even before. Plus... he's hot."

I nod, pleased with his answer. I can't help but smile at the last bit. What question would he ask? I can't think of anything he would want to know.

"My best friend is hot," I confirm. This is probably the only time I will agree with him; not probably, it definitely is.

"Who was the last Gamma and why would the mention of him cause Gabe to shut down on me?"

EXCHANGE

Adea

I am aware a question is coming, but I am not prepared for such a loaded one. I'm not expecting that. I scratch my head, as I try to figure out how to answer that.

"First off, that is two questions. I promised to answer one, so I'm going with the first. The last Gamma was Olivia, and she was a she, not a he."

"I think I should have been able to choose the question you had to answer," Leo huffs. "I would have preferred to hear the answer to the second question."

"I'm sure, but I think that's something you should ask Gabe." Silence falls for a moment before his gaze turns to Gabe again. His eyes follow him as he jogs in place, and my heart warms, only a fraction, but it warms.

"I did," he says.

My mouth drops. "What?"

"I did ask him about the last Gamma."

"Why would you do that? Did someone tell you to?" I ask, suspicion seeping in. The thought of someone taunting my best friend and forcing him to dredge up those memories is pissing me off.

"No, well yes, but no. Darci was interested in knowing who she was replacing. Mingling isn't her specialty, so she asked me. Gabe was the only person I was talking to, so I figured I'd ask him. I didn't think it would hurt but… apparently, it could. I wanted to get to know him, but the question basically ended our conversation, and he withdrew from me," he says seriously.

"Well… that'll do it," Korra whispers. I fight the urge to laugh; Leo would think I am laughing at him.

"I see…" This is one of our first decent conversations, and it is beyond weird. I steal a glance his way, and see the sadness there. My heart melts knowing he is trying to get to know Gabe.

"Look," I start, "Since we're being chummy, I'd like to give you some advice." Leo dives me a look at the word 'chummy,' but I ignore him. "Don't talk about the last Gamma around him. Don't mention her. In fact, avoid that topic unless he brings it up."

He nods. "Do you have another question for me?" He asks.

I laugh at the slight hope I hear in his voice. I shake my head. "Nope."

His shoulders slumped in defeat, and I wanted to laugh. Will Leo treat me nicer now that he knows I am his Luna? If Leo is possibly involved with Gabe, I want us to get along, even if I don't like him.

I sense someone making their way in behind us, and I turn to find Brianna. I remember being in awe as she took down her opponent on the first day. Her long blonde hair is up in a ponytail, and her almond-shaped eyes are lined with wing-tipped eyeliner. I am itching to spar with her.

"I would try avoiding her until you have more practice," Leo murmurs from my left.

"And why is that?" I ask, folding my arms in front of my chest.

"You've had a week of training whereas Brianna," he jerks his head in her direction, "has been training for years. I was simply offering you advice about a comrade I've known for a while. What you do with that advice, is up to you."

His warning doesn't serve its purpose; if anything, it makes me want to fight her more. I watch as she walks past me. When she comes to a stop, I wonder if she wants to spar against me too. I am disappointed when she bows and continues onto the field.

"Although," Leo whispers, "I honestly wouldn't mind seeing you put on your ass, Luna." His words are taunting, but I won't let him get to me. So much for getting along. It's fine though. I already know I can handle him, so this is him being petty over a loss.

You can't help it if he's a sore loser.

***

Gamma shows up and makes everyone run laps. I was light headed by the time she called us back to the field. Everyone pairs off, and Leo and I are told to run more laps while Gabe spars first. I don't get to see the entirety of his fight, but I have faith he'll win. Leo glares at me, as we run more laps while everyone else pairs off and fights.

I ignore his glare, as I struggle to breathe. I am out of breath, but I push myself to keep going. The sun blares down on me, and I am starting to sweat. I push forward, and leave Leo behind. I do not have the ability to hold a conversation while running.

We run three laps around the field before Darci links us to come back. We jog onto the field, and Leo gives Gabe a high five as they swap. Gabe runs over to me, his cheek red from a hit. That is going to bruise.

"How'd you do?" I ask.

"Pretty damn well," Gabe says, "I'm killing it at this warrior stuff."

"Wow, someone's tooting his own horn," I tease.

A crooked grin spreads across one side of his face. "Toot toot."

I laugh out loud before I sit down, and try to calm my breathing. "Don't make me laugh! I can barely breathe right now," I whine.

"I can tell," Gabe laughs sitting down beside me. "I could hear your inner groan when Darci told you guys to run more laps."

I want to slap him for laughing at me, but I am too bothered to try. I want to save my strength for whoever I get paired with.

"I wanted to pair off with Briana," I say as my breathing slows, "but now I don't think I can hold my own. I'm already tired, Gabe." I whine, throwing my head back.

"Be careful what you wish for, Ady. Darci is going to pair you up with someone she thinks can match you. Let's hope Leo's partner puts up a fight. The longer the fight, the longer the break." He is trying to encourage me, but I realize I will need more than training to whip my butt into shape.

CRAZED

Adea

There isn't a single breeze in the air; no reprieve from the angry sun blaring down on us. I can feel beads of sweat forming in places I don't want to acknowledge. Of course, Gabe sits unaffected beside me while I am slowly going crazy. My chest still dips and expands with each breath. I itch to get up and move. I know it will only make me sweat more, but at least I'd be busy doing something instead of cooking beneath the sun.

We sit in silence, watching as Zoe squares off with a brown-haired guy from Tier 2. He has a muscular build, although small for a werewolf, he still towers over Zoe. I wonder why Gamma would pair the two. Zoe is a Tier above him, and I am curious who is being tested here: Zoe or him? Is it strength versus agility?

Her opponent has speed, and there is strength behind his punches. I question whether she would be able to avoid him for long. Zoe is quick, and blockeseach of her opponent's punches. He looks irritated as he mixes his punches with kicks and she blocks those too.

How long will she be able to block his attacks? She throws a jab that connects with his nose. I can hear the sickening crack, as his nose breaks. I lean forward excitedly; she has a hit on him. She steps back while he grabs his nose.

Zoe stands there until he looks up at her. The look in his eye shows he is taking it personally, and he is ready to continue. Her face gives away nothing, as she stares at him. She doesn't taunt him and doesn't show any reaction to his anger. She just stares at him as she waits. I blink, and he moves.

He shoots towards her, cutting the distance between them, and she is unable to block as he hunches down and throws an uppercut into her gut. He moves with a speed he hadn't shown earlier. Her eyes widen, as surprise spreads across her features. She doubles over, and he straightens. The roles are reversed now, as he stares down at her.

She is a Tier above him, but he clearly holds the advantage at this point. He leans in until his lips are an inch from her ear. He whispers something, and the cruel smile tells me it isn't something nice. She lifts her head, and the woman I'd seen last week is nowhere in sight; you know, the one who remained expressionless while she fought.

Time stands still as she locks eyes with her opponent. The look in her hazel eyes is crazed, and a small smile pulls up at the corners of her lips. Brown-haired must not have been expecting her reaction because he hesitates for a second. That second is all she needed; the speed she shows means she's been holding back. I don't know what he said, but shit was about to go down.

She moves then, punches flying. Because he faltered, he is

caught off guard, and takes a jab to the chest, a punch to the shoulder, and she jumps aiming for the side of his head. He blocks that one, but is on the receiving end of her fury.

All he can do is attempt to block her attacks as they rain on him. He isn't able to do anything else; there is no opening for him to fight back. Even as he blocks severe hits, he isn't able to block all of them, and he is beginning to tire. Every other hit makes contact, and I am in awe at her speed.

He focuses on blocking his face and head, but she is landing punches to his gut, his ribs, and his body. It is hard to keep up with her moves, and I am entranced, too afraid to blink and miss something.

Zoe punches him in the stomach, and he groans, lowering his arms, leaving his face and broken nose open. I might have hesitated, but she does not., She socks him square in the nose. There is no sound, no movement from him, as his eyes roll back in his head. His body falls back until he hits the ground.

Her opponent is out cold. My eyes darted around to see if anyone else near her had witnessed her fight. A couple of people who had finished were watching with wide eyes. Gamma stands with her arms crossed, and a smile on her lips. She'd been testing Zoe, and she passed.

Gabe whistles beside me, and my eyes find Zoe again standing above him. Her leg twitches like she is fighting the urge to kick him while he is down. My mouth still hangs open as I watch her. She spits beside him before rubbing her stomach absentmindedly. I read her lips as she murmurs 'Prick'.

Feeling my gaze, she looks up, and our eyes meet. My shoulders tense. The crazed look is gone, and her hazel eyes squint as she gives me a smile. Automatically, I return it nervously before she turns away.

"She's… a badass," Gabe says quietly.

"Right? Remind me never to get on Zoe's bad side," I murmur. "I hope I'm never paired with her. I doubt she'd go easy on me because I'm her Luna."

"I think she was okay in the beginning. It wasn't until sleeping boy wonder gave her lip that she lost it." Gabe tsked, as he leaned back on his hands. "It's always the quiet ones that are crazy."

"Mm-hmm… let's not call her crazy, yeah?" I laugh. I glance at Zoe now speaking with Gamma.

"You're right," Gabe says, closing his mouth and pretending to zip it and unzip it. "She was speedy though! I'm not going to lie, I thought he had her in the first half. I thought she was a goner."

GABBY

Adea

"As soon as she started throwing hands, I knew sleeping boy wonder was done for," Gabe continues. "She looked like Sukuna, the way she was going at him; it was the wide eyes. She moved so quickly it looked like she had four arms!"

"Sukuna?" I ask.

"From Jujutsu Kaisen?" Gabe asks incredulously, as if he is someone I should know.

"You know I don't watch anime, Gabe," I huff.

"Ugh," Gabe huffs in return, as if I am somehow burdening him by not knowing who this guy is. "He's a curse, or demon, for your uneducated mind to kind of understand, and he's got four arms. I'd let him do whatever he wanted to me with those arms," Gabe groans.

"Gabe!" I exclaim while a smile spreads across my face.

"What!? Don't play coy with me. He's daddy, and you'd agree with me if you knew what he looked like. You know what? I'll bless you today, I'll show you a picture when we get back to the packhouse."

"I'm good," I laugh. "I'll take your word for it."

"Nooo, don't be like that Ady. I need you to fangirl with me!"

"I'm good," I confirm.

"You're missing out!"

I give him a look that tells him I am more than okay with my decision.

"Well anyway, Zoe was moving like him, and I was impressed," Gabe says. "I'd be down with sparring with her. I'm always up for a challenge."

"I'll pass," I say. "I choose life." Gabe bursts out laughing, and I roll my eyes. I'm Serious, but okay.

When he stops laughing, we sit in silence for a few minutes. It isn't until I start watching Leo, that I realize I have my best friend alone. This is my chance to ask him about last weekend. Zoe's fight distracted me, and I'm not sure how much time we have left without Leo.

"Are you going to tell me what went down this past weekend?"

My eyes wander over to Leo holding his opponent in the air before throwing him down. The guy grunts before rolling out of the way of Leo's kick that is aimed for his head.

Gabe isn't watching him. Instead, his eyes are on the blue cloudless sky. The light mood and joking atmosphere are gone, and he doesn't look at me, and doesn't show signs of hearing my question.

He swallows slowly. It looks painful, as if words are trying to come up, but are getting stuck, and he can't get them out. I'm not expecting a choked-up Gabe. He blinks a few times, and I know he is trying to keep back tears.

What the hell happened?

And whose ass do I need to kick?

NO ONE hurts my best friend.

I expect him to play coy with me, maybe call me crazy and dangle the truth in front of me before recounting in very clear detail everything that had happened. He turns his head so he is looking at me. My best friend stares at me with hurt-filled eyes, and I bite the inside of my cheek. This is the last thing I ever want to see in his eyes.

"Oh, Gabby," I say, grabbing his hand. "What happened?"

"I slept with Odis."

When I say my jaw drops, my jaw DROPS.. It almost hits the ground.

"You slept with Odis?" I ask gently.

"Well, fucked. We fucked," Gabe says as he nods. A humorless laugh escapes, he just has to set that straight. "… and I want it to happen again… and again. I want it to happen a lot of times."

"Why aren't we squealing about this, and why is it bad?"

His eyes water, and he purses his lips together. I squeeze his hand, waiting for him to continue. "It wasn't bad… like at all. The sex was mind-blowing. What happened after was bad… he said it shouldn't have happened. He regretted it.

"At first, I thought it was because of the pack, or maybe I was a shit lay. I wasn't asking him to be my boyfriend, but after he fucked me three different ways til Sunday, he instantly told me he wished it hadn't happened."

"Did he say why he felt this way?" I ask.

"He said it was because of… her. He said we were betraying

her by being together. When I thought it was almost like she brought us together," Gabe says quietly, with a one-shoulder shrug. "Was I being selfish in hoping she brought us together?"

"No, baby. That wasn't selfish. I would have thought the same thing if I were in your shoes. I knew Olivia and him had a past… I didn't know how deep his feelings ran for her." Gabe holds my hand tightly, as I continue, "I don't understand why he thinks it's a betrayal. I would think Olivia would want you to be happy, would want Odis to be happy."

"I wasn't asking him to take me as a chosen mate. Goddess, I wasn't asking him for anything. I… I just felt happy and… it has been so fucking long since I felt happy, Ady," Gabe's voice cracks, and I want to bring hell down on Odis. "I let myself be selfish, and I liked it. I liked every moment with him…. until he left. He left mid-fight. He left without fixing it. He just left, and it hurt as much as his words did."

"I'm sorry," I say as I wipe a tear from my own cheek. "You deserve to be happy, Gabe. You didn't deserve him treating you that way."

Gabe gives me a sad smile, and my heart breaks because the way he looks at me tells me he thinks otherwise. Goddess, I've never wanted to hurt someone as badly as I do at this moment.

LIFE

Adea

"I don't understand why you guys can't be a thing, see each other, date, choose each other as mates."

"It's not that easy," Gabe sighs, leaning his head back and raising his eyes to the sky. "It's more than Olivia. I think his position as Beta is also a part of the issue, and children. Sure we could mess around for some time, but eventually he would need to produce an heir. If I said I would be okay with having a piece of him, would that make me pathetic?" Gabe asks, looking at me.

"No, Gabby, that doesn't make you pathetic, not one damn bit. It tells me how much you like him," I say, "but you need to like yourself too. I was excited at the thought you might be getting back out there, but I don't want you doing something that's going to hurt you. I want you to value yourself and your feelings. I hate seeing you sad; it physically hurts me."

"It'll be okay," Gabe starts, "I'll be okay." It doesn't sound like he believes it himself, but he looks at me reassuringly. Gabe smiles at me and squeezes my hand again. "I've got a lot on my mind right now, but I'm thankful for you."

"Of course," my voice cracks, as I look him in the eye, "You can always talk to me, Gabe. I'll always be here for you. If you need a night together, I'll let Ethan know we're having a sleepover, and we can talk all night like we used to."

"I know I can always talk to you. You're my best friend, Ady," Gabe flashes me that crooked smile I love so much. "Thanks for listening to my little breakdown in the middle of training." He laughs, darting his eyes towards the field. "But… I don't think Alpha would appreciate his mate in bed with another man."

"I can have a sleepover if I want," I gripe. "It's been a long time since our last one. He just needs a little convincing," I say with a mischievous smile. My eyebrows bounce suggestively, but Gabe shakes his head.

"I appreciate the thought, Ady," he says with a smile. He leans over and gives me a bear hug. "But I choose life."

I can't help but sniffle and laugh. I wipe a tear as he uses my earlier words against me.

***

"Since I came in first in the competition, don't you think I should go up a Tier?" Leo crosses his arms and glares towards the field. He'd beaten his opponent and joined us mid-hug.

"It's not like I can kick my Luna's ass to go up a Tier. I think my situation deserves an exemption." Does that mean he changed his mind on trying to fight me? "Not that I'm saying I won't," Leo shoots me a side glance, "At this point, I have to ensure I don't lose my job over it."

"I look forward to it," I roll my eyes.

So much for that.

"Correction," Gabe says with a bit of sass, "WE, came in first." He points back and forth between him and the giant standing, while we sit on the grass. If we'd had more time, I would have asked him about what his thoughts on Leo were.

"Yes, we came in first, but the issue right now is: how can I bump up a Tier. I'm not okay with being Tier 3 for the rest of my life."

"If you would have just won the first time around, you wouldn't be in this predicament." I smile wickedly as Leo reels on me, and I feel a sense of triumph as he levels me with a glare that would make anyone else look away.

"I don't know what's going on here, but it needs to stop, now." I can feel Gabe's eyes on the side of my face, and I know Leo can too. He is the first to look away; his eyes finding Gabe and turning his head to face my best friend.

"I don't know what the hell that was about," Gabe starts, "but you need to remember your place, and remember who she is." I smiled victoriously as Gabe glares at Leo.

"But she—" Leo is cut short by Gabe.

"Figure out what you can do with Darci. She might excuse this, and pair you with someone else. If she doesn't excuse you, you can ask Ady for a rematch. If you win you get to bump up a Tier. If not, you need to accept your rank."

Gabe smiles as he looks at me.

"We may be training together right now, but we are not equals. She is above us, and I won't take you disrespecting my best friend and our Luna."

"And you," Gabe turns on me and my smile vanishes real quick. "Don't provoke him. I know you're angry, but he's not the one you're angry at." His words douse the flames that had begun to grow. He's right, I shouldn't take my anger at Odis out at Leo... even if he is asking for it.

"My apologies, Leo." I turn my attention back to the giant. "As Luna, I should know better."

"Mm-hmm," Gabe looks between the two of us before he looks past Leo.

"Looks like your wish came true," Gabe murmurs.

"What?" I ask.

Gabe nods his head towards the field. I follow his gaze, and find Briana staring at me. I audibly gulp.

"Oh yeah, you're up," Leo says. "Gamma told me you'd be up as soon as Briana ended her opponent. She was confident she would win."

He reaches out his hand for me, and I stare at it a second before I grab it. He pulls me to my feet, and I purse my lips to the groan that wants to escape. I give Gabe a look, and he laughs as I give in to my fate.

BRIANA

Adea

Each step I take brings me closer to Briana. This morning, I woke up ready to get back to training. Now that I am facing Briana, I am more than just a little nervous. She wears a mask of indifference, as I stop a few feet from where she stands. She has the body women die for: she is tall and slender.

I can feel the eyes of some of the pack members who have already finished fighting, or are on a break, on my back. I don't have confidence going up against Briana, and I feel more pressure knowing they are watching.

Just what I need.

"You're right to worry about her," Korra says. "I can sense how strong she is."

"Thanks for the encouragement," I reply sarcastically.

"You wanted to get stronger," Korra points out.

"WE need to get stronger," I remind her. "The dreams may have lightened up a little, but I haven't forgotten about Shane."

"I haven't forgotten the asshole either," Korra says.

"If we're ever taken by him, I need to know it won't be because I didn't fight."

"I know," Korra says. "Come on, let's try not to get beat too badly."

"Oh, thanks, Kor."

"Glad I could be of help," she says happily.

Briana's stance changes, and I know our sparring session is about to start. I can feel the danger in the air. The sun is high in the sky, as I face Briana. Her almond-shaped eyes are calculating as she watches me. When she doesn't move, I grow too anxious to stand still. I inch closer, and keep my arms up defensively in front of my face. I've already seen her in action, and I know how fast she was on her feet.

I jab with my right, and keep my left arm up. Then I jab with my left and keep my right arm up to guard my face. Briana dodges both and returns with a jab of her own. A crack sounds, as her fist connects with my nose. I am blinded by a white flash before I try to blink it away and focus on where she is.

Fuck, that hurt.

She doesn't stop there. She takes a step forward, her shoulder following through, and her elbow comes flying forward. I'm not fast enough, and her elbow slams into my temple. Pain, followed by a headache, explodes on the left side of my face. I grip my head with my left hand, as I try to move back and out of her reach.

Briana follows my movements and stays close. She doesn't let me get away, and I am struggling to find an opening. I drop down into a low squat, and throw punch after punch into her stomach. Left, right, left, right. She doubles over, and tries to guard her stomach, as I throw what strength I have into each punch.

I am knocked back as she hits me with her left hook. I'd hit her, but I didn't do enough damage. I stumble backward, but thankfully I find my balance before I fall onto my ass. When I look at my opponent, her arms are up, and she stares at me like a predator staring down their prey.

My breathing is labored, and I try to block out the pain. My head is throbbing, and it is getting worse with each passing minute. I step towards her, and throw my shoulder into a punch, as I try to hit her in the face. She steps back, and quickly dodges it. She doesn't say anything, doesn't taunt me, she only watches me. It feels as if she can see my attacks before they come.

She twists her body, and out of the corner of my eye, I can see her left leg coming up towards me. I can't get out of the way quick enough, but I manage to move back a few inches. Instead of my neck, her foot connects with the right side of my face. More pain explodes across my cheek. Her foot slams into my cheekbone and I know it will bruise.

I am not a match for Briana, and I knew going in who would win this match. I had wanted to avoid fighting her because I know she is an amazing fighter. I had deluded myself into believing that if I ever went against her, I could at least hold my own. Turns out I can't.

My face whips to the left, and I stagger as I try to stay upright. I had been so ready to get out of bed and get to training. This has only proved that I still have a ways to go. Briana watches me, and her eyes fly to my hand, as I make the decision to try again.

I lunge at her, and attempt to punch her again, but it is as if she knows what I am going to do. She side-steps me as the world spins out of control. My opponent's face blurs, as she closes in on me. Briana quickly slaps my failed attempt of a punch down with her left hand, as if it were a pesky fly.

I audibly gulp, as I am left open. She doesn't hesitate, and she punches me in the face. My head bounces back, and I stumble backward for the second time today. My eyes roll into my head, and I close my eyes, trying to fight gravity as it pulls me down. Briana doesn't waste any time.

She doesn't let up; she goes in for the kill. Her fist shoves into my stomach, and I wheeze, as all of the breath inside of me comes rushing out. My back hunches over. My body curls around her tightened fist. My mouth hangs open, and saliva drips down and hangs from my jaw. Light explodes and covers my vision. The last thing I see is Gabe running towards me before I fell.

DOWNPLAYED

Adea

All I can see when I open my eyes is white. I squint, trying to understand what I am looking at. I am laying down, and there is a white ceiling above me. I am disoriented, trying to make sense of where I am, what day it was, and I wonder what in the fuck happened.

After a few moments of blinking and staring at the ceiling, I realize I am in my room. The sun is setting and is casting shadows that run along the walls. It is night, not morning. I don't understand why I am here, or why my head is throbbing. As the fog starts to clear, bits of my day flash through my mind.

I remember breakfast with everyone, Leo fighting, sitting on the grass with Gabe, and walking towards Briana.

Briana.

I sit up in bed abruptly. Instantly, I am hit with pain all over my body, starting in my head. I flinch from the bruising in my stomach, and I fight the urge to touch it. Remembering my nose,

I tenderly touched the bridge, and breathe a sigh of relief. It has been pushed back into place and is healing.

Next, my fingers graze over my cheek, and I check my other cheek. One side is more swollen than the other, and I know I looked like I've been chewed up and spit out. I had been sparring, if you could call it sparring, with Briana.

More like you were fighting for your life.

Yeah, thanks, Kor. I was there.

My wolf chuckles at my response. Briana kicked my ass and then some. I hope I never have to fight against her again. I knew she was strong, and even though I lost, I'm glad I was partnered with her. She only proved how much stronger my foes can be, how strong I need to be. She set a goal for me to strive towards. Despite the pain, my hands ball into fists, and I smile. I am excited about the path in front of me. I feel hope knowing I am getting stronger.

A flash of movement to my right causes me to flinch back and cry out. My body cries out against the sudden pull. A scream that wasn't my own bounces off the walls. My eyes take in the blonde hair first, and drops to the eyes, wild with fear. Relief hits me and I can't help but laugh as I stare at my best friend. He is screaming like he is being chased.

"Goddess, Ady!" Gabe grips his chest, leaning back in his chair, his shoulders drooping with relief. I am still laughing as I stare at my best friend. "I dozed off for a minute, and forgot where I was."

"That sounds like the drunk you, Gabe," I tease, wiping my eyes.

"Well, I'm as sober as a horse. I haven't had a sip since your ceremony, and I should probably refrain from liquid courage."

"I've missed this," I say leaning back against the bed frame. "Late-night talks, jokes, and fun with you."

"They were simpler days, weren't they?" Gabe asks, sitting forward and leaning his elbows on the bed.

"Days when all I worried about was what we were making for the packhouse meals, and how to avoid Shane," I say, slipping into a daydream of earlier days. Gabe sighs beside me. "You are always there for me, Gabe. A lot of my happy memories are with you."

"I know. I'm an amazing person, and everyone wants me in their life."

"Hey now," I say and lightly slap his arm.

He chuckles and stares back at me. "Other than partying, drinking, and sleeping around… I had happy memories with you then too… little sis."

He reaches out and curls a strand of hair around his finger, "Being your one, and only, bestest friend in the entire world… I feel I owe it to you," he slips the strand of hair behind my hair, "to tell you, you look like absolute shit,' He says. He flashes me his sweet, crooked smile while he spits anything but sweet words.

"Well, excuse me," I say, with a little more than an ounce of sass. "I just got my ass handed to me on a silver platter from the strongest warrior in our pack. I wouldn't be surprised if only Ethan rivaled her strength. Also, I wouldn't expect you to look so pretty after a fight with Briana."

"Don't worry you're *pretty…*" Gabe blinks and gives me a side glance, "… little head over me. Unlike you, I know I could hold my own against *Briana*." Gabe's nose is in the air at this point. "I don't know if you noticed during the competition, but… I'm pretty strong, Ady. After seeing her in a fight with you, I know I'd be just fine. Seeing her put you on your ass only made me want to fight her more."

"If you hype yourself anymore, I might throw up," I tease.

"When I do go against her, I'll get revenge for you," Gabe says honestly.

"Oh, my knight in shining armor," I sigh. My best friend chuckles, leaning back in his chair.

"But all jokes aside, I was so worried. You scared the living shit out of me. I'm glad you've finally come to," Gabe says.

"Did you realign my nose?" I ask.

"Goddess, no. Doctor James left an hour before you got up. He helped you with that, and checked you over before he left."

"I'll have to thank him," I roll my eyes. "What about Ethan?"

"Okay, so hear me out," Gabe says.

I groan. "This already doesn't sound good."

"I wasn't going to at first because I didn't want to be the bearer of bad news," he says defensively.

"But?" I press.

"In the end, being the great friend that I am, I did. I may have downplayed your injuries though."

"How so?" I ask.

"I may have told him you slipped and fell? He freaked out when I told him I had to call the doc for you, but I reassured him that you were in bed resting. I convinced him it wasn't worth him leaving what he was doing. I told him I'd be by your side until he came back."

STUBBORN

Adea

The next time I wake up, the room is dark; a little bit of light shines through the windows from the crescent moon. I remember I had another hour of jokes with Gabe before I started to yawn. Gabe demanded I rest. He caressed my hair, and I quickly dozed off. There is no longer a blonde in the chair by the bed. My eyes take in my mate's large frame; the moonlight highlights his chiseled chest. His head rests against the chair at his back.

"Ethan," my throat is dry, and my voice comes out choked. He sits up quickly, and grabs the water off the table. He slides onto the bed, and helps me sit up. I take the water with a slight smile, which he doesn't return. I tip my head back, and drink the water down; my thirst isn't quenched until I finish the cup.

My mate takes the cup from me, and places it on the table. He takes a deep breath before exhaling deeply, and turns to face me. The angry expression on his face leaves me quiet. I don't know what to say. I search his face for an explanation; I don't want him to be angry.

"What were you thinking?" Ethan asks, his voice low and accusing. The muscles in his jaw flex, as he clenches his teeth.

I know I look like shit, but my body is healing. I'd been training, he knew that, and despite how I look, I feel a lot better than I had a few hours earlier.

"What do you mean?" I ask.

"Don't play with me, Adea. Don't act like you don't know what I'm talking about," Ethan growls. "I don't have the patience for this. Gabe said you were fine, but when I get back, the first thing I see is you passed out. Why wasn't I told of your condition? I should have been called the moment you were knocked out on the field."

"I was resting," I say. I rest my hand on top of his. He doesn't move to hold my hand, but he doesn't move it away, either. I knew he'd be upset, but I'm surprised he's angry. I thought I would be able to heal a bit before he got home, but I'd been wrong.

"I've been sitting by your side for the last few hours. You never woke up; you didn't so much as stir. Before Gabe left, he assured me that you had woken up." He closes his eyes and inhales deeply. "He brought you to the room, and you were still passed out. Why didn't Doctor James tell me? Why didn't you tell me when you woke up? Why did Gabe keep this from me? How can I leave you in his care, if I can't trust him to keep you safe?"

"That's not fair, and you know it," I say. "I'd trust Gabe with my life. I asked Gabe not to make a big deal of it."

"When was this?" Ethan asks. "Before or after you passed out?"

"Gabe knew what I would want."

"What about what I want?!" Ethan says angrily. "Look at you! I didn't assign them as your bodyguards for them to sit by while you get beat up!"

"Where's Gabe?" I ask.

"I sent him to his room when I arrived," Ethan says.

"What did you say to him before he left?" I ask. Ethan looks at me with an expression I hope isn't guilt. "What did you say to him?"

"I was angry. I dismissed him from his duty for today. I told him we would speak tomorrow."

"I was training, Ethan. I wasn't in any danger. I woke up in bed, and Gabe explained what happened. I didn't think… I should have linked you. I'm sorry," I say. His shoulders drop an inch, and I know his anger is dimming. "Don't be mad at me."

Ethan sighs and shakes his head slightly."I'm not angry at you," he says quietly.

"During training, I am not their Luna. I am just like every other warrior out there who needs to test their limits and be tested. It was not their place to step in during training. Had she been trying to kill me, yes, but I was in no real danger, Ethan."

"I understand that, but this," he says, waving at my body, "is too much. I can't stand to see you like this. There was no reason for it to get this far. Gamma should have stepped in."

"Why?! I don't get to have special treatment. She assigned me to someone she knew would be a challenge. I got my ass kicked today, but that only shows me how much harder I need to work."

"Stop being so stubborn, Adea!" Ethan says in frustration. "You will always have someone by your side, me or your guards. I've seen you fight, and I know you can handle your own. On top of you being able to put up a fight, why can't you trustus to protect you?"

"It's not that I don't trust you," I say, caressing his cheek. "I don't just need to be able to put up a fight. We've talked about this before. Can you honestly say that I could hold my own against you in a fight?" I ask. Ethan blinks, and I know, by the expression on his face, that he knows I couldn't.

"Shane may not be an Alpha anymore, but he has alpha blood in his veins. I need to be strong; I have to be able to fight. I want to be able to defend myself against the strongest warrior we have. If I'm ever in the position of weakness against Shane, I need to know I'll be able to defend myself. I have to be able to take him down."

"Okay," Ethan murmurs, holding my hand and kissing my palm. I look at my hand, and realize I am trembling. "Just please… I can't come home and see you like this. Don't let it get this far… next time."

"Next time?" I say hopefully.

"Next time," Ethan nods. "But you need to promise me you'll tap out or something when you know you've lost."

"I promise," I smile. I flinch slightly when the pain in my cheek gets worse. The swelling has gone down, but it is still bruised.

Ethan lifts the blanket and slides in beside me. His arm wraps around me, and I rest my head on his chest. He lifts me, as if I am as light as a feather, and he lays me down. He presses a kiss lightly to my temple, and his fingers caress my arm.

"I love you," Ethan says.

"I love you," I whisper, falling asleep to the thrum of his heart.

BLESSED

Shane

Fury blossoms beneath my veins, and I roar my rage to the heavens, as I stand above the bodies. There had been no other choice, no other way, no other path I could have taken, but it still rattles me. Emotion bubbles in my chest, and threatens to make my eyes water, and pull me to my knees. I refuse to cry, and I stifle the thought to cry for the lives I'd taken tonight.

The Goddess has blessed my path, and I can't stray from it, even if I want to. Earlier, I had set out with my men with the intention of killing my father and taking back what is rightfully mine. I've been denied my birthright for far too long, and I can't let another day go by. I deserve my pack. I deserve my queen. I deserve my family. I need it. My actions here prove I'll do anything to get what I want. Nothing will prevent me from getting it back.

Tonight, I've risen above my asshole father, and I've accomplished the goal I'd set my mind on the past few months. I finally killed him. With him out of the way, I will take his place, no, my rightful place. There is no time to mourn, no time to cry for my loss, and no time for the guilt over my actions to bring me to my knees. My chest hurts and my mind struggles to make sense of the flashback that hurls through my mind.

***

Not bothering to close the door behind me, I stepped into the living room, and only had a few moments to look around before a loud noise dragged my attention to the stairs. My mother rushed to me with open arms as she ran down the stairs.

Her eyes watered, as she took in my face. She'd gotten tinier, if that was possible, and her hair had grown longer. She sobbed as she crashed into me, her arms wrapping around my shoulders. I wrapped my arms around her tiny frame and hugged her back.

Heavier footsteps rushed down the stairs, and I locked eyes with my father. It had only been a few months, but he'd gotten older. He was still a large man, but his eyes looked tired, and his face was gaunt. The mistrust and disappointment in his glare would have bothered me, had I been the young pup he remembered. I was no longer that little pup.

"Get away from him, Rose!" My father ordered. His back straightened, and his eyes grazed over my body searching for a weakness. When he found none, he met my gaze, and a low grown sounded from his chest.

No greeting for the son he threw out. My mother ignored him; she looked up at me, and her hand caressed my cheek like she did when I was a child. "He's home, Josh. We haven't seen him in months. Let me hold our son," she cried. Tears filled her eyes as she searched my face. For what, I couldn't say.

"He's no son of mine, and he's here during an invasion," my father hissed. "Our people are being slaughtered. We're being attacked by rogues! Who do you think led them here? He's here to kill me, and take over. Now, get away from him, Rose!" Mother's expression didn't change; she continued to caress my cheek and gave me a sad smile.

"I have missed you every day that you've been gone, my pup. I love you.

The front door slammed against the wall, as Devin ran past me in his wolf form. My mother watched as he ran up the stairs. She gave me one last look before she stepped away from me. When she was far enough away, my father grabbed her and dragged her over to the couch.

"You lost your right to this pack when you were exiled," Father said.

"You mean when that prick took what was mine?" I growled.

"Adea is his mate! She is his, and his alone!"

"She's MINE," I growled. "You didn't hesitate to get rid of me, you listened to his ruling. Are you not an Alpha? Do you not make your own rules?"

"Our kind has laws we must live by," Father started.

"Excuses," I spat. "No one could separate me from my family, and I'm not letting you keep me from what's mine." I ignored my mother's gasp, and kept my eyes on my father. "I, Shane, the rightful heir of the Half Moon pack challenge the Alpha." He swallowed, and I reveled in the small sign of his nerves. "I'm not the small pup you can slap around anymore, am I?" I asked.

"You were a failure, and I did my best to break that part of you. Build you up into the leader you were supposed to be. I should have gotten rid of her when I noticed your scent on her. Maybe this could have been avoided."

"You couldn't have changed it. She belonged to me long before you

smelled me on her."

"I demand you let your mother go," he said.

"She's safer here."

I didn't wait for the response I knew was coming, I darted forward and my claws extended. I dug them into flesh, and my mother's scream echoed, as I ripped off my father's arm. He cried out in pain, and he reached with his other arm to grab the bloody stub that was left. I threw the limb to the ground. His breathing sped up and he shut his eyes tightly. Footsteps drew nearer, and my father's eyes flew open, and he glanced at her.

"Stay back," he ordered.

Maximus took over, and I released control of my physical form. I shifted into his wolf form. My father looked up at me with a look of a dead man, as I stood firmly on all fours. I opened my jaw wide, and I lunged for the man who had fathered me. Good fucking riddance. The satisfying crunch of his defeat was music to my ears.

UNAWARE

Shane

One second I'd ended his life, and the next, my mom's scent filled my nostrils, the metallic taste of blood on my tongue. Blood splashed along the wood floors, and stained the walls. It stained the couch. It was done, but what was this feeling? I dropped my gaze, but Maximus closed his eyes, blocking the view from me.

I didn't need to see to know; it didn't block out the feel of her small body. It didn't stifle my mother's scent, as it blended with the metallic taste of blood. As realization dawned on me, I choked. I didn't see her get closer, I didn't see her move at all. At the last minute, she'd pushed him out of the way and thrown herself in the way.

How had I not seen her? How did I miss her? I had lunged at my father; he'd been distracted, focused on his arm. I remember he'd looked at her to tell her to stay back. Had she stayed still? She must have ignored him. My mother jumped in the way; she took the blow that was meant for him. It should have been him. Before I knew what was happening, my wolf clamped down on her. It was too late.

Liquid splattered, and it didn't matter how hard Maximus tried, he couldn't block the taste of her blood from my tongue. She'd known, when I tore his arm off, that this would only end with my father's death, or my own. My mother's body fell limp, and my father's howl of agony filled the room. The loss of his mate tore his heart in half and ripped part of his soul from existence.

My father shifted back into his human form. He tore his eyes from my mother, and his eyes glossed over. He lunged at me despite only having one arm; the other lay on the floor. He moved without hesitation, but the anguish from the loss of his mate was clearly etched on his face. I wanted to mourn her, but that would have to happen later.

This wasn't what I wanted. It wasn't my intention to kill her. They had banished me from my home, stripped me of my title, and thrown me away. I was torn from everything and everyone I knew. This pack was rightfully mine, this home was where I belonged. I never thought the day would come when I would have to take what was mine and what I deserved by force.

Maximus loosened his jaw, I heard the sound of her body as it slumped to the floor, and we roared. I flew over my mother, I lunged towards my father, and I cursed the Moon Goddess. She'd paved the path for me tonight; she'd forced my hand. While she sat up there and watched. I wasted years of my life trying to do things my father's way, but I should have known better. Maybe, if I'd fought back earlier, things wouldn't have turned out this way. There was only ever my way.

The loss of my mother tore into my chest, tunneled deep, and made a permanent mark.

How was I going to explain to Mavy what I'd done?

How would I explain what had happened?

I crunched down on my father's head. I yanked, and the sound of flesh and bone tearing met my ears. I tossed his head to the floor, and it rolled before stopping by my mother's body.

***

The silence in the room is louder than the sound of my heart beating. I am pulled to the present, as a man runs into the living room and stops when his eyes drop.

He is covered head to toe in blood. I barely recognized him: Liam.

"I found her," he breathes. He holds his arm flush to his body, and he bows his head. I roar for the second time since I stepped through the front door. My claws sink into flesh, as I shift back into my human form. I demand one of the pack slaves bring me shorts, and within minutes I have shorts on.

Liam rushes outside, and I follow his lead. My father's pack has been caught unaware; his warriors weren't ready for us. When I rushed their border with my men, no one saw or heard us. A burst of adrenaline filled my veins, as wc rushed over the land I called home. No one knew of us until we made it to the packhouse, and by then it was too late.

Everyone had been sleeping in their beds. Liam had attacked the Deltas and the Gamma first. I trusted Devin to take out my father's Beta. If he wanted that position, he would have to challenge him for it.

One of the rogues I'd asked to join my team holds my baby sister by the neck. He is skinny, has black hair, and stares at my sister with a look I don't like. She scratches at her neck, and claws at his fingers, but he holds her tight. I take off into a run, and her eyes widen when she sees me. I take in her shocked expression, as it blends into confusion and fear. As I get closer, her expression is one of understanding.

"Release her," I order.

He hesitates, and that's all it takes for me to separate his head from his neck. Blood spurts out like a firework fountain going off. I block my sister from the sight, as he drops to his knees, and falls to the side. She's gotten thinner since I've last seen her. She has dark bags under her eyes, and she's chopped her hair short.

"Shane," Mavy whispers. I pull her up into a bear hug and hold her tight. Tonight, I claimed my birthright, my pack, and took back my family. It has taken me too long to come home, but the title of Alpha is officially mine. Half Moon pack is mine.

BETTER

Adea

I stand in the shower, head bowed, as a river of water cascades over me. Scorching, hot water heats my skin. My body warms, and the temperature in the bathroom rises. Facing the wall, the water washes down my body, cleansing me of outside thoughts. Four walls make up a safe place from my thoughts, fears, and worries. Here, I am able to focus on the feel of the water, the sound it makes as it splashes against the floor.

I push my hands through my hair and lift my face to the shower head. I sigh as heat hits untouched skin. I drop my head back and enjoy the sensation. I still haven't looked in a mirror; I know it is bad, and don't need confirmation. My body is healing slowly.

Ethan has been fussing over me, and while I love that he cares, it makes me feel weak. I am thankful for him, but need to get back on my own feet. He tried to come in with me, like he's been doing the last couple of days, but I assured him I am stronger and can handle washing.

Two days had healed the smaller cuts and bruises, but I still have some severe wounds that have made progress towards healing. I turn the water off, and the scorching pressure against my skin stops. I'd woken early, and spent the last hour in the shower. I know I won't be able to train today, but I am determined not to miss it.

Gabe and Leo have kept me company the last two days while Ethan was at work. I am more than thankful for the werewolf healing. If I'd been human, these injuries would have taken weeks, maybe months. I can't imagine being stuck in this room for that long. I am slowly becoming irritated; I want to get back out there on that field.

I can't stop thinking about the last training session. Flashbacks of my fight with Briana keep replaying in my mind, over and over again: Gabe and I had a heart-to-heart in the middle of training; Leo had won and made his way over before it was my turn to spar. Briana is a top fighter, and I wonder why she didn't participate in the competition. It would have been a close call between Gabe, Leo, and Briana.

Ethan knocks on the door, and I assure him I am fine. It is time to stop wallowing in the shower. I begin scrubbing down my body and washing my hair. After I'd woken up in bed, bruised and hurting, Gabe had been there to confirm that I'd been knocked out. When I woke up later in the evening, Gabe was gone, and Ethan had been angry. I understand why; coming home to a hurt mate would shock anyone.

Since then, I stayed in bed, ate, and bathed. Ethan wouldn't let me leave; he said I needed to heal. Putting down the shower scrub, I run my hands through my hair, and rinse the shampoo out. I wash off the soap from the rest of my body, and enjoy the last few minutes of hot water.

Electricity shoots through my body at the thought of sparring with Briana again. I need to sit in on training, even though I can't participate right now. I can't miss the opportunity to watch her train. If I can get a feel for how she fights, I might be able to spot her weaknesses, and I can get a better understanding of how to beat her.

Defeating her is another stepping stone towards being confident in fighting against Shane. I haven't, for a moment, let myself believe in the silence that has followed Olivia's death. He is still out there, and defeating her is a sure way for me to prove to myself that I can stop history from repeating.

The images of being unable to fight him off make their rounds through my mind. I doubt I will ever forget the fear of knowing there is nothing I can do to free myself. My hands clench into fists. I will make sure I do everything in my power to avoid being in that position again. If I have no choice but to be in that position again, I will make sure I'm not the same, weak person. I won't go without a fight.

A chill travels down my spine, and tears start to blur my vision. I'm not going to cry. I bat my eyes quickly, and duck my head under the water. I won't cower under him; I won't let him win. Instead of discouraging me, it pushes me to be better, to be stronger.

Turning off the water, I step out of the shower and grab one of the towels I've placed on the sink. Tenderly, I dry myself off before tugging on the black shorts and oversize v-neck sweater. The mirror is fogged up, and I am thankful I don't have to see my black, blue, and yellow reflection. A part of me whispers that it doesn't matter how much I try, I'll never be able to change anything, but I ignore it.

I've been working hard to heal you.

I know, Kor. Thank you for your help.

You don't look as bad as you think you do.

I think there's a deeper reason here, Adea.

Are you my therapist now?

I think we should talk more about Shane.

I don't think we need to. I've thought about him enough, Kor.

My wolf huffs, and I roll my eyes. I grab a second towel from the sink and begin drying my hair. Korra doesn't say anything else, and I am thankful she doesn't. When I am satisfied with my hair, I dry my neck before brushing my hair. There is no use in trying to be pretty today. I put my hair into a tight, low bun, and flattened down my baby hairs that tried to stick up in random places. I throw the towels in the hamper, and when I am ready, I open the door and step out.

EMERGENCY

Adea

The cold air kisses my skin, and goosebumps rise all over my body. It's one thing I don't like about hot showers, but what's a girl to do? The room is filled with the light from the rising sun.

Ethan stands by the table. He is distracted by a message on his phone, and I get a second to take him in. He is dressed in black slacks, and a white button-up shirt. His sleeves are folded, and my eyes linger on the exposed tattoo sleeve. His full lips lift at both corners, and dimples in his cheeks tease me. I walk across the room quietly, taking in the rest of him. My eyes trail up his strong smooth chest. His hair is slicked back. His strong jawline is as sexy as the first time I'd seen it.

My mate turns towards me, and his eyes trail seductively down my body. We haven't touched each other since the morning I got my ass kicked. I've been so hurt, and Ethan insisted on not hurting me. I told him he wouldn't, but he won't listen. I love how he loves me. Will I ever be good enough for him? The fact that I get to spend the rest of my life by his side makes my heart explode.

Silence fills the room as I reach him, and he stares down at me. Can he read my thoughts? His eyes follow my movements, as I reach up and poke one of his dimples. He smiles wider, the action only deepening the dimple. I doubt a day will come when I won't swoon over his smile.

"You're beautiful," Ethan breathes. His fingers caress my cheek gently, but I don't flinch. My swollen cheek has almost completely healed, and it doesn't hurt anymore. I lean into his hand; it is warm and firm, like him. He leans down a few inches until his lips are by my ear.

"If you were completely healed, I'd take you, right here, on this table, right now," Ethan growls. His breath tickles my ear, and I turn my face so I am facing him and kiss his cheek.

"Don't threaten me with a good time," I say cheekily. "And… I didn't hear a reason for you to hold back."

He straightens his back, and gives me a look. Ignoring it, I stand on the tips of my toes, and wrap my arms around his broad shoulders. His warm cinnamon scent fills my nose, and clouds my senses; it is as sweet as him.

One of his arms snakes around my waist, and pulls me close. A noise between a gasp and a grunt escapes past my lips. I press my soft chest against his hard one, and can feel the sexual tension start to build in the room.

My eyes zero in on the top three buttons of his shirt; they are undone. I smile, as a devilish idea crosses my mind. I lean forward, and press a kiss to his exposed skin. His breathing grows shallow, and I pepper his skin with kiss after kiss. Ethan groans, and something hard bulges against my belly.

"Well, that was fast," Korra purrs.

"I know," I sigh.

"I miss Elijah," Korra pouts.

"I'll talk to him about planning a run so the two of you can get some time together."

I smile proudly at the effect I still have on him. Ethan's head drops back slightly, and I take that as a welcome sign. My hands slide down from his shoulders to his chest. When he doesn't say anything, they slide lower, and it is my turn to groan as my fingers graze over muscle, and dips in between ridges.

"Adea," Ethan growls. "I will not take you while you're hurt. You're testing my control, and I'm not as strong when it comes to you."

"I don't know what you mean," I say, as my kisses turn to licks. "What are you doing today, my King?"

"I'm meeting Beta Odis in the lobby, and here you are, tempting me into bed. If it wasn't important, I'd listen to the siren's call, and have my way with you."

"I've got plans too," I murmur, "but what's important enough to keep you from taking me?"

"Adea… it's business… I have to attend to," Ethan murmurs.

"Mmm, what kind of business?" I ask.

"Well," he sighs. "An emergency meeting has been called. All of the Alphas from the surrounding packs have been summoned. It's crucial that I show. I can't miss it."

"What's it about?" I ask. I stop teasing him with my lips and mouth. I lift my head to look my mate in the eye as he speaks. Something has to have happened if an emergency meeting is called.

"I'm not sure. I won't know until we get there," Ethan says. "Odis has been pressing me to hurry up, but I wanted to make sure you were okay before I left."

"I'm fine," I laugh. "I was only showering, love."

I stand, watching my mate for several long seconds as our breathing slows, and a smirk spreads across his lips.

"What?" I ask.

"Someone's being obedient," Ethan says. I pushed against his chest, and took a step back.

"I'm not a child." I sigh. I turn from him and started pacing. "I'm honestly worried. I hope it isn't a war. What do we do if it's a war?"

"Hey," Ethan says, grabbing my arm. He pulls me back towards him. "You don't have to worry. There are a few things it could be: an issue with an heir; possible rogue attacks; a new pack could have formed or maybe an issue with one of their mates."

"That last one doesn't seem like a reason to call the neighboring alphas to a meeting," I say.

"The point is," Ethan says, wrapping me in an embrace, "it's nothing for you to worry about." Leaning my head against his chest, I sigh. I hoped not.

RESPONSIBLE

Adea

The sun is blinding, and I know it is going to be a hot day. My mate kisses me, and heads for the door. I lean back on my hands, and watch as Ethan grabs his keys, wallet, and phone.

A part of me wants to drag him back to bed, but I know he needs to leave, and I have plans of my own today. I sigh as he bends down and slides his foot into his shoe. His sexy toosh teases me as he slides his other foot into the other shoe. He straightens, and fastens one of his buttons.

"Be safe," I murmur. Ethan's hand freezes on the door handle. He turns his head to look at me and smiles.

"Don't worry," he says, "It's just a meeting. I have Odis with me and we'll be back right after."

Ethan opens the door and walks out. Gabe and Leo are standing guard right outside, and he doesn't bother closing the door. He knows I won't leave them out there.

He glances at Gabe, but doesn't say a word. Silence hangs in the air between Ethan and Gabe; I can feel it, and I know Leo can too. Ever since I'd gotten hurt, things have been awkward between the two of them.

My mate nods to Leo, and heads out. Leo remains impassive during every exchange between the two. I know where Leo stands, and for once, we agree on something. People get hurt during training, especially while sparring.

For Ethan to expect Gabe to keep me from getting hurt while training isn't reasonable. It isn't something Gabe can do. Getting hurt is expected, but Ethan still hasn't forgiven Gabe. I don't understand why he doesn't hold Leo to the same standard.

As soon as the elevator doors close on Ethan, Gabe strides in like he owns the place. Leo follows after him, his eyes on Gabe's behind. His eyes slide past Gabe, and I gave him a knowing look. He smirks at me, not caring that he's been caught.

"Good morning, Adyyyy," Gabe says cheerfully. He jumps onto the bed beside me while Leo closes and locks the door. Gabe is wearing dark blue slacks and a white polo shirt. My eyes dart to Leo, who is wearing the same. Gabe pulls me in for a bear hug, and squeezes tight before letting go.

"Hey boy, hey," I say.

"Why didn't I get one of those this morning?" Leo pouts.

"Well hey to you too," I say sarcastically. He gives me a little head nod before focusing on Gabe again.

"Uh, because you're not my bestie," Gabe says. "Duh."

"I can be your bestie," Leo says.

"That position is filled," I say with an ounce of sass. "But um, what's with the matching outfits? Are these one of your uniforms?" I ask.

"Do you like it? The suit was too stuffy to wear today. I googled the weather for today, and it's going to be hot as balls out. I wanted to wear something a little more laid back, and not as suffocating today. We were given suits, slacks, and different colored polo shirts to choose from for uniforms," Gabe says. Leo walks over to the table and sits in the seat.

"So what's the plan for today, oh great Luna?" Gabe asks.

"Well," I start. "You know how I love doing nothing."

"No, no I don't. You can't stand staying still," Gabe says suspiciously. His brow furrows and his eyes squint as he eyes me.

"Rude," I laugh. "I'm going down to the field to watch today's training."

"You're not serious," Gabe says.

"I'm very serious," I counter.

"Ady," Gabe says.

"Gabby," I reply.

"I don't even know why I'm surprised. You actually want to go to the training," Gabe said.

"Yes," I affirm.

"You do remember your mate, right?" He asks.

"Yes," I say and nod.

"You know, the Alpha that wants to kill me," he says.

"He doesn't want to kill you," I say, rolling my eyes. Gabe glares at me.

"Yes, well said Alpha isn't happy with me. If it weren't for us being the bestest of friends, I'm sure I would be six feet under by now. He's pissed, and you want me to take you where he doesn't want you to be?" Gabe asks.

"He never said I couldn't go to the training field," I say.

"He didn't say 'don't jump off a cliff' either, but you're not doing it," Gabe says. I ignore that.

"I'm not going to participate, Gabe, I'm only going to watch."

"Mmm-hmm," Gabe gives me a look that says he doesn't believe me for a minute. I give him my best puppy dog eyes, and he sighs, his eyes slowly shifting to Leo. He hasn't said a thing about it, but Gabe isn't going to let him sit out on the topic.

"You're not going to help me out here?" Gabe asks. Leo leans back in his chair, turning his head, and his eyes trail over Gabe as he sits cross-legged beside me on the bed.

"Nope," Leo says. Gabe huffs, but Leo just smiles at him. "I'm her guard, not her master. My job is to guard her against threats, wherever she goes. As long as she's alive and breathing, I'm good."

"See? There's nothing to worry about. Besides, Ethan just left. He'll be gone for a while. I doubt he'll be back until late tonight. I'm just going to watch Briana," I say. I cross a letter x over my heart, "I swear, I will only watch."

"Ugh," Gabe relents. "Fine, but while you're watching Briana, I'll be watching you. No funny business, Ady, and don't try me. If I even SUSPECT you of thinking of joining-"

"I won't!" I exclaim.

"I wasn't finished," Gabe says "I'll throw you over my shoulder, and whisk you away from the field. I'll bring you back here, and we'll stay in and watch Netflix instead."

"Gabe!" I gasp before I burst into laughter.

"You laugh now, but I'm *so* serious," Gabe says.

Leo gets up and opens the door. I hop up from the bed and prance behind him. Gabe groans, getting to his feet, and follows me.

"When did *I* become the responsible one?" Gabe grumbles.

RUN

Gabe

Noon is the hottest time of the day here in Desert Moon. Sweat beads and slowly drips down my forehead. It isn't even noon yet, but the sun blazes down on us with a burning passion. The three of us are excused from training until Ady is completely healed, but Leo isn't having it.

As soon as we walk onto the field, he winks at me before he makes a beeline for the group of people awaiting Darci's command. After they warm up, Leo is paired with some guy from Tier 2. His muscles glisten with sweat, and tense as he spars with his opponent.

I'm not as invested in the training session as Ady. I sigh as a cool breeze tickles the back of my neck. I sit cross-legged on the grass. There isn't any shade, so we have no choice but to sit in the uncomfortable heat. The occasional cool breeze is like a cold cup of water in a desert.

Ady stands next to me, but she isn't paying me any attention.

The field demands her attention, and I grumble from where I sit, but don't bother her. I know she is serious about getting stronger. A part of me knows she still fears Shane.

She is focused on Briana as she fights one of the other girls in Tier 1. I know there aren't that many girls in Tier 1, but I've only started training with them, and am not sure who is who yet. Leaning my head back, I look up at the cloudless sky. I am transported back to this morning.

***

I hadn't slept a wink last night, and to top it off, I woke up before sunrise. It was as if I'd hopped into bed, blinked, and morning had come. I tried to go back to bed, but couldn't. Finally, after multiple attempts, I bolted from bed. Every part of me screamed that I was wide awake. I dragged myself from bed and got dressed.

If I couldn't sleep, I'd go for a run. I needed to do something, or I'd go crazy. I grabbed gray shorts to put by the door, so when I returned, I wouldn't walk through the packhouse naked. The last thing I needed was to catch Odis in the elevator butt naked. The longer I stayed in my room, the more I thought of Odis.

Ever since that night, my thoughts of him had only multiplied. My heart wouldn't listen when my mind told it he rejected us. I couldn't even have a meal at my table without thinking of him spreading me out like butter. I'd get hot and bothered, only to get frustrated and grumpy. Beta Odis had too much power over me, and he didn't even know it. It pissed me off.

Slamming the door behind me, my body itched with the need to shift. My wolf was on edge, and we were both ready for a run. As I headed down the hallway, I was so lost in thought, I ran into Leo. I didn't think anyone else would be up this early, but here he was. He asked where I was going, and when he found out, he invited himself.

My protests fell on deaf ears, and, after a few tries, I gave up. I was wasting time here when I could be out there, being wild and carefree. I didn't want him to pry into my personal life. I didn't want to flirt, or pretend everything was fine. I didn't want to act like I was fine right now. I didn't want to think. I preferred to be alone, but I knew that wasn't going to happen.

Maybe I gave in because, deep down, I knew I needed a friend, wanted it. After making him swear he wouldn't ask me any questions, or bother me, I continued my mission towards the elevator. All I wanted to do was run, feel the earth below my paws, and let Felix take control. My hands trembled as the elevator descended.

Odis was beginning to slip back into my thoughts. I wasn't going to keep acting like a wounded puppy; it was pathetic, and I knew I needed to get my act together. My heart swore it knew Odis didn't mean it, but my mind told me not to be stupid. I was Ady's bodyguard now, and life didn't revolve around a man who didn't want me.

I was bound to see him more, now that I would accompany Ady whenever Ethan was absent. I couldn't have this awkward as shit tension between us every time we saw each other, or were in the same room together. I wasn't going to chase after him. As much as I wanted to, I wouldn't. I wasn't a love-sick puppy, and I knew my worth.

As soon as the elevator doors opened, I sprinted out and across the living room. I waited until we were outside, threw my shorts by the door, and shifted. I don't think I could have waited any longer. I wouldn't have been able to keep walking until we got closer to the forest. I wanted nothing more than to slip back and let Felix drive.

Reading my mind, Felix stepped up and surged forward powerfully. He didn't bother looking back at Leo; time waited for no man. It wasn't long before Leo's wolf, Brutus, could be heard running up behind me. We were used to running alone; Brutus only pushed Felix to run faster.

Normally when I run, I go to the forest by the packhouse, but ever since she'd been taken, I hadn't gone there, couldn't go there. It was no longer a go-to spot, and I wracked my brain as I thought of where to go. Brutus kept up behind me, and Felix got an idea. I saw where he decided on, as he darted for the other end of the pack's territory. We would make our way around the city.

JUNK

Gabe

My wolf and I hadn't spoken much since our mate had died. He'd been quiet, and I had been too busy wallowing in my own pain. I didn't see his pain, or acknowledge the fact that he'd lost his mate too. I didn't check on him, and a wave of guilt washed over me. I'd been a shitty friend to Adea, and I'd neglected my wolf.

I promised myself I'd make it up to Felix when we got back to the packhouse. He loved these runs even more than I did. I would make them a priority. We would never get over Olivia, but I hoped he could speak to me if he needed to. I would be better;, I wouldn't be that friend who put their feelings before those important to them.

The chilly air pulled me from my thoughts for a few moments. It felt amazing, my cheeks were cold, and my eyes were dry. The sun was starting to peek over the horizon and cast shadows along the territory. It wasn't hot yet, and the early morning cold air froze all of my worries and anxieties.

Felix made his way along the border, his eyes trailing from all of the open areas of the land to the dark shadowy parts. I didn't keep track of time, but I could tell hours passed. The air grew warmer, and the city began to get busy. Felix turned around, and we headed back to the packhouse.

My heart sank. It was over as soon as it had started. If I didn't have Ady, I think I would seriously consider living in my wolf's skin for a few months. It was frowned upon, and lone wolves were considered rogues. It didn't make me want to do it any less, but with Ady in my life, I wouldn't leave her. I had a job, too.

I pushed back the thoughts of Odis that were already resurfacing. Felix lowered his head; we were low to the ground, as he pushed harder against the wind. I would just focus on Ady, her recovery, and being there for her. She'd been injured pretty badly, but her wolf had been working hard on healing her.

Felix and Korra never ran together either. Maybe I'd ask Ady if she wanted to go on a run sometime. We'd take Leo with us too, since Felix and Brutus got along. As the packhouse came into view, I readied myself for reality. I'd have to do what I said I would: I'd get my shit together, and put on my big boy pants.

As we came to a stop, Felix whined before saying goodbye to Brutus. Brutus wagged his tail, and once again, I was happy Felix had found a friend. Pulling myself from the backseat, I regained control and thanked Felix. I shifted back into my body.

I stood naked in front of the packhouse, but I didn't try to cover myself. We were pack members, and it was normal for us to see each other naked. Leo was quiet behind me as I made my way towards my shorts. I didn't glance back at him. I knew if I looked, I might give him the wrong idea.

What if we gave him the wrong idea, Gabe?

I knew there wouldn't be anything wrong with that. There shouldn't be a problem with him getting the wrong idea. Hadn't I told Ady that I was going to get back out there? Yet, here I was trying to stop a hunk from "getting the wrong idea"? I shook my head. I'd let myself think that. Even though deep down, I knew as much as Felix knew, I didn't want to give him the wrong idea because of a certain someone.

Bending down, Leo whistled as I grabbed my shorts by the front door. I couldn't help but smirk. I rolled my eyes as I stepped into the piece of clothing. When I asked about the whereabouts of his spare clothing for after the run, he shrugged and told me he didn't bring any. He planned on walking butt naked through the packhouse, but I fought him on it.

The only reason would be that he wanted me to get a good look. Thankfully though, I'd won the argument, and I convinced Leo to grab a pair of shorts on our way down this morning. I stared at him victoriously as he pulled them over his ass. He let his junk hang for a moment before he tucked it in, and I shook my head.

It was his turn to smirk, and he laughed as I gave him the middle finger. It didn't matter that we were shirtless and weren't wearing any shoes. Our naughty bits were covered, and he wasn't bad company when he kept his mouth closed.

I thought that would have been enough; there was no reason it wouldn't be. As we walked into the living room, I was almost too slow to stop my jaw from dropping as we came face to face with Odis. Leo had thrown his arm around my shoulder and decided to open his mouth for the first time since we'd shifted back. He cracked a joke about me staring at his junk.

Averting my eyes, I avoided Odis' gaze as we walked through the living room. Leo didn't greet him. He straight up ignored him as we passed him, and I wasn't sure if he did it on purpose, or if he really didn't see him. I don't know why he was there that early, but it wasn't any of my business. I wasn't going to try and explain myself either. We weren't even talking, and he'd made himself perfectly clear, hadn't he?

I held my breath as we headed towards the elevator. We didn't have time for breakfast since we'd gone for a run. Thankfully, we wouldn't be going to train, so eating breakfast for energy wasn't a priority.

***

A scream brings me back to the present. I sigh, leaning back on the grass. My eyes scan the group before landing on Briana. Adea and I both watch as she breaks her opponent's nose. He throws his hands up and steps back; he was forfeiting.

FALLEN

Ethan

Alpha Rich is the one who had called the emergency meeting. Beta Odis thinks it is in response to another rogue attack. On the drive over, he expresses his worries about our previous efforts to keep the rogues out. We aren't the only pack who had been attacked in the last year. The number of packs being targeted is only increasing.

Thankfully, I've been working on a new system that would alert us when anyone was within fifty feet of our borders. It is being tested by a few packs at the moment. This is the reason why I don't think the emergency meeting is about the rogue attacks. Since the last meeting, we've been working on protecting our pack lands. My gut tells me this is about something else entirely.

We aren't the first to arrive on Alpha Rich's territory. There were a few other vehicles and people getting out of their cars. As we walked down the meeting hall, the hair on the back of my neck is standing up. Odis opens the door, and a total of sixteen men are sitting around the table: eight alphas and eight betas.

I walk into the meeting room, and take my seat around the table. Odis sits by my right. The seated men greet me before continuing their side conversations. A few of the seats are empty, and I wonder where the missing alphas are. Alpha Rich waits a few more minutes for the others who walked in after me.

By the time Alpha Rich gets to his feet, all but four seats are filled. The side conversations come to an end, and everyone seated shifts their attention to him. Alpha Rich found his mate later in life, and they had their pup at an older age than most did. His son will be nearing adulthood in the next year. Many of us have known him since we first took over our packs. He's someone who has helped us in our early years.

"I want to thank all of you for coming here on such short notice," Alpha Rich begins. "I know emergency meetings tend to come during the worst times, but I'm glad to see all of you. There's no way to say what I'm going to say lightly, so, I'll be blunt. Late last night, there was an attack on Half Moon pack, and they have fallen. Alpha Joshua was killed, and so was his mate."

The room is quiet as the words sink in. An Alpha only falls when he is challenged to a duel, if a sibling or family member decides to fight for the spot of Alpha, or ... if his pack is ambushed.

"If this took place late at night, I'm assuming Half Moon was under attack," I say.

"Does that mean one of us attacked Half Moon?" Alpha Jake asks, the alphas seated stare at the empty seats. "And now there's a new Alpha? Or was the pack disbanded?"

"Is that why we started the meeting, despite the absence of some alphas?" Alpha Darius asks.

"Yes, and no," Alpha Rich says. The room breaks out in murmurings and whispers. "Let me finish." Everyone in the room falls silent.

"We don't know the full story, and I don't think it's safe enough to send any of our Deltas over to investigate. From what we have heard, this is what we know: Alpha Joshua's exiled heir showed up in the middle of the night, but he wasn't alone. Although we don't know where these wolves came from, he led a pack. Alpha Joshua and Luna Rose were not the only deaths. Everyone who was loyal to his parents, and those who held a position of power were slaughtered, along with their family."

"It appears we have a new Alpha in our midst," Alpha Jake says. A few of the alphas cast side glances his way.

Goosebumps litter my arms, and bile rises in my throat. The unease I felt on the drive over only grows. Not only had that sick fuck killed his parents, but he'd also killed their Beta, Gamma, and Deltas. He could have stopped there but he didn't. He killed their wives and children too. Anyone he saw as a threat was killed. My anger brings Elijah forward, but I maintain control. I don't want to think about what this might mean for my mate.

"Are we going to just welcome him to the group?" Alpha Jake asks.

"Shane is the new Alpha of Half Moon. He has already assigned a new Beta and Gamma under him. His Gamma informed us early this morning of the change in Alphas. The Alphas missing today went to congratulate him on his victory," Alpha Rich says.

"Disgusting," I spit.

"Agreed," Alpha Darius says.

"They were scared for their own packs, and went with their tails between their legs," Alpha Jake says. "Cowards."

Alpha Rich ignores us and continues,"I called you here today to inform everyone of the new Alpha. From here on out, Alpha Shane will be joining our meetings. We will need to make room for him and his beta at the table. Despite his methods, he owns a spot at the table, and I believe we would all like to continue our peace treaty. He accomplished his goal by claiming his birthright. We shouldn't have anything to worry about from him."

"'Shouldn't have anything to worry about from him' doesn't guarantee anything," Alpha Jake says. He is more than apprehensive of Shane, as am I.

"What will we do if he tries to impose on other Alpha's territories?" I ask. Alpha Rich arches a brow at me, and folded his arms in thought. His gaze moves around the room.

"Is everyone here worried Shane might move on to attack other territories?" Alpha Rich asks.

"It wouldn't be wrong to assume that. Look at the missing alphas. Where are they?" Alpha Jake asks.

"We all knew Alpha Joshua as a kind man. Such a violent takeover makes me wonder about the sanity of the new alpha," Alpha Darius says.

ALLY

Ethan

"Had Alpha Joshua reached out to us, we would have reacted to the situation the same way we've all agreed to. The right way to handle an attack on our neighbors is to go to their aid. We would have aided and assisted him in defending his people because that is what our laws say we must do. If Shane had challenged his father the right way, then we would have stood back and let them fight. Since he attacked him and won, he has taken over the pack, and is now the rightful Alpha of Half Moon," Alpha Rich declares.

"Not just anyone killed him," Alpha Jake says. "A son killed his parents last night, and now he rules over their people." Many of the alphas murmur their agreement with Jake.

"We don't know Alpha Shane, but we will need to welcome him," Alpha Rich reiterates. "The moment we bend our rules is the moment everything slips into chaos."

Alpha Darius gets to his feet. His brown hair has been buzzed short since the last meeting, and his hazel eyes trail slowly over everyone. He makes and holds eye contact before moving on to the next as he addresse everyone.

"If Alpha Shane, or any other Alpha sitting here, were to be attacked by Half Moon, or any other pack, I would do everything I could to defend you. My warriors and I would show up and fight alongside you. We have been at peace for years, and I won't have it fall apart because my pack didn't hold up the deal. We have all sworn to help each other, and I hope you would do the same for me," Alpha Darius declares, his eyes flaring with passion.

I want to say I would do the same for him, but I can't think straight.

The rest of the table murmurs their agreement, but I couldn't help the unease I feel. I had exiled Shane from his pack, and it was because of my ruling he had lost his birthright. He screwed up, so I don't regret any of it. I am uneasy because of Adea. From what I remember, he felt no remorse for what he'd done. There was only anger.

"If I make speak," Odis's voice booms. The chair next to me squeaks against the floor as it is pushed back. Beta Odis stands, his head bowed in deference, until Alpha Rich gives him permission to continue.

"We have had issues with Shane on multiple occasions, and I worry for the safety of our pack."

"The Desert Moon is, by far, the largest pack. What do you guys have to worry about?" Alpha Jake asks. He is the Alpha of the Lunar Moon pack. They have a fairly small pack, so I can understand why he is so irritated. He is worried about his own pack.

"I'll briefly explain, for those who do not already know. For those who do know, I apologize for taking up your time. Shane assaulted my Luna on our pack lands after she found her mate. He didn't care that she'd already been claimed by Alpha Ethan during the ball. He had a previous relationship with her, and didn't take the news well. He ignored the laws of our kind, and assaulted her," Odis says.

"On your pack lands? The disrespect," Alpha Jake growls. "I would have removed his head from his body, had he done that on my lands. Anyone that touches what's mine doesn't deserve mercy, or grace."

"Well, we followed protocol by holding a trial. In order to keep the peace, things must be done properly. Alpha Ethan had a history with Alpha Joshua, and even though it was hard not to kill Shane while he was in custody, he graciously let them choose, death or exile their pup. They had worked with each other a few times and peace between our packs should always come first," Odis says.

"It doesn't matter how long you've known someone. You've been far too merciful, Alpha Ethan," Alpha Jake says. He glances my way, and I growl at him in warning.

"Being stripped of his title, and being exiled should have put an end to it, but that wasn't the last we heard of him. A few weeks after he was exiled, he kidnapped our previous Gamma. She was held and tortured for weeks. We only got her back after she'd been completely broken and had switched sides. It wasn't long after that when we realized what had happened," Odis continues.

"And what happened to the traitor?" Alpha Jake asks.

"We held a trial for her, and she was executed," I say, answering for Odis.

"Her death was a heavy blow to our pack. Since then, we've done our best to keep our lands safe and secure. The news of him killing his parents, taking over his pack, and rising to power is unnerving. I believe we have more than enough reason to think Desert Moon may be next on his list," Odis says.

The other Alphas nod in agreement, and some began to look worried. The idea of one pack not being safe makes it probable for the rest of the packs.

"Half Moon has a large number of wolves in its pack. If a time comes where Desert Moon is attacked by Half Moon, will you come to our aid as well?" Odis asks.

Alpha Darius stands up first and nods to me. He slams his arm across his chest, and his ally Alpha Viktor gets to his feet. The other Alphas stand up until Jake stands as well, and they are united in their decision.

"We stand with you," the Alphas declare together.

I am worried for my Luna, but I am confident in my strength. Knowing they have my back brings me a small sense of relief. Standing to my feet, I cross one arm diagonally across the front of my chest.

"Thank you," I say. "Everyone should tighten their borders, and prepare their soldiers just in case. We don't know what Alpha Shane is thinking, or where he might attack next, if he plans to. Stay alert, and contact us if you need help. We will come to your aid if needed."

TENSE

Ethan

As soon as everyone is seated, the meeting continues. Since we are all gathered, everyone gives their reports on how their packs are doing. After everyone has given their report, hours have passed.

When everyone is done, I stand and update the packs on the progress we are making on the new system. If it continues to do well, Odis and I will travel to each pack and install it into the packs who want it. The rogue issue isi something we all had been grappling with ,and from what I know, everyone is on board with the new system.

After the meeting, many of the alphas hang around to chat. A handful of them excuse themselves. I'm not surprised. This meeting was called on such short notice, and we are all eager to take the news back to our packs.

A few of the other alphas approach me. Some want to plan a group date, saying their Lunas are dying to get out and make friends. I am wary of taking Adea away from our territory right now with everything going on. I know she'd like the idea, and tell them we'll have to plan something when it is safer.

Others approach me wanting to find ways to strengthen our alliance. To this, I offer to invite them onto our territory for a meeting. I don't think my mate would appreciate me leaving the pack so soon after this meeting.

Before I met Adea, I was always working, and while it is my duty, I am in need of some downtime. All this work is keeping me from the important people in my life. I haven't had any time to hang out with Odis, go running for fun, or make love to my mate. My wolf whines in agreement.

Now, with the news of Shane taking the title of Alpha, I need to break the news to her. I also have to break the news of Alpha Joshua and his mate's death to her. I don't know much about her relationship with them, but I know it will hurt her.

I wish I could go over there and kill him, but I can't move first. I would not only break the pact with the other packs, but I would lose their loyalty as well. There are a few other alphas that expressed their desire to move against Shane, but I know better. I won't ruin my relationship with Alpha Rich. I know how he runs things, and this is the way it needs to be.

We are stronger united. At least, that's what I keep telling myself. Closing my eyes, I push back the images that threaten to have me relive what I've seen. Anger, and the need to protect her resurfaces.

I fight the growl that begins building in my throat, but fuck if I'm notwondering why the fuck I am trying to stay calm. One of the hardest things to do is fight my wolf when he wants the same damn thing I do.

I want nothing more than to find the piece of shit, and watch him cry as I tear him apart, piece by piece. He's caused my mate an insane amount of damage. He hurt and bruised her. To this day, she still fears him, and Goddess I swear I'll kill him.

I don't know how I am going to hold back from killing him at the next meeting. Sitting at the same table as that dickhead is a dilemma. I don't know if it is possible, but he needs to be alive by the end of the next meeting.

My muscles are tense at the thought, but I'll deal with it when the time comes. Until then, I need to figure out how to get my wolf, Elijah, to go along with me. He is protective of Adea, as much as he is of Korra.

We haven't talked about her nightmares recently, but I know she is still having them. She still wakes up in the middle of the night. Some nights, when I couldn't wake her, I hold her close, and do my best to calm her.

My muscles crack, as my hand crushes into a tight fist. Adea is mine, but the thought of seeing that fucker pisses me off. The images I've tried so hard to push back come crashing to the forefront of my mind.

The asshole was on his knees in front of her the night of the ball. That night, before he stood to his feet, the fear I'd seen on her face set a bomb off in my head. Now, it cripples me and steals the breath from my lungs.

If I'd been only a little later stepping outside, he would have claimed her. I would have had to kill him… I *should* have executed him at the trial. The words the other alpha had spoken repeat in my mind. They are right; I know they are right, but it is too late.

I can't go back in time, no matter how much I want to.

I've never asked her how long that had been going on. I don't know how long she'd suffered in that packhouse under him. As much as this needs to end, it has to wait. I have to wait.

Elijah tenses and snarls within me. Odis clears his throat, and I almost get whiplash as I turn my neck to face him. My gaze lands on him, and my eyes glow in the reflection in his eyes.

"You need to relax, Alpha," Odis says quietly and lowers his head. Remembering where I am, I push Elijah to the back of my mind.

"My apologies," I say to the Alphas standing by me.

I wasn't there for her before the night of the ball, but every time after, I'll be there for her. I will continue to be there for her, and stay by her side. I'll do everything in my power to keep him from her.

There is nothing I won't do for her.

PERIL

Adea

Briana won against her opponent again today, too. If I had forfeited that day, I could have avoided being knocked out ,and I would not have had to take a break. I will be participating today. It was a mistake I won't repeat again. Next time, if I know I cannot not win, I will tap out and continue trying.

I've watched Briana during her sparring sessions, I never see a single opening. The entire time she faces her opponent, despite knowing he isn't as strong as her, not once does she drop her guard. It is frustrating, to say the least, but I can't help but admire her.

After grumbling about it for a good amount of time, the idea hits me like a lightning bolt out of the sky. Briana doesn't have any weak spots or openings, but I could create one. If I could do that, then I could land a hit and weaken her, or possibly take her down. I need to create an opening.

I watched her for hours, and she is always blocking her face and nose, so there's no hope in trying to hit her with a jab. She's stealthy and quick. She easily blocks every attack that targets her face. I am not exceptionally fast, so I already know my attack wouldn't connect.

There's also her temple. I could go for it, but with how quick she is, it is highly likely she would be able to dodge it by back stepping it. As for her ears, she could and, likely would, block it. Her arms are always close to her body ,so her ribs and gut are always protected. Hoping to land a punch would be just that, hope. It won't be possible unless I can dismantle her defense.

My goal in watching her today is to find an opening, just one, and I come up with nothing. What I find is that her defense is without fault. Although she doesn't have any openings, that doesn't mean she is invincible.

No one is invincible ,and if she doesn't have an opening, I will have to create an opening to get an in. Briana's hands and arms are always close to her body, and fast enough to block any attacks on her face.

Assessing her lower half, I notice she uses her legs a few times to grab her opponent's attention while she goes for the kill with a jab or an uppercut. She doesn't use her lower half as often as she does her arms.

I'm not sure of where I can create an opening, and I think about it throughout the entirety of her sparring match. It isn't until after her opponent submits, that I get an idea. Since she isn't as active with her lower half, I think of possibly striking her in the knees.

As I think it over, that thought does start to sound like a good fucking idea. If I can get a direct kick to her kneecap, I can dislocate her joints with a round kick. I doubt I can bust a kneecap, but I can still try.

I will have to be precise, and use enough strength, but if I can direct it to an open area that is easily broken, I know the chances of creating an opening for me to put her down are higher.

An alarm should go off in my mind about hurting her. None do. . I'm not worried about hurting her, because she hadn't worried about me. She didn't hesitate, either; she knocked me out without a second thought. She also has her wolf, who will come to her aid with healing.

My mind focuses on her knee again. If I could bust her kneecap, or cause her some sort of pain, she might drop her guard. Even if she drops it for only a few seconds because of the shock, it will create the opening I'm searching for.

In the event that I only hurt her and don't bust her knee, I would need to ensure she's down. Following through with a jab to the nose or to the temple would bring me halfway there. While a right hook to the jaw would hopefully finish her off, and would guarantee a win for me. Korra agrees with my line of thought, and with that it is decided. I should be fully healed by the next practice next week.

Briana nods to her opponent, and I watch as he backs away from her. She then walks over to Gamma Darci ,and they begin talking. My brows furrow in confusion as I try to think of a time they have interacted before. When I come up empty, a slew of thoughts pass through my mind.

Is she close to Darci?

Was she close to her before they came here?

Has she ever lost a match since she joined Desert Moon?

They had come from the same pack, and could have interacted many times before. Before I can think more on it, Gabe nods at Leo as he makes his way to us. He finished his match, and doesn't want to stick around to watch everyone else as they finish sparring. He didn't hold back, and knocked out his opponent in today's session.

Gabe is more than happy with the idea of leaving. It is a hot day, and since he hasn't sparred with anyone, the princess wants to get out of the sun. Jumping to his feet, Gabe bumps against me before grabbing my hand.

"Feed me, oh revered Luna. Your subject is famished, and in danger of peril," Gabe says while pretending to fall against me. I can't help but laugh and shake my head while Leo gives us a look. When we are spending time together without the seriousness of their job hanging over our heads, they get to relax a bit.

CONFUSED

Adea

Gabe pulls me from the field, and with a nod to Gamma Darci, the three of us leave. I squeeze Gabe's hand and smile at him as Leo follows from close behind. I'd been so focused on Briana that I haven't paid any attention to Gabe. I've made today more stressful than it needed to be.. I have a plan in mind, and I can think more about it later tonight.

For now, I will focus on loosening up and hanging out with my best friend. Leaning into him, as he had done earlier, an idea comes to mind. I throw my weight against him, and he stumbles as he tries to hold me.

"Damn, Ady! What are you trying to do? Squish me??" Gabe asks. The incredulous look on his face has me bursting out in laughter. I almost tear up.

"Help," I gasp, "gravity is increasing on me." I push the back of my hand against my forehead and close my eyes.

"I have no strength and could have dropped you!" Gabe

laughs, pushing me to my feet. Throwing him a smile, I interlock my arm with his and pull him along.

"You two are so childish," Leo murmurs from behind. I don't bother to turn around, but I do face my head to the right and stick out my tongue. I know he can see me, but I don't care to see him. I turn up my nose and continue forward.

"We didn't get to eat this morning," Gabe whines. "As your bodyguards, we need strength. Isn't that right, Leo?" Gabe asks as the field disappears behind us.

"If you say so," Leo says. "I can run on no food for a couple of days without getting weak," he boasts. I don't need to turn around to know he is puffing out his chest like a gorilla. Gabe rolls his eyes, and I stifle a laugh.

"Not everyone can work without food, Leo. I was a cook before I came to this pack. Food is my life. It's what I live for," Gabe says dramatically, lifting a fist in front of his chest. Leo doesn't say anything, but I hear him chuckle from behind us.

"Why don't you stop lurking behind us, and walk by our side, Leo?" Gabe asks, peering over his shoulder at Leo.

"I'm not lurking," Leo says huskily. "Plus, I don't mind the view. Haven't I told you this before?" He asks.

My cheeks flame and my eyes widen as I turn my head to shoot a glance at Gabe's face. A small smile pulls at the corner of his lips, but he shakes his head.

"Get your ass up here, pretty boy," Gabe says. Leo doesn't say anything, but he picks up his pace and walks by Gabe's side. He glances around us and searches the area. Even when he is joking around he is still working. I realize I was still tense, as I feel my shoulders relax. I am starting to get used to Leo, and with the way things started between us, I never thought this would happen.

As we cross over the courtyard, one of the Deltas assigned while Odis is away steps forward. I can't remember his name, but I recognize him from Olivia's trial. He bows his head slightly before speaking.

"How can I help you, Luna?" He asks.

"We're going for lunch. Can someone bring one of the cars? I don't care which one it is," I ask politely.

"Before I do that, I'm on orders from the Alpha to ask you: where are you headed?" He asks. I am a little put off by the fact he has to know where I am going, but I also understand that, as Luna, my moves are watched.

"The three of us haven't had breakfast, and just came from training. My guards are running on empty, and they need fuel," I say.

"I've recently received word from Alpha Ethan to keep you near the packhouse. Would it be possible for you to stay here?" He asks.

I am confused as to why Ethan would reach out to the Deltas, and not to me. He was at a meeting and hasn't told me anything about this. Did something happen at the meeting, or is he just being cautious? Before I can ask, the Delta speaks again.

"I can have something delicious prepared for you here, Luna," the Delta says. I want to refuse, and ask why I need to stay in the packhouse. I don't want to be a bother and have the cooks make something for me outside of the normal eating hours, but I also know what it means to get orders from the Alpha.

It will only make things harder for him if I decide to leave anyway. Despite wanting to go to my favorite place and eat one of those delectable waffles, I sigh in defeat. It's not his fault that my mate spoke to him about this new plan without letting me know. I flash Gabe an apologetic smile, and he pouts, but doesn't say anything.

"That sounds like a great idea, thank you, Delta," I say, squeezing Gabe's arm.

"Please follow me," the Delta says. He bows his head slightly, and turns on his heel. We followed him as he heads for the kitchen.

"I don't want to eat in the kitchen. We can take a seat out here, can't we?" Gabe asks. The Delta stops a few feet away from the kitchen door and turns to face us.

"Of course. You guys can sit out here. I will have a small table brought out for your meal," the Delta says before heading into the kitchen. Gabe pulls me towards the couches, and plops down on the one closest to the door.

"Since we won't be leaving the packhouse area, we can at least get a change of scenery for our meal," Gabe says, patting a spot beside him. I smile and sit beside him.

FLIRT

Adea

Gabe and I watch Leo as he takes a seat on the couch across from us. He looks bored, and I wonder more about his background. Gabe leans forward, his eyes on Leo, Leo's eyes on Gabe. Leo's eyes ignite with something I recognize instantly as lust. Gabe's eyes have a look of curiosity.

Who is Leo? After a solid five minutes of Gabe and Leo eye fucking each other in silence, I decide to step in. Gabe laughs at me, like it isn't possible for them to go at it right here on the couch.

"What do you do for fun, Leo?" I ask. "When you're not saving the world and fighting innocent young women?"

"You mean when I'm not kicking ass?" Leo replies with a cocky smirk. "The same thing I did before I came here: work out. I like challenging myself on a daily basis, and I don't like losing." He gives me a look that tells me he hasn't forgotten how he'd lost to me, but he doesn't comment further.

Gabe rolls his eyes. "Well, before I came here, I liked to go out."

"Mm-hmm," I laugh. Leo's eyes snap to me.

"Tell me more, Tiny," Leo says.

"Gabe liked to have fun alright," I laugh. "There was never a weekend where he didn't 'go out'". I wiggle my eyebrows and use air quotes when I say 'go out'.

"You were a party animal?" Leo asks Gabe. "I wouldn't have guessed, Mister Straight and Narrow."

I choked on my spit. Gabe gives me a shocked and betrayed look, and it only makes me struggle even more.

"What's that supposed to mean?" Gabe asks me.

"Oh come on," I laugh and lean into him. "When you weren't being the bestest friend in the entire world you were … what's the term? Fucking bitches." Leo has the widest smile on his face as he looks at Gabe. He is seeing him in a new light, and he definitely likes it.

"Oh," Leo growls. "Am I attracted to this?"

I burst out laughing so hard there is a pain in my stomach.

"That's in the past," Gabe says. "That was a long time ago!"

"Not that long ago," I cough out. He gives me a look and I look away.

"It was," Gabe says, looking at Leo. "I don't sleep around anymore."

"What changed?" Leo asks. My mouth drops, but I give Gabe a side glance. His eyes have a glazed look in them, and I know what, or who, he is thinking of. The look is gone as quickly as it comes. I am about to step in and change the topic when Gabe leans forward.

"What changed me from a playboy to who you see now? I found my mate, and I did a 360," Gabe says. He looks into Leo's eyes, and Leo looks into his. I am relieved to see that Gabe doesn't look sad.

"I didn't know you were mated," Leo says slowly. I can see the wheels in his head turning as he tries to rack his brain of a mate. His brows furrow.

"Don't hurt yourself there," I say with a laugh.

"Ha to the ha," he says. "I don't remember smelling anyone in your room. I've also never seen you with anyone ,other than me and Tiny here. Unless… is the Beta your mate?" Leo asks. His eyes widen at the thought.

"Wow, you really went everywhere with that bit of information, didn't you?" I ask.

"No," Gabe says, tilting his head away and exposing his neck for Leo to see. He no longer had Olivia's mark. "No, Odis is not my mate," Gabe laughs, but it doesn't quite reach his eyes. "You didn't smell anyone in my room because there hasn't been anyone for a while. She died."

Leo's mouth opens and closes., Once. Twice. He looks like a fish, and if it wasn't a serious thing, I would have laughed.

"I'm sorry to hear that," Leo says.

"Are you?" Gabe asks. A small smile plays on his lips as he watches Leo's flustered state.

"Am I glad that you're single now? Yes. Am I glad your mate died for this to happen? No," Leo says seriously. I don't know about Gabe, but my heart fluttered for him. Leo continues, "Now, I've been in a few relationships. I've dated women and men, but it was never anything too serious. I prefer to keep things simple, and people get too clingy. It never worked out because I want to sample everything, and don't want to be tied down to one person."

"The two of you sound similar," I say. I bump shoulders with Gabe, and his shoulders droop a little, relaxing..

"We do," Gabe says.

"You know what's better than one?" Leo asks.

"Uh-oh," Gabe says.

"Two," Leo says with a wink.

"That was terrible," Gabe cringes. "Were you trying to flirt there?" When Leo nods, Gabe laughs. "You need to work on that."

"I know," Leo smiles. "I'm a little rusty."

"I'll say," I laugh. I am definitely the third wheel in this conversation, but I don't mind. I like knowing Leo can make Gabe laugh. My best friend has made it clear to me that Leo isn't who he likes, but that doesn't mean anything. The person he likes is being an asshole, and Gabe deserves to be treated well. No one knows what the Goddess has in store for him.

"Are you still in mourning?" Leo asks. My eyes widen as I look between him and Gabe.

"No," Gabe says. I don't know how true that is, but I am glad he said that. It means he is trying, and I am always rooting for him. Leo doesn't even bother trying to hide the smile on his face as he watches Gabe. "Don't get cocky," Gabe rolls his eyes. "I'm single , but it doesn't mean I'm interested in mingling."

"Mm-hmm." Leo is smug, leaning back against the couch.

DEEP THROAT

Adea

Gabe fights the smile on his face, but I can't help the one on mine. My eyes dart to Leo, and the smile on his face says he doesn't believe Gabe for one second.

"Or maybe the opportunity hasn't presented itself to you yet," Leo says. "Maybe," he continues, leaning forward, his forearms on his thighs, his eyes trained on Gabe, "you'd mingle if a hot muscular sexy man gave himself to you."

Gabe doesn't flinch, or show any sign of being affected by Leo's words. He just stares back at him like they are talking about the weather. I feel warm, and I fight the urge to fan myself as I watch them.

"Maybe," Gabe says, leaning forward, "not."

The sexual tension is so thick, you could cut it with a knife. If it goes on any longer, the electricity in the air will combust. Just when I think it can't get any hotter, the kitchen door swings open.

All three heads turn and watch as the Delta steps out, pushing a cart of food. The tension is forgotten and mouths water as eyes search the cart hungrily. As he gets closer, I make out a platter of steaming hot paninis.

One half of the tray is turkey, and the other is beef. My eyes scour the rest of the cart, and I notice another platter of chips, a large bowl of soup, and a salad bowl. There are also two jugs: one of orange juice, and the other is water.

"Thank you, Delta John," Gabe says as the Delta comes to a stop before reaching the couches.

Well, I now know his name, so I can avoid the awkwardness of asking him for it. Delta John tells him it's no problem as he grabs a folded table from the bottom of the cart. He unfolds it, and puts it in between our couch and Leo's couch.

After the table is set up, Delta John turns back to the cart and begins unloading the cart. I swallow the saliva pooling in my mouth as the smells fill the air. When everything is set up nicely in front of us, I force myself to tear my eyes from the food.

"Thank you, Delta John. Everything looks and smells amazing."

"No worries, Luna. I'm glad it's to your liking. Please link me if you need anything else," Delta says, and with a slight bow, he excuses himself.

I don't bother waiting and grabbing a plate. I fill my plate, grab a bowl and fill it with soup. Gabe has been complaining of hunger this whole time, but I don't realize how starved I am until the food is in front of me.

When Gabe and Leo are done filling their plates, I am already halfway through my sandwich. I am about to take another bite when my eyes catch on Leo. He is staring at Gabe while he shoves half of his sandwich in his mouth. The way he is doing it while maintaining eye contact makes the act of eating a sandwich so much more sexual than it should have been. It isn't the first time today, but I choked on my spit, and pour myself a glass of orange juice.

"Are you okay?" Gabe asks, slapping my back.

"Yeah," I cough. "I didn't realize Leo's mouth was that big."

Gabe snorts and Leo smirks. Shaking my head, I pick up my sandwich and take another bite. I don't think I've ever seen Delta John work the front lobby before, but whenever I see him working it, I will be sure to ask for another sandwich.

"This panini might be better than sex," I groan.

"You're lying," Gabe says. "You're just really hungry. The three of us know nothing is better than sex, and I know big Alpha isn't doing it wrong." I blush and decide against answering that question. Instead, I pick up my soup, and start scooping delicious bites of broccoli potato deliciousness into my mouth.

The three of us scarf down the rest of our food. I try to savor it, but I'm so hungry, and I don't bother trying to eat nicely. We're all hungry.

"So, Leo," I say. I make a dent in my soup, as I shoot Gabe a mischievous glance. "Is there anyone here you're interested in?" Leo swallows his food and licks his fingers. His shoulders shake as he chuckles, and he levels me with one of his cocky smirks.

"I don't know if deep throating my sandwich didn't make it obvious," Leo says. "Or the clear 'fuck me' eyes I was giving Gabe while I did it, but I'm more than interested in your best friend. He's on my radar, and I've honed it on him."

Before my jaw can drop, or I can have a reaction, the front

door swings open, and all three heads turn. A woman I don't recognize walks in first, and behind her walks in a child. He's got blonde hair, tanned skin, and long eyelashes that fanned his cheeks.

I don't need to rack my brain to remember who he is. I instantly remember him as the child I saved. Seeing him brings me back to the first week or two after I came to Desert Moon. A rogue attack had taken place, and I remember not being able to stay still. I made my way to the daycare when I found out where the attack had taken place.

The woman stops behind the cart and bows to me. I give her a curt nod, but can't stop staring at the little boy by her side. The little boy looks up at me before looking at Gabe. I hear Gabe gasp, but I don't have to ask him why. I look at my best friend; his eyes are wide, and his lips are parted. The little boy looks back at me. The gray eyes that stare back at us belong to Olivia.

WHO?

Adea

For a moment, Gabe and I stare at the little boy in shock. The last time I'd seen him had been a while ago. And it was *before*. Before Olivia, before the Ceremony, just before. When Odis showed up at the daycare with wide eyes and his heart thumping, I figured he was his little brother or a family member. I didn't think of the color of his eyes and I didn't try to piece together who he looked like.

It feel like I slammed into a brick wall, and Olivia wasn't even my mate. I don't know what this is doing to Gabe, or what he is thinking. The woman hesitates, and I realize she's been talking. I don't hear her, and when I turn to Gabe, he is still staring at the boy. So I know he missed whatever she said too.

I apologize for my rudeness, and ask her to repeat what she said. The woman hesitates for a moment, her forehead crinkling, her eyebrows furrowing , and looking between me and Gabe.

She opens her mouth, closes it, and opens it again. The two of us are still and silent while we wait for her to speak. Leo is the opposite; he's completely oblivious to us and the atmosphere as he chows down on another panini. As the crunch of his bites fills the air, Gabe pulls his gaze from the little boy, and looks to Leo before looking back at the woman.

If this child is who we think he is, why didn't Gabe know of him? This woman has to know the connection between the child and Olivia. By default, she must also know who Gabe is, and what this child would mean to him.

"Do you mind if Paul sits here? I picked him up early from daycare and he hasn't had lunch yet. I figure he'll be safe here with the Luna and her bodyguards," she says. "I shouldn't be too long," she says apologetically.

"Of course! We don't mind at all. We missed breakfast and are grabbing a late bite to eat. We are still eating, and won't be leaving anytime soon. Paul is more than welcome to sit with us. He'll be safe with us," I assure her. "We do have more than enough food though; this is all for us, and there is a lot to spare."

"Oh no, Luna, it's okay. I promised him chicken nuggets and fries. I'm going to throw some in the oven and will be right out," she says. "Paul, greet your Luna."

Paul looks at me curiously, dips his head, and keeps eye contact with me. Gabe is trying and failing to be indifferent about Paul. The woman leads him over to the spot next to Leo. He jumps onto the couch next to him, and his blonde hair bounces up and falls over his forehead with the action.

His eyes trail over Leo, and a look of wonder crosses over his features. From a child's perspective, I can see why they would think highly of Leo, but he definitely doesn't need the ego boost.

Leo is still oblivious to Gabe's reaction, but flashes Paul a smile.

The woman excuses herself and dashes to the kitchen. After she disappears, I turn my attention back to Gabe. His face is a mixture of shock and curiosity. Gabe and I sit quietly and watch Paul as Leo pours him a glass of orange juice while he waits. They're busy talking; Paul asks how he got so big, and if he's a superhero.

Leo throws his head back and a boisterous laugh leaves his chest, cutting through the air. I'm glad he's good with kids because Gabe is still in shock. I pull myself together and clear my throat as I sit at the edge of my seat.

Leo tells him he is, indeed, a superhero, but Paul can't tell anyone. Paul swears on the Moon Goddess that he'll keep Leo's secret, and I can't help but melt. The pureness I see in Paul's eyes is the sweetest thing I've ever seen.

"Hey, Paul," I say in greeting. He turns to face me with his big gray eyes. The way he looks at me makes me feel like he can see into my soul. Children have that ability. I have no idea how to talk to kids, and I don't know what to say. I do know that if Gabe wasn't in shock, he'd want to know him; he'd have questions.

"Yes, Luna?" Paul asks. tilts his head and blinks.

"You can call me, Ady," I tell him. He smiles, and the little dimple on his cheek makes me smile. He's such a cute kid. I fight the urge to reach forward and ruffle his hair.

"Yes, Ady?"

"Do you remember me?" I ask him. He blinks before he nods furiously.

"Yep! You saved me from the stinky wolf," he says. "I remember… he smelled me and was getting closer. It was a looooong time ago, but I remember how happy Odee was."

"That's right, he was very happy you were safe."

"Odee?" Gabe asks, his voice choked. He finally finds his voice. Paul turns to look at him. His expression is curious.

"My dad," Paul says. "He's the best! He's big and strong and has the biggest muscles I've ever seen. No one can beat him... but," his eyes go to Leo, "I think the superhero might be bigger than my dad," he whispers.

Gabe's eyebrows furrow, and I know he's thinking all of the worst things. I decide against asking any more questions, and am ready to talk about school when Leo opens his mouth.

"Your dad's name is Odee?" Leo asks. "That's a weird name," he laughs.

The door swings open again, and in walks Ethan. Relief hits me and I feel myself physically relaxing, knowing he's safe, knowing that he's home. My mate smiles, making his way to me. He doesn't close the door, and Beta Odis walks in behind me. My eyes find Gabe and I don't know what he's thinking.

COMPLICATED

Gabe

Dad. He said dad. His dad's name is Odee. A four-syllable name. There are a lot of four-syllable names. In this pack? One that starts with an O? One that I had been screaming the past weekend? Oh, my Goddess. It could just be a coincidence. A coincidence? I almost snort. I think not.

How did this happen? When did this happen? If this is what I think it is why didn't I know? I didn't know this whole time. No one told me anything. Why didn't anyone tell me?!

I am sitting in a sinking ship in the middle of the ocean. The walls are caving in on me, and the water is starting to seep in. My worries and thoughts are starting to fill the room. It is quickly rising, and I'm not sure I can keep calm.

The day the rogues attacked and Ady had saved him: I remembered that day because I had been there too. I was there with her, I'd walked up to her while she held him. She'd been holding him that day. I'd seen them, seen him, and hadn't thought anything of it.

I also remember seeing Odis. He'd come in hurried and worried. He'd been looking around like a mad man. He only stopped to check on his Luna because he'd been calling her his Luna even before the ceremony.

I remember thinking it was weird the way he'd searched Ady and the child for wounds. I figured it was because he was doing his duty. He wasn't mated and wasn't seeing anyone at the time, so I never thought… I had brushed it off thinking the child was his little brother.

I don't remember seeing the child's face then. Even if I'd seen his eyes, would I have known? Or would I have thought it was a coincidence? Would I have even noticed that his eyes are a perfect replica of hers? How could I have dismissed her likeness? It is so obvious.

Still, I cannot grasp the reality of the situation. No matter how clear it is. Desperately, I am trying to hold onto the truth, and instead, it is spilling through my fingers.

Olivia, my Olivia, my mate, had a child. Why hadn't she told me? Wasn't she a virgin? Wracking my brain, I flip through the memory of our first time. She had told me I was her one and only.

I would have known, I should have known, I wouldn't have… I wouldn't have… did I see what I wanted to? Did I only feel what I wanted to feel? Did she only tell me what she wanted me to know? Did I only accept what she said without question?

She couldn't have been… this has to mean she'd been with Odis. I knew he felt something towards her. I knew there was more there, but I didn't… I couldn't have… When did they split up? Was it because of me? Did I ruin a family?

No. Stop. I'm getting ahead of myself. I won't jump to conclusions. This isn't okay. Nothing will make this okay. Can anything make this okay? What would make keeping him a secret okay? What could make me okay with this? What could make me okay with the child?

Why did she keep this from me? Did she think I wouldn't understand her? Did she think I wouldn't want her if she had a child? Would it have mattered? I don't know. I would have still wanted her. I would have been willing to… to work something out. Why wasn't I included in this?

She was mine, in her last days. She'd been mine. Why? Why had she… Lies, she'd lied to me. Why? Why had she lied to me? I've been mourning my mate. I've missed her with every fiber of my being.

How well could I have known her, if I hadn't known about him? Had I even really known her? The thought causes a stab of pain in my chest and my throat to tighten. I am second-guessing my time with her, analyzing my relationship with her, and wondering how much I really knew about her.

If I had a child out there, I would have told her. She would have known from the start. I wouldn't have kept anything from her. I didn't have any secrets from her. I told her… I told her everything I thought was important to know.

Yet, she hadn't done the same with me. I feel yet another sharp stab of pain in my chest. What did that say about me? How important could I have been, if this was kept from me? I don't know what to fucking think.

The evidence of her lies sits across from me.

What if she had a reason? My wolf pushes the whispered words past my thoughts and into my head. What reason would make this okay? Was there a reason that could make this anywhere close to okay?

No. There isn't. No reason will change the fact that she hid him from me. Nothing will make it okay that she lied to me about something this serious. As her mate, I deserved to know there was a piece of her out there in the world.

I should have known. I should have been told. With her gone from the world, he is all that is left of her. No, stop. I cannot go there. That isn't the only issue here. Odis is a whole other fucking issue that I am not sure I can unpack today.

Without care, my mind stares into the abyss that is Odis. He had said we were a mistake, and now I understood why. He had a whole fucking life before I found her. Another stab to the chest has me feeling like my heart is splitting again. This is more complicated than I'd thought. I am barely able to keep myself from diving into that issue.

SECRET

Gabe

It isn't jealousy that has me ready to break down, it is the feeling of betrayal. Paul isn't a baby, he's been on this earth for years. If his nanny hadn't brought him here, would I have ever known? Would Odis have kept me at arm's length to keep him a secret from me?

The child isn't the issue. I don't have a problem with him. It's the fact that I didn't *know* about him. I never would have known about him, if not for this chance meeting. I still am not sure how I feel about this.

I am mad, but not about him. I'm not mad that there is a history I didn't know about. I'm not mad that the history I thought I knew isn't real. I'm notmad that there is a shit load of time that is unaccounted for. I'm not mad that she kept him a secret from me.

I *am* mad that, now that I know and have questions, I can't fucking ask her. Why has this been kept a secret from me? Why didn't she have pictures of him? Why hadn't there been any signs of his existence? Why didn't we know him? Why didn't she introduce me to him?

My head is spinning and I don't know if I can stomach any more of this. I have so many questions, and the two people I want to ask actively kept this knowledge from me. Did Ady know? No, if she'd known, she would have told me. Her mate definitely knew, but he didn't have to tell me. The people who should have told me didn't.

Leo's laugh echoes off the walls at the same time that all of the breath in my lungs leaves my body. The thoughts swirling in my head promise a headache. Questions I know I may never have answers to flash through my mind.

Denial slaps me across the face. Maybe I am seeing things wrong.

Or maybe you are refusing to see reality. My wolf, Felix, is quick to hit me with reality. The obviousness of Paul's paternity stares me right in the face. As much as I want to, there is no denying it.

A muffled voice can be heard, and even though it sounds far away, I know better. Closing my eyes, I struggle to focus on where I am. I can't just keep staring at him; I am probably making the poor kid nervous.

The voice must belong to Leo or Ady, but I can't differentiate between which one. It is as if I am hearing everything with my hands over my ears. Ripping my gaze from Paul, I turn to look at my best friend by my side.

"Your dad's name is Odee?" Leo asks. I can finally hear him,his voice cutting through the tornado of thoughts that are starting to drown me.

Ady's eyes are wide with worry, and I can feel her concern for me radiating off of her in waves. My best friend's lips open slightly, and I know she just wants to know what I am thinking.

Even as I look at her, all I can see are the pair of gray eyes I know are sitting across from me. She is about to say something when the front door swings open, interrupting her. Turning towards the front door, I follow her gaze.

My best friend's mate walks in, but I only glance at him for a second. The smell coming through the door tells me who's about to walk in after him. My heart skips a stupid little beat and I don't even flinch when Odis walks in.

His hair isn't as neat as it usually is; it falls forward over his forehead. His facial expression doesn't say that he's stressed, but the look in his eyes betrays him. They went somewhere, but when I try to figure out where they went, I come up blank.

A meeting.

The meeting. Right, I'd forgotten all about it. Ethan had been summoned to an emergency meeting. Judging from his face, and his lack of a smile, something bad must have happened.

Odis doesn't see me at first. He doesn't see anyone but his alpha. His eyes are on his back as he walks in. When Ethan starts walking towards Ady, Odis' gaze lands on his Luna. I want to run and hide.

I don't want him to see me, but I'm a deer stuck in the headlights. We haven't said a word to each other since that night, but his eyes drift from Ady to me. I hate the way my stupid heart does a somersault in my chest, despite the betrayal I feel.

Ethan leans down and kisses Adea breathless. I don't need to look at them to know; the smooching sounds fill the room. My eyes lock on Odis', and I want to hate him. The way he looks at me sends my body into overdrive.

Shit, I want to blame him, but I can't. He isn't my mate, isn't my anything; never was. My mate isn't here anymore, and he's all I have. I want to blame him, I want to yell at him, hit him, cuss him out.

I want to run to him and take all of my hate out on him. As much as I want to do that, I can't, can I? It's not his fault that I didn't know about Paul. It wasn't his job to tell me about him.

At the same time, I want to run into his arms and cry. I want him to make this make sense. I want him to wrap his arms around me, and beg me to hear him out. I want him to tell me everything. I want him to make this okay. I want him to tell me he wants me in his life.

I swallow the painful lump in my throat as his gaze drifts from me across to Leo. I keep my eyes on his face, waiting for him to see who else is here, waiting for the pin to drop. His body tenses, and his eyes widen as they drop down to Leo. I've never seen him so shocked.

THE GUN

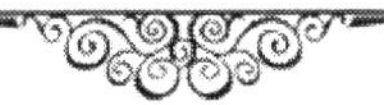

Gabe

Never have I ever seen Odis look as shocked as he does now. Paul hasn't seen Odis yet; he's too busy looking at Leo in awe. Odis comes to a stop, and I watch as his expression shifts from shock to confusion. Every fiber in my body tells me to get up and leave, but I can't Not yet.

A warm hand touches the top of mine, and I turn to find Ady's hand squeezing my own. Her mate stands by her side and stares at me with an understanding look. I swallow back the sour taste of their pity.

I wait. I wait for something, as I track his every movement down to the slightest changes in expression. I watch as Odis' eyes leave Paul, and slowly slide to me. I don't know what I wanted to see, but what stares back at me isn't it. It isn't enough.

He takes a step forward, his eyes searching my face as his lips part. I don't know what I expect him to say. At this point, I don't know if I'm ready to hear what he has to say. What could he say that would make this make sense? Odis comes to a stop by the couch Leo and Paul occupy.

"Paul," Odis chokes out.

My eyes fill, and I realize I am not even worth an explanation. He isn't going to try and explain. I continue to watch him as he turns his head away from me. His eyes fix on Paul again.

Nodding my head, I answer whatever question I'd had in my head. The sooner I face the truth, the sooner I can move on from him. The sooner I see last weekend for what it was, the sooner my heart will stop beating for him.

Hearing his name called, Paul turns and finally notices his father. The little boy jumps to his feet and jumps into Odis' arms. With happy eyes, and a bright smile on his face, he doesn't bother hitting the breaks as he crashes into Odis.

Paul smacks face first into his stomach. Odis immediately wraps an arm around him. When Paul lifts his head and stares up at Odis, his eyes are warm and his smile is genuine.

"Hey, little man, what are you doing here?"

"I finished school early," Paul says.

"Where's nan?"

"She's in the kitchen," Paul answers.

Paul's little arms are unable to wrap all the way around Odis, so his fingers cling to the fabric at Odis' sides. Odis grips his hands and lowers himself to his knees until he is at eye level with Paul.

I am a bystander who is unable to look away. Odis proceeds to ask Paul about his day, and their conversation continues. He doesn't spare me another glance, and the mask I'd had in place for the little boy has completely slipped off. I am unable to hold back my feelings.

What did I think was going to happen? That the hopeful scenario I'd played out in my mind would happen? That he'd run to me, and actually explain who Paul was, why I didn't know about him, and beg to be in my life? I can't help the chuckle that breaks free.

Before you get all crazy on them, don't you think you're jumping the gun?

Are you actually telling me to remain calm right now, Felix?

There's more to the story. Don't you think? Why else wouldn't you have known about our mate having a child?

How would I know IF NO ONE HAS TOLD ME ANYTHING?

You know what I mean. Don't get curt with me. I'm in the same boat as you. She was my mate too.

I know…

Why don't you wait until you guys can talk?

Why would I get my hopes up? We haven't been able to. He said it was a mistake!

Gabe… Doesn't Paul's presence prove that there is more to his rejection?

We still haven't been able to talk.

Why are you waiting for him to come and talk to you? We don't need to wait for him to be ready. We can make it possible ourselves.

I don't want to seem desperate. I won't. I've already offered myself up to him, and you saw how it turned out. It didn't go well. I can't go through that twice in less than a week.

Gabriel, we don't kn-

I don't care about what he has to say! I can't… I won't sit around here any longer.

Felix tries to say something else, but I don't give him another second to try and convince me of anything. Squeezing Ady's hand, I am on my feet in a flash. Turning to face Ady by my side, I blow my head to her and her mate. I know she'll understand why I have to leave.

I just need to get away from here, away from him and the boy with her eyes. Without bothering to look at him, I pass Ady, and head for the door.

I hear her calling my name from behind me but I keep going. My feet carry me to freedom, throwing open the door, I run outside and shift. I run past the packhouse area. I run until the buildings blend into a mixture of colors.

***

Odis

Staring at Paul, I try to focus on the conversation we're having. He starts talking about a superhero I have to fight so he can see who's stronger but I can't focus. My attention goes to Gabe as he jumps to his feet and says goodbye to Ady. He forgets about his duty but Leo is here so she's still guarded. I watch as he heads out the door without a second glance my way.

Plastering on a small smile, I drag my eyes from the door and focus on Paul. My wolf is screaming for me to run after him but I silence him as Paul's nanny walks out. She's holding a plate of Paul's favorite foods he's only allowed to eat on weekends. Her eyes slightly widen but she gives me a nod in greeting.

PRETENDING

Odis

After she pulls Paul to a sitting position by Leo, she serves him his food and drink. There isn't a fruit in sight but I keep my lips sealed. I watch as Paul thanks the Goddess for her food and asks her to bless his Nan who made it. He thanks the Goddess for keeping his Odee safe and my heart warms.

Sighing, I stand to my feet and run my hand through my hair. There's a fuck load of things I want to say and do but I can't. There's also a shit ton of bigger things I have to worry about other than chicken nuggets and fries.

Focusing back on Ethan, I find him sitting on the chair with Adea in his lap. He cradles her in his arms as if she were made of glass. My shoulders sag with the news we heard at the meeting.

Despite what the other alphas said, I would be prepping our soldiers for battle. Our guards need to be up and everyone needs to be alert. From what I remember of the new "Alpha", he was weak and unhinged.

We don't know him, we know nothing of him. Even after exhausting our resources to find him after we lost Liv, we couldn't find him. He was a weasel and knew how to hide. Our scouts scoured the surrounding territories and even went outside of our area to find him. I was at a loss for words or what to do when they came back empty-handed.

We had no space and no room to worry about anything else. We may not know what his plans are or how many warriors he has but he's already shown his hand. We know what he wants and I won't let our people be taken by surprise. No, we would be prepared.

With the news of a new alpha at the table, I had a lot on my plate, I had a lot of things to do. I also needed to fill in our new Gamma. I don't know if I can wait for Ethan to tell Adea first.

Even though I have a lot of things I need to do, I couldn't stop thinking about the man who had just run out the front door. Every part of me wants to take off after him, find him, and explain. I know what he's got to be thinking and my heart hurts with the pain I saw on his face. I hurt knowing the betrayal he must be feeling.

We haven't made up and it's all my fault. I know it is but when it comes to Gabe, I don't know what I want to happen. What could happen between us? I'd already drawn a line between us.

Despite what I want, I won't be the man who does things without thinking. I'll never be him again. I need to think things through before I make a move. What I have in mind would be the complete opposite of that.

I can't ignore the guilty voice that whispers in the back of my mind. It tells me I've already done what I wanted to do. I've already done those things and I've taken what I want.

It tells me that I'm full of shit and at this point, I'm pretending. There are consequences for my actions and this one will be losing him. It whispers that I'm the same person who threw away his chance at a family.

I'm repeating my mistakes. I bite back the growl that threatens to make its way from my chest and into my throat. I am not that man anymore and I'll be damned if I lose Paul to anyone. He's all I have left.

It reminds me of what I've lost and the life that I've lost. I'm nothing more than that. My wolf, Troy, tells me I know better than to listen to it. Haughtily, he reminds me I should be listening to him because he knows all.

You can't be trusted either, you like him.

I'm an extension of you, of course, I like him.

You've only proved my point!

All I'm saying is, maybe your thoughts are wrong. MAYBE you should try sitting down and talking to him because all I see is a scared man. You're running away and telling yourself that you're doing what's right. When the right thing to do would be to take responsibility for what you've done. Face him like a wolf and tell him how you feel, what you're thinking, and what you want.

And then what?

And then you hope it isn't too late.

You're telling me to rip myself open and present my most vulnerable sides to him?

Yes.

Even though he might not want me anymore?

Yes.

Even though I don't know what he'll say?

Yes.

Even though I don't know what he'll do or say?

It doesn't matter how many times you change the question, my answer is yes.

There's a fuck load of things I want to say and do but at this moment, I can't. Paul comes first, he always does and I won't have him be present during any of it. He is too young to understand why he doesn't have a mom. He doesn't know anything about Liv other than what he remembers, which isn't much.

After what happened, Liv wouldn't see him anymore. She refused to and I accepted that he was mine and mine alone. He's too young to understand what Gabe is to me and I don't even know what to do about him. I've been ignoring him and I know I'm a piece of shit for it but what else am I supposed to do?

Say I was to take Troy's advice, how would that go? I'm a single father to a son that was his mate. What am I supposed to say? Oh hey, now that we've fucked, let's co-parent and live happily ever after?

Yeah, the fuck right. After everything I've seen and been through, I know that's not a possibility. I won't lie to myself and I won't lie to Paul so I can get what I want. Even as I think these thoughts, I haven't stopped looking at the door.

DENIAL

Odis

Luna Adea and Ethan were making eyes at each other as they slipped into their own world. They shared touches and whispered sweet nothings to each other with the three of us around. I wasn't one for PDA and I drew the line at kisses. That was my cue to look away and I had no choice but to give my attention to Leo and Paul.

What I wasn't expecting was the ease Leo had with Paul. He was smiling and talking to Paul like they have known each other for years. I expected that from Paul he was an easy child and got along with others well.

Leo didn't look at me and I was fine with that. He kept smiling and laughing. Maybe he hadn't picked up on the awkwardness in the room or maybe he just didn't care.

Adea asked Leo a question and they started engaging in conversation. I wasn't sure what they were talking about but my mind wouldn't focus. As much as I tried, it didn't matter how hard I tried, my mind drifted to a crooked smile and a smart mouth.

The look on his face when I walked in was pure devastation. As much as he tried to hide it, I saw it. I can't even begin to try and fathom what he's got to be thinking.

When he left he didn't say goodbye or even acknowledge me. I mean, I didn't expect him to say goodbye and I didn't deserve him to look my way but I'd hoped.

With how quick he left, there was no way he didn't know. One look at Paul and anyone would see her in him. I was thankful he was Liv's mini-me. I could see her n him every day or at least the girl I once knew.

On the outside, I was calm and collected but on the inside, I was a raging hurricane. I struggled against the need to take off after him, instead, I had focused on Paul.

That was my goal, focus on Paul and don't look at Gabe. I was too afraid of what I'd see. Now that he was gone, my mind had followed him. He was upset, probably angry. I tried to tell myself that he needed some time to think things through. Running will help him burn off the steam from his anger and a breath of fresh air will calm him and his wolf.

Does that mean we're going to go after him?

Maybe.

You know you're going to go after him, let's be honest.

I'm just thinking about him…

While you are in denial just remember that time is the best gift we can give.

Before I can respond, Nan reaches over and takes Paul's plate. It's empty except for a small ketchup smudge. When she returns from the kitchen, she wipes up his mouth and pulls him to his feet.

"It's time to go," Nan said gently.

"Aw, no, please?" Paul begs.

"We've got to clean the house before it's time for your nightly routine," Nan said.

"Five more minutes?" Paul pleads. When she shakes her head he tires for less. "Four more minutes?" He pulls his fingers up and shows her four fingers. Nan doesn't break from schedule often and she already did today with him getting off early. It's not happening.

"Sorry, dear. Say goodbye to papa," Nan said. With that it's final but I know he'll try again.

Paul turns to me and walks towards me with heavy little feet. Crouching down, I open my arms and pick him up in a big hug. Nan walks up behind him and gives me a knowing look. I nod to let her know we're on the same page. Looking behind his shoulder, Paul sees Nan.

"Aw," Paul pouts. His big eyes grow sad and he pushes out his bottom lip. It doesn't work on me but it doesn't stop me from smiling. "Please, Odee?"

Shaking my head, I squeeze him tighter. "You heard Nan and you already know you have a lot to do today," I said. "How about this? Tonight, I promise to be home before you fall asleep. I'll tuck you in and sing sunshine," I said as we pulled apart.

"Promise?" He asked. He had passed his baby stage but I could still hear a lisp with some of his words. Offering my pinky finger, his little face lit up and he brought his up. Our pinky fingers curled around each other and we sealed it with our thumbs.

"Promise."

Nan took a step forward and I put him down so his feet touched the floor. His shoulders slumped slightly before he waved goodbye. Turning, he reached up and grabbed her hand. After he said his goodbye's to Adea and Ethan, he flashed Leo a smile and followed his nanny out.

Are you planning on going home late?

Ignoring my wolf, I try to sit still. I don't know when it happened but I've already decided to find him. I give Paul and Nan a few minutes before I'm up on my feet. I don't know if it was Troy trying to convince me or if subconsciously I knew I was going to.

There's been enough time that I know I won't run into them if I leave now. Nodding to Ethan and Adea, I excuse myself. I don't miss the way Luna ignores me but there's nothing I can do about that.

Leo glares at me as I take my leave. It's as if he suspects where I'm going and a small smile pulls at the corner of my lips. Three sets of eyes follow me as I leave and I know they know. They have to.

Forcing myself to walk and not run out of the packhouse, I eventually make it out the door. I shift without hesitating and rip through my clothes. I don't have any extras planted by the door but I can link Jamie to help me out.

READY

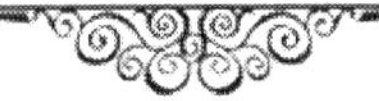

Odis

My wolf, Troy, hadn't said anything since we'd left the packhouse. As soon as we started running towards town his emotions began to blend with mine. He didn't need to say anything. I could feel his hope as if it were my own.

I know these lands like the back of my hand but I have no fucking clue where he could have gone. When I can't smell his scent in the air, Troy whines.

All I know is I'm doing what feels right and right now? Finding Gabe feels right. After we search the city, I realize there are too many sections and I can't think of a reason why he would come into the city.

Could I link him? It would save me a lot of time but I didn't want to bother him or let him know I was coming. What was I going to say when I found him? I hadn't thought that far ahead yet.

If I were trying to get away and be alone, I'd go through the desert area. I'd want to go to less populated areas and I wasted time here in the city.

Troy takes off and we trail around the city while I try to pull myself together. I'm sloppy when all I need to do is put together a plan that'll help find Gabe.

I needed to think smarter, not harder. Searching the entire territory would be a waste of time and I might miss him. Where could Gabe end up going? After a long night of running…

It's obvious he'll go to the packhouse but it's too public to have a conversation. Where would Gabe go? I'm hit with an obvious idea almost as soon as the question fills my mind.

Troy turns on his heels. I think I know where he'll go and Troy agrees with me. We're heading back in the direction of the packhouse and nerves fill my belly. I'm sure he'll be there. I'm just hoping he didn't already.

When the forested area beside the packhouse comes into view we pick up our pace. As we enter through the forest the cool shade of the breeze sends a shiver up my back. It's a welcome and even though it's dark here I know it'll only be this way until I get to the clearing.

I've found myself here on more than one occasion. Picking up his scent, I knew I was right. He had either just been here or he was still here. I knew the forest called to him as much as it did to me. It was a place outside of the packhouse I could come to when I wanted to be closer to her.

Odis, Didn't I tell you that time was the best gift?

You're looking for him just as badly as I am.

Because I want to see him… That doesn't mean we should see him. Are you finally ready?

I don't know, Troy.

Maybe you should ask yourself this before you throw yourself at him… again. From my point of view, it looks like you're running around like a chicken with its head cut off.

What does this have to do with what we're talking about, Troy? And I wasn't going to throw myself at him.

I'm saying you're running around like you don't know what to do but deep down you do. If you weren't going to throw yourself at him what are you going to do? Do you have a plan?

I-I

Exactly. You don't know what you're doing. Isn't your motto: Think first?

Yes, I'm thinking.

Are you though?

I'm thinking that I want to see Gabe.

You're being reckless. I know how you think, you need to know what you're wanting, it's INGRAINED in you. What are you going to do when you find him, O?

Don't you think I know? I'm going to tell him about Paul and I'm going to explain.

And? I'm going to tell him… I'm going to tell him that I haven't stopped thinking about him. He's been on my mind every single moment since I had him underneath me.

So, you're going to go from Paul to confessing?

Yes-NO!

Then what's the plan? I'm going to explain about Paul.

You're going to tell him about Rick?

Yes.

What else?

What do you want to happen after you've told him everything?

Are you going to tell him you want more with him?

Isn't that what telling him I've thought of him every day?

Don't answer my question with a question. That won't get us anywhere. What do you want to come from this conversation?

I want...

I don't fucking know what I want but maybe I'll have an answer when I speak to him. Light almost blinds me as the trees open and I find myself in the clearing.

Spotting Felix, my heart pumps twice as fast as I slow to a stop. He's sitting with his head on his legs. When he senses me he turns and sees us and my wolf and I both look back.

His tail drops and he sits up. Now that I've been seen, I have no choice but to walk forward. I've been looking for him and now I have him in front of me. Felix shifts and Gabe is left in his place.

"What do you want?" Gabe asked. He didn't beat around the bush and he wasn't going to bother with pleasantries. I wasn't angry at his tone, I should have been but I was too bothered trying to fight the need to look at his naked body. Troy let go and I shifted back.

"I... I want you, Gabriel."

He hesitated and clenched his jaw as he stared at me. He didn't bat an eye and my words didn't soften his gaze. He was really mad.

"You don't get to fucking do that," he said while shaking his head. Besides... a lot of people want me, Odis. Why should I care if you want me?"

OVERBEARING

Odis

The growl that left my throat was possessive as I took a step toward him. My natural instincts told me to make him submit. The thought of him with anyone else had plagued my dreams more than I cared to admit. I didn't need him reminding me of his options but maybe it's what I deserved.

After what I did, I know I didn't have a right to feel the way I did but it didn't stop me. Seeing him with Leo every day has rubbed me the wrong way. I wasn't blind I saw the way Leo looked at him.

That on top of the challenge in his voice just now had the wolf in me demanding to dominate him, to make him mine. Right now I just wanted to talk to him. I was here for a reason but that didn't mean I'd let him get away after judging me.

"You want me, that's why you should care," I growl.

"Don't you fucking growl at me," Gabe said. He folded his arms in front of his chest protectively. I didn't miss the way his eyes sadden for a second before they flip to protective anger as he glares at me. "You don't know a damn thing about what I want. I don't know why you've come to find me. You've had multiple times to talk to me this week. I don't know what you were hoping to get from me today but I have nothing to give."

He's right, I know he's right but I never seem to say the right things or do the right things when I'm around him. All that comes out of my mouth is the wrong thing and I don't want to fuck this up again.

"I… I just want to talk," I said. Lowering my voice, I close my eyes and breath deeply to calm myself. As much as I want to claim him, that isn't what I came here to do. If that happens again, he'll just think he's a piece of ass and that's not what he is.

That's not what he is at all. He means… more and I haven't had more for such a long fucking time. I'm scared of what that could mean for me and Paul. I'm scared of what that could mean with Gabe.

"So talk," Gabe said. He wasn't going to make this easy for me but I liked him even more for it. He wanted to make me work? I'd work. I'd do whatever he wanted me to do. I wanted to make things better between us but where do I start?

"I wanted to explain," I started. The mask of indifference Gabe had been wearing drops for a second and I'm able to see what's behind it. His eyes widen and an expression between hurt and hope flashed across his features before the mask settled back into place.

"Well? Go on," Gabe said.

"I know you must have some… questions about Paul," I began, "I'm sure you've made some assumptions and I wanted to clear the air. Paul is Olivia's biological son." Gabe's chin trembles slightly but he clenches his jaw and stifles the movement.

"It wasn't hard to come to that conclusion. I can see the pieces of her in him," Gabe said. "I'm not angry that he's Olivia's. I'm pissed that I didn't know about him until now. Why don't I know about him? Why didn't she tell me about him? Why haven't you told me about him?"

"Before I can answer those questions, I need to tell you a few things first," I said. I wasn't sure how this would end but the best place to start was at the beginning. His arms drop in front of him as he waits for me to begin.

"I've known Olivia for years and I've loved her since the moment I saw her. We became best friends and were inseparable. We spent most of our days together. I couldn't get enough of her. It wasn't like how it was when you came here," I said as I glanced at the sky. I was completely immersed in my memories of her.

"We did everything together until she met this guy named Rick. I called him Rick-the dick. She met him at a human campfire party and he was the only other wolf there. She said there was an instant attraction but I think it was the phase she was in. Teenagers find older guys more attractive."

"I hated him before I even knew him. She started hiding things from me and acted like she didn't want to be around me for too long. Whenever we were supposed to meet she would give me these shitty excuses and our relationship grew distant."

"I didn't want to be that overbearing best guy friend so I backed off and gave her some space, even if I hated the distance. I couldn't help the feeling of something being wrong and I was right. Something was very very wrong."

"It wasn't until they'd been dating for six months. I'd met him a few times and I was right to hate him. He was full of himself and I couldn't stand him. At this point, we only saw each other maybe once or twice during the week when he approved of it. We'd gone from seeing each other every single day to a handful of times."

"One of the approved days we were having lunch at a cafe. She was quieter than usual and she went to bite into her sandwich when her sleeve drooped. I didn't notice at first because my eyes were always on her face. I started noticing the changes in her appearance and the clothes she wore."

"When my eyes dipped to her wrist my heart fucking dropped out of my chest. There were black and blue bruises blotches starting at her wrists. Without a moment of hesitation, I reached out, grabbed her arm, and pulled her towards me. Lifting her sleeve there were bruises going all the way up her arm."

PROVE IT

Odis

"I saw red. I didn't bother listening to the excuses she tried to come up with. They were lies, all fucking lies. I found Rick-the-fucking-dick and I beat him within an inch of his life. When he left town she finally opened up to me. She told me about all of the things he did to her. It made me sick and for the longest time, I blamed myself for not doing anything in the beginning. The things he did to her, Gabe. It tore my heart out."

"Things were hard for a while after because he fucked her up. I got her to start training and she grabbed onto it with her all. It made her feel like she had some control of her life. It felt like things were finally going to start getting normal or… as close to normal as they could."

"I'd always known I couldn't live without her but I wanted more. I knew she wanted to wait for her mate but for me, it was always her. I asked her to go steady anyway and she said yes. She let me have a piece of her I didn't deserve. Shortly after, she told me she was pregnant and it wasn't mine."

"Why did she keep it from me? I'm her mate, shouldn't I have been told?" Gabe asked.

"That first question in itself is a very long story but to cut it short, she didn't want him. She couldn't stand the sight of him and when it came to it, she didn't want to parent him. I think she kept him a secret from you… because she wanted to keep that torturous part of her life hidden from you. I'm not saying it was okay but… I know why she did it."

"As for why I didn't tell you, it wasn't my place to tell you because… there was nothing between us. The two of you were mates, I wasn't your mate and I wasn't her mate. If I had jumped in I would have come across as the crazy ex. You would have thought I was trying to come in between you two. Liv and I had already come to an agreement before you came into her life. Your presence didn't change that agreement. She had no contact with him. Paul was mine and mine alone."

Needing to be closer to him, I take a step closer. He's got a distant look in his eye and I know he's processing all of this information. I'm sure there was a better way to have this conversation and maybe if I'd taken the initiative to introduce him to Paul we could have done that.

***

Gabe

I don't have to look at him to know he's staring at me. Everything in me wants to reach out and touch him. My mind is reeling with everything he just told me. I thought I knew my mate but maybe I only knew what she showed me. I couldn't ask her anything because she was gone and I couldn't be mad at her. Did this make me love her any less? Definitely not.

"Are you okay?" Odis asked.

"What do you think?" I shot back. I was still angry at him. This didn't change anything between us. This didn't repair anything. I was still hurting because of him. I needed to run, I needed to get away from here. Odis stared at me with what I thought was longing but I couldn't bring myself to believe it.

"Tell me what I can do to make this easier," Odis whispers. He reaches out and caresses my arm. I ignore the goosebumps that spread up my arm.

"Nothing will make this easier. It's just life," I said as I batted his hand away. "I just need time to… I don't know."

"I wanted to say I'm sorry," Odis said.

"About what, Odis?" I asked. "It didn't look like you were sorry for anything this week."

"I know… I… I was sure that I needed to think things through first. I'm sorry for how I treated you."

"So now that you've said sorry do you think it makes everything better?" I asked.

He walks me back until I'm up against a tree. The rough bark scrapes my back and it stings but I don't bat an eye at the pain. Saying sorry doesn't fix everything. I glare at him as he leans down and presses a kiss to my chest. The sensation causes my skin to break out in tingles. I want nothing more than to give in to him. His hands slide down to my chest and he starts to pepper kisses.

"I know nothing I say will make it better," Odis whispers. He lifts his head and looks me in the eye. "Let me show you how sorry

I am. I… I'll show you how sorry I am every day until you can forgive me. I don't know what will happen but I want to be with you."

My breath catches in my throat. My heart wants me to believe him and ride off into the sunset with him but my mind says differently. Life doesn't work out that way and I can't ignore the alarm bells going off. My mind is telling me I can't let myself be stupid enough to believe he's finally saying what I've been wanting to hear.

Putting distance between us, I take a step back holding eye contact with him. The look he's giving me almost deters me from what I'm about to do. I can't think straight when he's touching me.

It's not as easy as saying I don't want the kid and he's not yours anymore. Paul is Olivia's and I can't ignore that. As much as I've been wanting what he's willing to give me now I can't. I can't let myself think with my dick right now.

"You want me to believe you but how do I know you're not just saying this because of how you're feeling? How do I know you're not just going to change your mind like last time?"

"I'm here… asking you for more."

"Us being together like that was you asking me for more. It wasn't just physical between us and I thought we were on the same page. I gave you what was left of my heart and you shattered it. I'm not going to lie, I want to believe you. Hell, I want you but I'm not going to be let myself believe you want me all of a sudden."

"Let me show you-" Odis starts but I cut him off. I can't listen to him anymore or I'll change my mind.

"I don't trust you."

"Gabe, please," Odis begs.

"Where was this version of you when you took me every way you wanted? It hasn't even been that fucking long and you want me to believe you've done a full 360?" I ask, shaking my head.

"I-I wasn't sure…," Odis said.

"You're going to have to show me with your actions that you mean what you say. I can't just take what you're saying and believe it after the way you've treated me. You're going to have to prove it to me because I can't trust you."

It hurt me to deny him but I was done being played with. Turning from him, I shift and run. From behind me, I swear I hear him say he's going to prove it to me.

FAVORITE

Adea

So much had happened in the few minutes that was supposed to have been our meal. Paul and his nanny came, Ethan and Odis came back, and Gabe left. I'm fairly sure Odis left to find Gabe. I had hopes he'd gone after him and tried to make up with Gabe but I don't want to get my hopes up.

My mind was on Gabe and I hoped he was okay. Paul was a huge blow and I wasn't sure how I would handle the same situation if I was in his shoes. I knew how he felt about Odis and all I could do was hope it worked out for him. I sat cocooned on Ethan's lap as he kissed my neck.

He was my peace and I loved him to death but we were not alone in the sitting room. There were three of us here and I did not want to start making out with him in front of Leo. As if reading my mind, Ethan straightened up and turned to my guard.

"Did anything happen while I was gone?" Ethan asked. He switched into alpha mode so quickly I couldn't help but smile.

"No, Alpha. There's nothing to report," Leo said.

"I know that now I'm back I would normally give you the rest of the day off but I need you to work the rest of your shift."

"Understood, Alpha," Leo said. "I wasn't expecting to get off early."

"I plan to spend the rest of mine with my mate," Ethan said.

He stood to his feet and lifted me with him as if I were light as a feather when I knew I was anything but. I was more than ready to go back to our room but I was confused as to why he was keeping Leo on.

Normally when he came back from a meeting or from work, Leo and Gabe were dismissed. With Ethan by my side, I didn't need any more protection. Did this mean I needed more protection? I wouldn't ask him right now and decided to wait until we got into our room.

Ethan carried me to the elevator and Leo pressed the button. The ride up was uncomfortable and quiet. I tried to get down but Ethan only held on tighter. Leo kept his eyes forward as the elevator moved.

"You know I can walk, right?" I asked.

"I know you can," Ethan said.

"So put me down," I said as I poked his chest with my finger.

"I want to hold you," Ethan said.

The elevator doors opened and Leo stepped off first. He waited outside as we walked past and Ethan walked to our door. It wasn't until we got to our door that Ethan put me down. He wrapped his arms around me as I opened the door.

Leo stood by the entrance to our room and didn't know what to say to him. Ethan didn't bother with words as he led me in and closed the door. He nuzzled his nose into my neck. I turned to face him and he led me back until I was up against the wall.

"Ethan! He's right outside," I whispered.

My mate smiled mischievously at me. I had to fight back the moan that wanted to escape as he ground his hips against my most sensitive area. We hadn't closed the door for two minutes and he was already hard. As much as I wanted this, the last thing I wanted was an audience while my mate took me up against the wall.

I don't mind at all.

Of course, you don't Kor.

I take offense to that, Adea.

I can't with you.

"So?" He murmured as he kissed my mark.

"Fuck," I said.

"He's not going to pay attention to us anyway," Ethan murmured as he nibbled on my neck.

"It's hard not to pay attention when the person you're guarding is moaning and screaming from the other side of a DOOR."

"I love making you scream." Ethan leaned back and looked at me. When I didn't crack a smile he kissed my nose. "Adea, I love you and I want to make love to you. I don't care if anyone hears as I take you. I've had you on my mind all fucking day and I'll lose my mind if I'm not buried inside of you."

"Oh how romantic," I giggle.

Ethan kisses me with a passion that has my knees wobbling. He lifts the hem of my shirt and I lift my arms into the air. He pulls them off and discards them onto the floor before turning back to me triumphantly.

I reach back to unclip my bra when his fingers wrap around the thin material between my breasts. In the next second, my bra is ripped in two and my breasts fling free. My mate lets out a growl as he lowers his head and takes one of my breasts in his mouth.

He replaces his mouth with his fingers as he moves to the other. My breathing comes out ragged as he explores with his tongue. Dropping to his knees, I run my hands through his hair as I watch him pull down my pants.

"Goddess, I'm a starved man Adea and you're my favorite meal," he groans as he lifts my leg, wraps it around his head, and grips my thigh. Leaning in, he inhales deeply breathing me in.

"Ethan," I hiss as I try to hold on to the last bit of restraint I have. We're still by the door and I know I won't be able to be quiet once his lips touch me. I start to push him back but his strength is unmatched and he doesn't budge.

I shivered as his mouth wrapped around my sensitive flesh. The last of my restraint is nowhere in sight as my hips bucked against his face. His tongue licked a line up between my folds. He chuckles as I arch my back and he knows he's won.

SERVE

Adea

Ethan's mouth wrapped around me and his tongue dipped in and out of my wetness. There was nothing slow about his movements and I was speechless as his tongue took me to places only he could. His tongue swirled around my needy clit and I was quickly losing myself.

Needing more, I pressed forward, grinding my hips against his face. I threw my head back against the wall as two fingers slowly slid into me, moaning as he filled me. The sweet sensations rippled through me as his fingers continued ravaging me.

A sweet feeling of euphoria clouded my mind as he continued filling me. Moaning and panting, my nails dig into the flesh on the back of his neck. He ignores my need for more as he laps up my juices like they're a gift from the gods. His tongue darted into me like he was dying of thirst and only a taste of me could quench it.

With every lick of his tongue, my body tightened as my orgasm started to build in my belly. Ethan licked and sucked my clit as his fingers slid in and out of me at a merciless pace. Just when I thought it couldn't get any better I felt a third finger pressed at my back entrance. I fought the automatic urge to tighten up as the finger breached past the first ring of resistance. Fisting a handful of hair, I forced myself to stay still. Clinging to him as he pushed on past the second ring of resistance. I groaned as he filled me. His tongue flicked over my oversensitive tip and I bucked against him. Crying out, his name on my lips as I came hard on his tongue.

I was a panting mess, my head still high in the clouds. His fingers didn't let up as my orgasm shook me to my core. I didn't even try to come down from the high. My belly and muscles were tight as wave after wave washed over me.

Ethan groaned as he continued lapping up my juices. My fingernails dug into his shoulders as his fingers slid in and out at a slow and hard pace. His tongue sensually licked up between my folds as he pushed his face into me.

"You taste so fucking good. I could eat you out every day of the fucking week and never get tired of the way you taste," Ethan said, his voice husky and full of desire. I didn't even bother answering as he forced me over the edge again. I was overstimulated and my body jerked slightly as he slowly pulled out of me.

Ethan stood to his feet and lifted me up off the ground. He kissed me and I wrapped my arms around him. Tasting myself as I kissed him back. He kissed me as he carried me. When he stopped before we got to the bed, I pulled away to ask where we were going when my back pressed against the cold glass.

"Ethan!" I gasped as I pressed my chest against his. The shock of it startled me from my orgasm fogged mind. "It's fucking cold!"

He didn't answer but the asshole had the audacity to chuckle. His strong firm hands gripped my waist tighter and he lifted me effortlessly higher until my breasts were pressed against his face. My mate growled as he licked a heated line across my breasts. He looked up at me, his eyes holding mine as he slammed me down on his hard length.

I groaned as he sunk into me and my eyes rolled in the back of my head as I took one hard inch after the other. He was thick as he stretched em wide and hard where I was soft. My head rested against his chest when he was fully seated. My breasts squished against his muscular torso. The feeling of him filling me was intense and I was full. He pressed into me and I swirled my hips needing more. I needed him to move and I needed him to do it right fucking now.

"You're so fucking perfect," he murmured as he pressed a kiss to the top of my head. "And mine."

"Yes," I breathed as I ground harder on him. "I'm yours and you're mine. There's no one out there who doesn't know I'm yours," I said exasperated. "Now please," I beg.

"Mm," he murmured, ignoring my pleads. "The whole world could know but a time where I'm not utterly obsessed with you will never come. The Goddess made you for me and I thank the stars for that every day."

"Ethan," I plead. "Please."

Finally taking mercy on me, my mate lifts me up and slides me down on him. His eyes never left my face when he pulls out. He watches my facial expression and the noise I make as he fills me in a way that I crave, that I need. My legs tighten around his waist and my fingers dig into his biceps as I try to balance myself.

He lifts me again, my face lines up with his neck and I take the opportunity to bite his mark. Ethan's head rolls back and he grunts when teeth pierce his skin. His head leans against mine and I suck on the sensitive skin around my bite.

"Fuck," he groans. I release him in time for him to bring me down hard on his thick length. He feels harder than before if that's even possible. Deliciously, he fills me but before I can enjoy it, his pace picks up and he's thrusting hard into me. I'm moaning as he uses me for his pleasure, our pleasure. I'd forgotten about the coldness from the window. My mind solely focused on what he was giving me.

"Ethan," I gasped as my orgasm began building. "Ethan, oh fuck, Ethan." I moaned as he hit that sweet delicious spot deep inside of me.

"I know," He mutters, his eyes on my breasts as I slide up and down his body. "I know."

His abs flex against my stomach as he slams into me over and over again. It's everything I need and my orgasm rips through me. He pulls down hard on me as he thrusts up at the same time. It's perfect and all too much at the same time. I'm coming and tightening around him. My mate thrusts into me once, twice, three times before he cums with a roar. He calls my name over and over again as he moves me on top of him. Our bodies are slick as I slump against him as he fills me.

TAPPED OUT

Adea

Ethan lifts me off the window and carries me over to the bed. Laying me down, he kisses me and flexes his thighs. I'm not at all ready for more right now and when he presses his hips forward I groan.

"Noo," I whine. "I'm all tapped out. He laughs against my lips and my wolf whispers for me to bite his lips.

I'm trying to calm him down and not encourage him to keep going, Kor.

Is that what we were trying to do?

Well... maybe for me at least.

"I know, I'm teasing you," Ethan trails kisses down my neck. "Wait here, I'm going to be right back."

He slowly pulls out of me and I moan. I'm still sensitive but I feel empty as he walks toward the bathroom. Closing my eyes, I start to drift off when the sound of the water running jolts me awake.

The door opens and closes a few minutes later and I can hear his footsteps as they grow closer. His warm hand is on my thigh now and I want to check and see what he's doing but I'm too bothered to open my eyes.

My breathing has slowed down and sleep is promising me sweet nothings. My thighs open wide and a warm cloth presses against my center. I sigh with the comfort it brings my aching lips.

My eyes flutter open and I watched the bulking figure above me. Gently, he takes care of me, wiping from top to bottom until I'm clean. He reaches over and picks up another towel. I feel all warm and tingly as he picks up a dry one this time and presses it against me before patting me dry.

When I'm all clean, he disappears before reappearing. The bed dips as he lays by my side and I let out a breath of contentment. His arm blankets me and his hand curls around my stomach. He doesn't disturb me but his fingers rub little circles on my skin.

"I love you," he murmurs.

"I love you too," I whisper. I peek over at him and he's watching me. Before I can say thank you a yawn takes over cutting it short. When I'm done yawning, I laugh sleepily. "Thank you for taking care of me babe. I appreciate you."

"You don't need to thank me for any of that. I'm just taking care of you. My queen deserves aftercare," he murmurs as his fingers slid up and down my stomach. He continues touching me until I fall asleep.

***

The first thing I see when I wake up is Ethan. His fingers drift up and are warm as they caress my cheek before brushing a strand of hair out of my face. His eyes lingered on my lips until they darkened and he leaned forward so ours could meet. When we separated, my eyes looked past him to look outside. The sun had fully set and the room was dark except for the gentle moonlight that filtered through the window and past the curtains.

"Why are you up?" I asked as my gaze returned to my mate.

"Go back to bed," he whispered.

"Mm, don't tell me what to do," I whispered back.

He was beautiful like this, his dark hair unruly from sex and his lips thick from the anything but sweet kisses we'd shared. His dark eyes calm and the beast in them finally satiated. High cheekbones and a jaw so sharp I was surprised it didn't cut my finger when I reached out and touched it. My fingers trailed to his lips and I replaced my fingers with my lips. Gently, he kissed me back as his fingers started to train down my neck.

"Ah ah ah," I said as I leaned backward. "I'm not going to let you distract me!"

"I'm not doing any distracting and you started it," he teased. "You're the one distracting me."

"Mm-hmm. You have to catch me up on the emergency meeting. I've been waiting all day for you to come home. You need to fill me in, Mister Alpha." I reached up and booped his nose. His eyes darkened for a split second, had I not been looking I would have missed it. "Was it that bad?" I asked.

The seriousness of his expression had my nerves flaring and more nervous than I had been all day. He swallowed and retracted his hand from my neck. *The way his expression turned grim told me that the meeting didn't go well. This wasn't going to be good but I couldn't figure out what could sour his mood.*

"I'm not going to beat around the bush, my love. Ever since what happened at the ball, I've done nothing if not try to protect you. As my Luna and lifetime partner, I thought I could keep the bad from you but I can't hide this from you as much as I would like to."

"Just give it to me, Ethan. I can handle it. You don't have to protect me. We are partners and we need to protect our pack. Whatever it is, we will work through it together." I reach over to him and grab his hand, squeezing it for reassurance.

"I was hoping we would have the evening in peace and I could put telling you aside until morning. Last night, Shane marched with a pack of rogues into Half Moon pack," Ethan said.

I gasped. I don't know what I was expecting but that wasn't it. My mind is reeling at the news. I wouldn't consider a handful of rogues a pack. There must have been a lot to have been able to take over Half Moon. I'm silent as I try to make sense of this. The packhouse, the people there, are they safe?

"Shane and his pack slaughtered everyone who worked directly under Alpha Joshua and Luna Rose. He also killed those loyal to him after he killed his parents," Ethan said.

POWER-HUNGRY

Adea

Shane killed Joshua and Luna. My throat feels like it's restricted and I can't breathe. My lungs refuse to take in air as I register the fact that the two people who took me in after the crash are now dead. We weren't close but they took me in when they could have killed me. They welcomed me into their home, gave me a roof over my head, and gave me a position in their pack which was unheard of for a rogue. No one did that.

"What about Mavy? I asked. The words sounded choked as the worst outcomes came to mind.

"There was no news of her but at this point, I would say no news is good news," Ethan said. "I'm sorry, my queen. I know this can't be easy for you and I wish I could make it better. That's not all, there's more."

"More?" I asked. What more could there be? I was afraid of his response but I needed it at the same time. I was sure my jaw had hit the bed. I knew he hated being the bearer of bad news.

"Shane has earned a seat at the Alpha table," Ethan said.

"You can't be serious," I said after I peeled my jaw off the bed. "That's ridiculous, Ethan."

"There aren't any meetings in the near future but a time will come when we will see him. You will see him at events and any meetings you attend. While there aren't any meetings in the near future that we know of yet, I'll try and excuse you from them for as long as I can but it's something we won't be able to avoid."

"How can he get a seat at the Alpha table when he murdered people?" I asked.

"It's a part of our laws. Although we have a peace treaty in place that we all need to abide by, Shane wasn't an alpha and didn't have to abide by it. He's taken over a pack and has rightfully seated himself as the Alpha of that pack. He hasn't said anything to us or sent word yet. Since his father is no longer here, we can't ask how far Shane got with his training. A meeting will need to be planned soon where he will need to attend. He will be sworn in and updated on the alpha laws."

"Ethan... I-I don't think I can face him. The last time I saw him," I started.

My mind instantly went back to the night of the ball. Images of Shane on his knees in front of me followed by the look on his face at the trial. Unadulterated hate as he glared at Ethan.

The fear I had for him before I came to Desert Moon was back. Thankfully, it wasn't as bad as it was before but it had slowly crept in. I have dedicated myself to training hard to get to a point where I feel I'm strong enough to protect myself from him.

I have gotten stronger but I am not where I need to be. I haven't even been able to rematch Briana. I don't have the confidence to go up against him yet. I'm not where I need to be and I fight to keep my breathing even despite the fact my mind and body are going into panic mode.

"I know and I'm going to do what I can to keep you out of it if that's what you want. Just know that eventually, we're going to have to face him," he said, his jaw clenched at the idea. "I don't want you to stress because you're not alone. I know what his return means for you. I want you to know you aren't alone and I'll be with you."

"And I love you for that," I say as a stray tear slides down my cheek. "I'm just a little rattled right now. Oh Goddess, Gabe, Olivia. After what happened, how can we... We can't trust him!" I exclaim. "The chances of the dream happening has risen. We can't cross out the possibility of a war with Half Moon happening now."

"I know, I know. I've already started on that. I'm going to have extra guards stationed at the border of our territory. I'll make sure our weak spots are covered. I doubt he would come the same way he did the last time but I'm not going to leave that spot open now. We know he's found entry there once before and it will be heavily guarded. Tomorrow, I'm going to speak with Odis on assigning a new team of warriors there and in the city. As for your dream, I haven't mentioned that to Odis and Darci."

"Do you have anyone in mind?" I asked.

"I'm thinking of stationing some of the warriors from the new recruits. Darci has given me a few suggestions. You've been training with them and I've heard from her that there. are some promising warriors."

"There are. I would suggest Briana and Zoe. Anyone from

Tier 1 and Tier 2 would be perfect," I said. My thoughts wandered back to Gabe. "I'll have to tell Gabe."

Ethan nodded. "The alphas may have welcomed him to the table but we won't be sitting ducks, my queen. From here on out, I'm going to have Leo or Gabe by your side at all times. Even when we're together. They are going to have to figure out who gets what time with you so you're always guarded. The Alphas don't think Shane will come after us but I don't believe that for one minute."

"I still can't believe he killed his parents. What could he be thinking?" I asked as tears pricked the corners of my eyes.

"People do crazy things when they're power-hungry," Ethan whispered. "What's scarier is what's motivating him to gain this power. I don't know what he's thinking or when he'll attack but we both know he hasn't given up on you."

AGAIN

Adea

The idea that Shane was still obsessed with me was daunting. It wasn't news but it was worrying. Now that he had Half Moon and the rogues under his command made him a threat to us and our pack.

"I know he hasn't given up on me," I said.

"I do think we're good for a few days but I don't think he'd have the balls to attack us as his first course of action as Alpha," Ethan said.

"Oh, he would," I said, remembering my dreams. "My dreams make so much sense now. No matter how hard I thought about it, I couldn't figure out how he was able to attack us. Especially when the trial left him without access to his pack. I couldn't figure out how he could attack us with the numbers that he did…"

"With his pack of rogues joining his numbers as Alpha of the Half Moon pack. He has a sizable force. We still aren't sure how many he has under his command for now but we know it's a hefty number. We've always known he was a threat but now he has the power to back it," Ethan said.

"I don't want to say we're safe from him just because he's new at being an alpha. He's unhinged and we can't take the chance that he'll catch us off-guard. We need to take him seriously and be on guard at all times," I said. I was sitting up in bed at this point. Ethan's hand wrapped around my arm and he pulled me back to bed.

"Don't stress about it right now, my love. It's late and we're both tired. We can worry about it in the morning,"

My mate said as he pulled me into his embrace. I wanted to fight him on it but decided against it. Choosing instead to lean against his chest. He was right, tomorrow was another day. These beautiful rare moments we had together were rare and few in between. I put off worrying about the threat of Shane tomorrow. Nuzzling closer, I nodded.

"You're right," I murmured.

"That I am," he chuckled. I hit my wrist against his chest. "What? I don't hear that often. I don't think I can remember if there was ever a time you told me I was right. I'll soak this in while I can," he said.

"Yeah yeah yeah," I laughed as his arms tightened around me.

"When I heard the news today, I couldn't stop thinking about you. I needed you. I needed to touch you and make sure you were okay," he said, his voice low.

I lifted my hand to his cheek, it was my time to caress him. It was my turn to comfort him. "I'm here and I'm fine."

He grabbed my hand and lifted it to his lips. "You're here," he said before he pressed a kiss to the top of my hand. We listened to the sounds of each other's breathing. The sound of his heartbeat was the last thing I heard before I drifted off to sleep.

***

Adea

The sun was high in the sky as I made my way out of the packhouse. Since Leo had stayed outside our door all night, Gabe was my guard today. Leo hadn't shown up to breakfast and I didn't blame him. I told Gabe he should take a plate up for him but he said he was on guard duty and would stop by later to give him some food. Odis looked like he'd seen better days. He hadn't bothered with a suit today and kept his eyes on his food. There wouldn't be much time today and I hadn't had a chance to talk to Gabe. The awkwardness in the air told me it would be better not to try.

Ethan had kissed me goodbye after breakfast and Gabe didn't look in Odis' direction when we left. Seeing my expression, my best friend linked arms with me and didn't say anything about it. Instead, we made our way down the path in the direction of the field.

Earlier that morning, Ethan told me he would fill them in on the emergency meeting. The Deltas would be called in as well so it was easier for them to implement changes within the territories they saw over. Ethan would also be speaking with Darci about where the new warriors would be stationed.

A lot of movement is happening in our pack today. We will be ready and it gives me hope that my dream will change. Switching my focus to the training session today, I would be leading today.

Darci would be late but I would need to break everyone off into pairs after we warmed up. My body had fully healed and I was ready to get back on the field. I had my sights set on Briana and I was determined to beat her.

As if reading my mind, Gabe leaned in. "Are you ready to get your ass kicked again?" He teased. I pinched him on the arm and he cried out as we turned the corner.

"Are you ready to sweat your butt off during warm-ups?" I teased back.

The field opened up in front of us and my eyes traveled over everyone as they got ready to train.

"Have a little bit of faith in me," I aid as I rolled my eyes. "I'm ready to divide and conquer today."

"That's the spirit," he said as if he didn't believe me. "Just make sure you remember how to tap out. Not that you're going to get beat up but you need to make sure you don't get to the point of no return like last time."

"I know," I laughed. "I won't let it get that bad again."

For the warm-up, Gabe and I ran laps around the field. He hates running the most but didn't say anything. Usually, I leave him in the dust but today he pushed forward and kept up with me. He said he had a lot to get out of his system.

GIVE

Adea

After warming up, my best friend followed me to the field. I called for everyone's attention and made an announcement. Darci would be late if she showed up at all. There were a few questions that I answered.

Everyone was split off into groups of two to spar. Gabe walked off the field and sat on the sidelines. He would spar with a man from Tier 3 that could use his help. Briana watched me as I made my way over to her.

Pushing all the worries of today behind me as I focused on Briana. I didn't have time to worry about losing. I stopped three feet from her. I had a game plan I wanted to execute. As long as I stuck to it I was sure to win.

"Are you sure you want to go against me again?" Briana asked.

Briana could be a model. Her blonde hair was pencil straight and the wind slightly blew her hair back so it flowed behind her. She wore athletic wear today, a workout tank top, and tights. Her small but muscular arms were what I could only wish for.

"Yes, I'm sure."

I know what she was thinking and I had to ask myself the same thing. Was I ready to get my butt handed to me again? I knew that was a realistic possibility but I wasn't going to let it deter me. Briana nodded.

She stood still, her shoulders tense, her hands hanging by her side. She was waiting for me to attack first. Running towards her, I threw a jab at her. Her hands instantly went up and blocked it.

Left, right, left, right. One after the other, I kept it going so she would think I was solely focused on her face. Eventually, I would need to bring up my leg and aim for her knee. For this to be successful, I would need to be quick, so quick that she wouldn't be able to see it coming.

Briana blocked each jaw and uppercut. I squat down a little bit and tried to hit her in the torso when she blocked it. Her elbow came down and landed on my nose. Blood gushed down my mouth and I could feel the liquid as it splashed on my chest.

This was her first attempt at hitting me and her attack landed. I knew it looked bad but I still had confidence in my plan. As long as I could give her a false sense of security, I would get her to lower her guard.

Then and only then would I go for her knee. I cocked my elbow back and thrust my fist forward, targeting her face. She didn't blink as she brought both hands up and blocked my attack with her forearms.

Briana didn't say anything as I continued throwing punches at her. She moved back and I inched forward. She jumped to the left and I was right on her. Every step she took, I mirrored. I made my moves predictable.

I knew she could predict my moves when our fight felt like a dance. Pretending not to notice, I punched her with my right arm. She went to dodge as I'd hoped she would. The position she had now would make elbowing her knee impossible.

So while her eyes were on my fist, I lifted my left knee into the air. Her head turned slightly, and her eyes widened as she noticed the movement but it was too late. I brought my heel down and forward.

My heel connected with her knee and a sickening crack filled the sky. Briana cried out as she stumbled back. She tried to stay upright but I knew she would still be able to fight. I pulled my fist back and swung it forward and down on her injury.

She cried out as she fell back. It was a dirty move but I needed to ensure she was injured enough to know she couldn't win. I needed her to tap out. Briana didn't move her leg as she rocked back and forth. Her fingers gently hovered over it. Turning her head up at me, she nodded.

"I give."

Relief and excitement filled me. I was on the verge of crying tears of happiness. I've gone over this plan over and over in my head. I say I was confident in my plan but a part of me knew there was a high chance it wouldn't work and I would end up having to tap out.

Leo was on Briana in an instant. Shocked, I stepped back. I hadn't realized he had arrived and I watched as she checked over her injuries.

"You did well, Luna. She is incapable of fighting," Leo said as he looked up at me. I wasn't sure if the look he was giving me was one that matched his words. He looked as if he finally saw me as a threat. "Good job."

"Yes, you did well," Briana said. "You had me completely fooled. I let down my guard."

"Thank you," I said. An apology was on the tip of my tongue but I didn't let the words slip. "I waited for you to let your guard down. It was taking a while and I worried you wouldn't. That or you would take me out first."

"Bravo. Very few people have been able to say they've taken me out. Especially to where I was this badly injured."

"That's enough. You're talking about your injury as if it weren't your own," Leo said. "I'm going to take her to see the pack doctor, Tiny."

I didn't bristle at his nickname. I was more surprised by the emotion in his voice. Gently, Leo's left arm slid beneath the back of her knees and she flinched. His right arm slid behind her back. When she was secure in his arms, he slowly lifted Briana in the air and she swung an arm around the back of his neck.

ENOUGH

Adea

"I'll come with you," I said. Leo was surprised as she looked at me.

"You don't have to do that. Gabe is still on duty, so you should stay here. I'll be back before his sparring session is up," Leo said. As if on cue, Gabe was by my side. I hadn't seen him get up or make his way over.

"I don't know how long I'm going to be or if I'll end it early," Gabe said. His eyes were on Briana and the way Leo held her in his arms. I could see the curiosity in his eyes but he didn't say anything.

"You can't end it early. Your sparring partner is in Tier 3 and could use some of your expertise. Help him out," I said. Gabe huffed but didn't say anything.

"Do what you want," he said before curtsying and strolling towards his partner. Turning to Leo and Briana, I gave him a firm look. I was going and that was that. Leo grunted and turned from me. I followed him as we headed off the field. I mind-linked the pack doctor.

Doc? Are you free right now?

Luna? What's wrong?

I need your assistance. One of our warriors was injured during training today.

I was worried you'd gotten yourself hurt again.

Oh no, I'm fine but she needs help. Where would you like to meet?

Meet me in my office. It's down the hall by the meeting rooms.

Perfect. See you there!

"I've mind-linked the doctor. He's free and said to meet us in his office," I said.

Neither of them spoke and we walked in silence. The two of them hadn't said anything and didn't have anything to say so I continued behind them. Leo must have shown up to the training to take over for Gabe. He would be covering tonight and I flushed as I remembered he stood outside the door last night.

"I've noticed you act differently around the other guard," Briana said, breaking the silence. Leo didn't say anything as he carried Briana. Before we left I had seen Gabe's partner lunge at him. I didn't have to worry about Gabe, the times I've seen him fight proved that. I was hoping he would give his new partner some pointers.

"I still haven't gotten used to this place. You and Gamma Darci fit right in," Briana said. Her tone was quiet but almost accusatory. I couldn't see Leo's face but from the back, I noticed how his shoulders tensed.

"We haven't been here long enough," Leo said, ignoring the last half of what she had said.

"Do you miss it?" Briana asked.

"Do you miss it?" Leo shot back.

"I asked first," Briana said. They were close and I wondered what they were to each other. Old friends? Had they grown up together before they came to Desert Moon?

"Why are you doing this?" Leo asked.

"Doing what?"

"Why are you asking me this?"

"I just wanted to know," Briana said.

"I'm not sure why you would ask that."

"We're close and I thought I'd ask. I'm curious," Briana said.

"I've got a position here-" Leo started.

"You had a position there too," Briana cut him off.

"Did I? Or was that just a title? Something that told me what I was and where I was stationed in life?" Leo asked.

"You had a position. I thought you of all people-"

"Had, Bri, HAD, and what about me? His voice was angry and I heard a hint of a growl in his tone. "That I what? We're here now and I don't want to think of 'before'. My life is quiet here and I would like to keep it that way. I want my past to stay behind me. Don't bring it up again."

"When did you change?" Briana asked. "What made you change your mind?"

"Did I say I changed my mind?" Leo growled. "I like it here. There's nothing wrong with me liking it. This is our home now and you should remember that.

"It looks like you have." Briana stared intently at Leo. His shoulders were tense and his head was down. She didn't say another word as Leo stared back at her.

"I haven't forgotten," Leo growled. "Keep bringing it up and I'll make you walk the rest of the way."

"It's not like I haven't been this hurt before," Briana said.

Well, that was awkward.

You're telling me, Kor.

To that, Leo went silent. He didn't look down at her, his eyes remained on the road in front of him. I couldn't see her face but I wondered what kind of expression she had. We walked in silence the rest of the way.

I ran forward and opened the front door open for them. Leo walked through and I closed the door shut behind us. Doctor James was waiting in the sitting room. He stood a few inches above me, he had beautiful dark skin and he was handsome for his age.

The last time he had seen me, I had been unconscious. I stepped forward and explained what happened to Briana as we walked down the hall. Leo followed behind with Briana until we came to a door. Opening the door, we walked into a roomy seating area.

"You can have a seat while I look over her," Doctor James said. Leo shook his head. Finally seeing Briana, she rested her head on Leo's chest, her eyes were closed. Leo turned to face me.

"We'll be fine now," Leo said. "I've got it from here. You can go find Gabe while I stay with Bri." I looked between the two of them, unsure if I should leave. "Alpha will not be happy if he finds you unguarded. I'm still reporting for evening duty. I'll find you after I see to her."

"Okay," I sighed in defeat. "Please take care of her, Doc."

"Of course, Luna. Enjoy the rest of your evening," James said. I waited for him to usher them into the backroom before leaving.

NEWS

Adea

When I arrived at the field, Gabe was just finishing up with his sparring partner. Looking around, I confirmed that Darci hadn't shown up. I tried to ignore the nervousness in my chest as my mind began to spiral into all the possible negative reasons for her absence.

There were a handful of people left but they weren't training, they were scattered on and off the field. Returning my attention back to Gabe, I smiled at my friend's lopsided smile. He thumped his partner on the back and waved him goodbye.

"See you, Ben!" Gabe shouted.

"You're such a flirt," I teased.

"Not even. I like men, not boys. He's way too young for me," Gabe said as he hugged me. "How are you feeling after putting Briana on her ass?"

"Honestly? I feel really great about it. I feel like…"

"Like you're a badass Luna who took down a fierce warrior?"

Gabe asked.

"No," I laughed, "I feel as if I can protect myself now."

The sauciness in Gabe's eyes disappeared and he looked at me with understanding. I didn't need to say why I needed to protect myself, he had his own issues with Shane. He knew why I felt the way I did, he knew what I was thinking without me having to utter a word.

"You've always been a strong woman but now you can kick ass," Gabe said holding the s. The sauciness was back. "Since we're being honest, I have a confession."

"Uh-oh," I said.

"I was honestly prepared to haul your knocked-out butt to Doctor James again. You've proved me wrong," he said sheepishly. He knew what was coming and dodged as I swung at him.

"Jeez. Thanks, you jerk."

"I'm also glad I won't have to explain to your mate why I didn't protect you during training," Gabe continued.

"Yeah yeah. I'm glad too," I laughed.

"I don't think you do. If it weren't for us being best butt buddies, your mate would have killed me," Gabe said as he grabbed his throat.

"He wouldn't have!"

"Mm-hmm. This whole situation could have been avoided if you had tapped out. I never want to see a repeat of that," Gabe said.

"Tap out, got it," I said in mock seriousness.

"It would make my life a whole lot easier," Gabe tossed his imaginary hair over his shoulders.

"Right, because my life revolves around you," I teased. Gabe flashed me another bright smile. "I'll make sure you don't have to haul me anywhere again. Speaking of, I'm glad Leo showed up when he did because I would have had you escort her."

"Mm, yeah, no thanks. We needed to put those muscles of his to good use anyways."

Walking into the kitchen, I did a full scan of the dining area. It was practically empty as we took a seat at the main table. Leo and Briana were nowhere to be seen. Ethan, Odis, and Darci were nowhere in sight and I hoped they were able to get something to eat while they were working. I thanked the kitchen workers as they placed hot plates in front of us.

"So, I have news," I said cautiously when the kitchen maid left. One of Gabe's eyebrows lifted and his fork froze mid-air as he gave me an out-with-it look.

"Go on."

"It's about the emergency meeting. Ethan told me Shane has taken over the Half Moon pack."

A look of confusion spread across his features followed by pain. He's made progress on moving forward with his life and I hate that I'm bringing it all back. Just when we thought we were healing and things were getting better, it got worse. We never spoke about what happened with Shane and Olivia. His hands balled into fists as he fought to remain calm.

"Why would they take him back?" Gabe asked through clenched teeth. "He stood trial and was exiled. Why aren't we going after him? There are laws in place, Ady. He kidnapped and tortured my mate. He hurt you and was exiled. If he had done to you half of what he'd done to her, he would be dead."

Gabe is pissed and he has every reason to be. Werewolf laws weren't the same as human laws. We killed all the time, yes there were consequences but as bad as it sounds, torture is a norm among our kind. Usually, it's used against prisoners of war or enemy packs. His mate's abductor is still out there.

"The laws tailored towards attacks are for allied packs," I say carefully. "In the middle of the night, Shane marched an army of rogues into Half Moon. He was only able to become Alpha after proving he was stronger than his father."

"How the hell?"

"We don't know how he had an army of rogues under his command but he must have gathered them together from the time he was exiled," I said.

"He's like a roach, fucking hard to kill. Is... is everyone alright?" Gabe asked.

"We received news of Alpha Joshua and Luna Rose's death from the Alpha meeting. We don't know anything about Mavy but Shane adores her and I'm hoping that hasn't changed. For the most part, the pack wasn't harmed. Only the ranked members were killed, those and the Deltas that were loyal to Alpha Joshua."

It's a lot of information at once. Our food remains untouched as Gabe and I sit in silence at the table.

"It's bad enough he's still out there but now he's back in power. If he was able to do what he did while exiled, imagine what he could do now that he has a pack to command," Gabe shakes his head. "What does this mean for us?"

"It means he's a greater threat than he was before. Ethan held a meeting today with Darci, Odis, and the Deltas. Our pack's safety is our top priority and Ethan's been working all day. The goal is to station more of our warriors around the borders."

"What of the forest?" Gabe asked quietly.

"We haven't forgotten about it. We're stationing the new warriors there."

"So we're suiting up for war?" Gabe asked.

BUBBLE

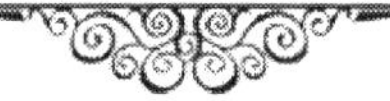

Adea

"We're not expecting war but we're taking precautions. We know how unstable Shane is and we don't want to take a chance of being blindsided if he decided something crazy. That's why we've started today on the off chance he makes a move."

"I know we're doing the best we can with the situation but I can't wrap my mind around the fact we're not going after him. The piece of shit we've been searching for has finally been located but we're not going to do anything about it? They're expecting us to just sit here?" Gabe shook his head, his eyes were wide in disbelief. "This is insane. When I see him, I'm going to rip his head off."

"When? Gabe, I know I have no right to say this but... I can't... I can't have you going after him for revenge. We need to do this the right way. I know, he didn't play by the rules and this is so shitty. I know this sucks and I'm sorry. You have no idea how sorry I am. I wish I could bring you justice for what's happened. I need you to believe me when I say he's going to get what's coming to him."

I was also trying to come to terms with Shane being back. Every time I thought of him it put my body into fight or flight mode. Images from my dream flashed through my mind. "I can't bear the thought of losing you. Please," I choke.

Gabe doesn't say anything but he grabs my hand and squeezes. Closing my eyes, I pushed them back. That was the last thing I wanted to focus on today. I could only handle so much and I definitely couldn't do this today, wouldn't. After we ate our food, we sat in the living room and waited for Leo.

A door closed and both of our heads swung in the direction of the noise. Leo strode down the hallway, a sly smirk spread across his lips when his eyes landed on Gabe. He took a seat next to Gabe.

"How's Briana?" I asked. His eyes were on Gabe as he answered.

"She's fine thanks to Doctor James. He said she'll need a few days to heal but he'll make sure to keep an eye on her to ensure it heals properly.

"What's with the sad face?" Leo asked Gabe. "Did you miss me?" He leaned into my best friend, who in turn leaned away.

"You're in my bubble!" I couldn't help but laugh. Trust him to act like a kindergartner who just found out boys have cooties. I was glad to see him smile. I wish I could make it better for him but I knew he just needed some time. "It's time for us to switch."

"Trying to get rid of me so soon?" Leo asked as he crossed his arms in front of him.

"Yes," Gabe said with a straight face. Leo pretended to be hurt as Gabe stood to his feet. He was quiet on the ride up. When we stepped off, we stopped at Gabe's door and he gave me a hug goodbye.

"Goodnight, Ady. Get some rest," he said.

"Goodnight, Gabe," I said as I squeezed him.

"Goodnight, Gabe," Leo said as he opened his arms. Gabe used his index finger to push Leo back by the forehead. "Rude," Leo muttered as Gabe opened and shut his door.

Leo walked me the rest of the way and stood by the door. I said goodnight to him and he nodded at me when I went in. Ethan was still gone after I took a long hot shower. I couldn't help but be disappointed. I had hoped he would be back. Sighing, I grabbed one of his shirts and pulled it down over my head. The material fell to my thighs and I wrapped my arms around myself. After turning off the lights, I crawled into bed and waited for my mate.

***

I woke from my sleep when the bed dipped. My eyes fluttered open and I tried to blink the sleep from my eyes. Squinting, I attempted to peer through the darkness. A large silhouetted frame hovered above me and I jerked back clumsily. I was about to scream when I inhaled. I relaxed when my mate's scent filled my senses. My mate was home.

"Goddess, Ethan. You scared me!"

"I'm sorry, my love," he murmured as he lay beside me. Ethan's large sculpted arms wrapped around my body and I sighed as he pulled me in close. Remembering that I had been waiting for him, I huffed.

"What time is it?" I grumbled into his chest.

"Late, go back to bed," he said as he yawned. It was infectious.

"How did it go?" I yawned as I asked.

"It's late. I missed you."

"Then make it quick. I'm not going to bed until I hear about your day," I said stubbornly.

"I said I missed you."

"I missed you too," I laughed. "Now tell me."

"Okay," he chuckled. "After I briefed everyone on Shane, the Deltas were dismissed. They went back to their section and gathered the warriors. I went with Odis and Darci one section at a time. We're working on a shift schedule. We want there to always be someone at the specified posts. Our people are on edge, seeing us prepare made some of them fearful. There were a lot of questions and Odis did his best to answer them. It took all day but after tallying our numbers, Odis feels confident. That's not counting the new warriors either. Darci is Gamma but she's been overseeing the new recruits. Tomorrow she's going to gather them up so we can get them set up. I wanted to get to it today but as you can see by the time we returned, it was too late."

"Wow. Well, you had a busy day and you were on my mind throughout mine. I was worried when we didn't see you at dinner. You've done an amazing job. Thank you for doing everything you can to keep our pack safe."

SQUELCH

Adea

"Thank you, My Queen. I'm just doing what needs to be done. I'll do whatever it takes to keep you safe," Ethan said as his arms tightened around me. We stared into each other's eyes. Leaning up, I pressed a kiss to his lips, and sleepily, he kissed me back.

"What can I do to help?" I asked.

"You don't need to worry about that. It's being taken care of. I heard about your training session today," Ethan said. He was trying to change the subject and I'd let it go for now.

"Yes," I laughed, taking the bait. "I beat her."

"You're going to have to give me a little more than that. I heard you didn't just beat her, you defeated her," Ethan said. "Gamma has said good things about her. She was a high leveled warrior before. I have no doubt she'll rise through the ranks here."

I was going to fill him in but he held me tight when I tried to sit up out of excitement. I accepted my fate and gave him a play-by-play of the fight from the comfort of his arms. He oohed and ahhed at all the right times. My mate was the perfect lover but I was lucky enough to also have him as my friend. It was the best thing in the world.

"I still can't believe it. I didn't think I would win. My best friend didn't believe in me. You think that he of all people would have been on my side." I pretended to pout and he kissed me.

"You can't blame him. You barely healed from last time and you were already back out there. Your opponent probably felt the same way." I opened my mouth but he didn't give me the chance to speak. "But if it helps, I believe in you and I was rooting for you today. I'm proud of you and the progress you've made in the short time you've been training."

"Thank you."

Emotion filled my chest at his words. I didn't know how badly I wanted to hear him say it. I wasn't even sure I would be able to beat her today but I convinced myself that I was. It was like a pat on the back.

Being loved and appreciated by him made me feel all kinds of happy. I loved the way he loved me. I only hoped that I was as good a partner to him as he was to me. Ethan's breathing hollowed and I knew he was starting to fall asleep.

"I love you," I whispered.

"Mm, I love you too."

I tried to slip out of his arms but they were wrapped tightly around me. I would not be deterred. I had an idea and I was going to act on it. My hand slid down his chest and he stirred. I listened as his breathing quickened.

"What are you doing?" Ethan said huskily.

"What does it look like?" I teased.

"Adea," he murmured.

"Sh, close your eyes," I whispered as my hand dipped lower.

"We should be—" Ethan trailed off as I felt the imprint of his cock.

Goddess, he was so big. It wasn't just his length, there was nothing small about him. I squeezed him with the tips of my fingers. I yelped in surprise and sat up. He shuffled as he pulled his pants down.

"Well, I'm awake now."

I laughed out loud as he lay back with his arms behind his back. He was so sexy and I kept my eyes on him as I made my way down his body sensually. I sat between his legs, my knees faced down and my backside rested on the bottom of my heels.

Sliding my hands up his thighs, he flexed beneath me. I slid my hands down his thighs and took my time feeling the sculpted muscles beneath my fingers. Lifting a hand, I reached forward until my hand brushed against his hardness. I wrapped my hand around the base of his cock.

It was hard and erect, of course, he was already hard. I squeezed him and smiled when I heard a sharp inhale. Leaning forward, I licked the slit on his tip and he let out a low growl of approval. I was hot and bothered as I stared up at him. There was something about making him feel good that made me feel powerful.

I licked my lips and dragged my wet tongue along the sensitive flesh on the underside of his tip. Ethan's thighs flexed and I couldn't help but smile. He wanted more and I obeyed. I dragged my tongue up his hard length.

"Fuck you're a tease," Ethan said under his breath.

"You know you love it," I whispered.

"Oh, I do," he growled.

Wrapping my lips around his tip and sucked while my tongue slid between the slit. Pre-cum had pooled there and I fought a moan as I tasted him on my tongue. My name was on his lips like a prayer and I decided to answer.

Lowering my head, I opened my mouth wide as I took him. He groaned as inch by inch disappeared into my mouth. When his tip hit the back of my throat, he cursed and fisted my hair.

He pushed my head down on his length, his tip slid down the back of my throat. I tried my best to open up for him but he was thick and I gagged. I didn't let it stop me. He lifted me up again and slammed my head down on his cock.

"Yes, fuck yes. Your mouth feels so fucking good," Ethan grunted as I bobbed up and down on his fat cock.

The squelching sounds of my lips and mouth around him filled the air. With each drop of my head, Ethan thrust upwards. "Keep going and I'm not going to last much longer." His hands gripped my shoulders. Ignoring him, I took him deep and swallowed around his length with each bob. Lifting me up, with an audible pop. I stared at him with wide eyes. His chest rose and fell with each breath.

"What's going on? Why did you stop?" I asked.

YES, PLEASE

Adea

The response I waited for never came. Ignoring me, my mate leaned forward and reached for me. His hands dipped under my t-shirt that hung around my thighs and slid up until he gripped my hips. He lifted me easily and I was pulled forward until my chest pressed against his. I was on top of him, my legs danged at his sides.

Staring down into his eyes, he lowered me until he was between my legs. When my legs touched the bed, I held myself up and he nipped at my throat. I lowered my chin and he kissed me. It wasn't hard or rushed, his kiss was slow and consuming.

"I'm going to make love to you the way only I can. I want to tattoo my name on your insides. I want to see the expression on your face you have as you take me. I want to see the look in your eyes when you come on my cock," Ethan murmured between kisses. His fingers trailed down my backside and he grabbed a handful of each cheek.

Um, yes, please.

"You've been bare this whole time?" Ethan groaned.

There wasn't any material separating his flesh from mine. I nodded as his fingers spread wide and squeezed. Rolling my hips, I teased his tip with my wetness. My hands were on Ethan's shoulders.

I fully intended to slowly slide down his length but my mate had other plans. Spreading my cheeks wide, Ethan slammed me down and in one swift movement, I was impaled on his cock.

I was taken by surprise and didn't have time to get used to his girth. I dropped my head against his chest, there was a rumble of pleasure. Inhaling deeply, I tried to adjust around him. I was aware of feather-light kisses on my forehead, cheeks, nose, and lips.

"Did I hurt you, My Queen?" He asked.

"Only in the way we both like," I murmured. Looking up at him, I pressed a kiss to his lips.

"That's why you're perfect," Ethan chuckled. "The Goddess made you for me."

Firm hands separated my cheeks and he lifted me up off his length and slammed me down on his hard length.

Full, that's what I was, I was so incredibly full. Usually, I liked to grind on top of him before I bounced on top but today, Ethan was in charge. Leaning back, I put my arms behind me, and when I felt his thighs below my hands I put my weight on them and lowered my chin.

Ethan's deep groan vibrated in his chest and my wetness glistened on his hard cock in the moonlight. Needing to confirm he was looking too, my eyes trailed up his chiseled chest to his face.

His eyes were locked on the part of his cock that pressed into my pussy and disappeared. Knowing he was as entranced as I was, I dragged my eyes from his face and focused on his thick length.

My eyes dropped to the space between us, his hard cock glistened as he rocked me back on his tip. I fought the urge to let my head drop and close my eyes. My mouth hung slack as he make us both feel good.

There was something about watching your lover disappear into your wet pussy. Every time I thought he was going to sink into me again, he didn't. Instead, he rocked me back and forth on half of his hard cock, only pushing an inch deeper each time.

I whimpered and moaned as the new position had his squelching into my wetness. The sounds of our lovemaking were erotic and made me want him even more. I dug my nails into his thighs but Ethan was relentless.

He was in control and I would feel good on his terms. His pace remained the same but he pushed deep into me as I rocked forward. He was hitting just the right spot and my thighs trembled as he fucked me hard and slow.

"You're so beautiful like this," Ethan's voice was low, his eyes flickered back and forth between my face and the space between us.

"Ethan, please," I begged.

"I love the feel of your tight pussy wrapped around my cock," Ethan growled. My fingers dug into his thighs as I tried to hold on tight as he impales me from the bottom. I was lost as he brought me to my orgasm.

The peaks of my breasts pressed against the fabric of the shirt. They bounced as he rocked me forward. Dipping his head, Ethan leaned forward and bit on my left nipple. It was all too much.

"Oh, Ethan," I cried.

"Come for me," Ethan said as he looked into my eyes. "Be a good girl and come for me."

The words were a match to gasoline. I cried out again, my pussy tightened around his thick cock. Ethan groaned as I orgasmed. He moved me faster on his cock, and I moaned as he fucked me through wave after wave of ecstasy.

"Ethan, oh," I moaned. "I'm—"

"I know," Ethan grunted as I squeezed him tight. "That's a good girl." Leaning forward, I brought my hands forward. I was going to rest my head against his chest but before I could I did a 360 as I was flipped and on all fours.

Ethan was hard inside of me and I squirmed underneath him. His firm hand was on my back, applying pressure, I dropped to my elbows before I leaned down until my cheek pressed against the cool sheet.

Ethan was still as he caressed my hair. It felt so good I closed my eyes. I closed my eyes and enjoyed the feel of fingers but they disappeared. Reappearing, his fingers slid down my back and my eyes flew open. I could feel the bed move as he leaned back. When I felt his hands on my backside, I wiggled against him.

BEFORE

Adea

It was probably not a good idea to provoke him while I was at his mercy. Or was it a good idea? I giggled at the thought when Ethan pulled out of me. I closed my eyes as he thrust into me hard. My sensitive pussy tingled painfully but the pleasure surpassed the pain. Pulling out of me, my body thrust forward as Ethan slammed into me. I hadn't been holding onto anything but with the pace, he was setting, I knew I would need to.

"Fuck," Ethan cursed. "This is mine, you are all mine."

He didn't hold back, as if he needed to convince me. We both knew I was his but I wasn't complaining. Ethan thrust in and out of me hard and fast. My breasts bounced under me and his balls slapped against my clit with each thrust in just the right way.

"All yours," I breathed.

I was quiet, all I could do was focus on the feeling of him in me. I don't know if he heard me. When he pulled out of me, I was ready. As he thrust home, I met him with a back shot. My belly tightened as my orgasm started building.

"Fuck, Adea. Fuck, yes," Ethan groaned.

Words were lost to me, all I could do was moan as he thrust deeper, if that was even possible. His hands gripped my hips and he pulled out to the tip and thrust into me again. I met each of his thrusts as I pushed my ass back.

I screamed as my belly tightened enough to hurt and my body spasmed as I came on his cock. It didn't stop me from making sure he came, I continued to I bounced back on his hardness, over and over again. Taking each of his thrusts as I tightened around him. Ethan's cock hardened inside of me

"Yes, baby. Just like that. Just. Like. That."

Ethan's grip tightened and he groaned as he came inside of me. He pushed his hips forward and I thrust back while I milked him.

"I love watching you take me," Ethan murmured. His thumbs massaged my lower back as he finished coming in me.

"Mm," I said sleepily.

After Ethan cleaned us up, he crawled into bed with me and we cuddled. He pinched the blubber on my hips and I bit his arm. We played in bed like flirty teenagers until we were out of breath and I gave in. Declaring he was the greatest Alpha in the world.

Pulling me close to his chest, he played with my hair and we started talking. Sleep was out of the question for the moment. We talked about things we wanted to do when the pack was safe. We talked about places we wanted to visit.

We talked as if Shane wasn't still out there. We talked about children and fought about what we wanted. Ethan wanted a girl and I wanted a boy. Before we wrestled, I told him he could have a girl if he wanted as if we could choose.

We've never really talked about children. It was normal for she-wolves to get pregnant a few months after they find their mate. The thought never really crossed my mind but I knew one day we would have children.

As Alpha, he needed an heir but surprisingly enough Ethan wasn't in a rush. He said he wanted to spend some more time with just me before we had a kid trying to squeeze in the middle of us at night.

We've been sleeping together a lot and I never thought about how weird it was that I hadn't gotten pregnant yet. We haven't been using anything, our kind doesn't try to stop the Moon Goddesses' blessings.

But now that we were talking about it, I wondered if I should worry. We were having a good time and I didn't want to bring it up. I made a mental note to talk to Doctor James. It felt good to lay in bed with my life partner and talk about the future and the things that we wanted.

***

That night, I had another dream. It wasn't like the normal dream I have. The dream was repetitive and it wasn't until I came to Desert Moon that I learned more. Since the new snippets, it hadn't progressed, there hadn't been anything new in months. Tonight wasn't like any other night, tonight, it was different.

This was before but it was also after. The air was chilly, the ground was cold, and there was something wet against my face. My body was heavy and for the life of me, I couldn't move. When I managed to raise my chest, everything hurt.

I was surrounded by darkness and -. Every lungful of air was accompanied by pain. In a panic, I thrashed around and my face pressed harder into the wetness below me. Something thick spread across my cheeks and I stilled.

Blinking, the smell of dirt and grass filled my nostrils and broke through my urgency. The smell of dirt and grass filled my senses. Despite the pain, a feeling of peace settled over me. I have no complaints if this was the way I left the world.

My body slumped against the earth as I gave up the fight. Memories flooded in, finding Gabriel's body, Ethan's heart, waking up beneath Shane. The reality of what happened unfurled in front of my eyes and a choked cry gets stuck in my throat.

Ethan. My fingers trailed up my neck to the rough broken skin from Shane's canines. Tears pricked the corners of my eyes as my hand dropped to my belly. My hand caresses my belly out of habit as I mourn the loss of my child and the loss of my future.

A deep sorrow settles over me and makes its way into my chest. I let my hand drop to the ground. Everyone I loved was dead, I had no one left. My hopes, my future, it's all gone. The only thing I had to be happy about was Shane's death. Even then, I wasn't sure if I really won. I may have killed him and put an end to his reign of terror but he took everything with him.

WHERE?

Adea

Blinking, the fog lifted and the view I was met with was the sun peeking over the horizon. I stared in awe at the hues of orange and pink that painted the morning sky. Sighing, I resigned myself to my fate. I wouldn't complain if this was the way I left this world. My chest shuttered and I fought to keep my eyes open..

In my peripheral vision, something was moving towards me and fat. Could I be so unlucky to be alive when an animal found my body? There was no fear as I thought of being consumed by a bear or whatever it was that was coming for me. My chest vibrates as I laughed.

If it was an animal, I'd leave this world as someone's breakfast. If it was a person, I didn't know who it could be. I couldn't think of someone who would run toward me with such urgency.

There was no one. Someone fell to their knees beside me and the lightest touch shook my shoulder. Their hands hovered over my body. A muffled voice urged me to speak or blink but I couldn't do anything. There was no point now anyway.

I could barely hear that but I think they asked me to stay. My lips parted as I tried to tell them that wasn't possible but no words came out. I couldn't even look at them. I could only see something black. Giving up, I continued to stare at the sky. Before everything went black, the sky grew closer as someone lifted me into the air.

***

Paralyzed, I was frozen as my body shook. Someone was shaking me and I couldn't do anything. I couldn't make a noise or answer. The voice was muffled, where I thought I heard a girl earlier, this time, it sounded male. I couldn't open my eyes but I could see the light on the other side of my closed eyelids. The voice became clear and I realized I recognized the voice. It was Ethan, he was calling me and the tone of his voice was worried, fearful even."Thank the Goddess," Ethan said. He was sitting up and I was laying in his arms. One of his hands cupped my cheek. Pushing his head against my forehead, Ethan sighed in relief. "Are you okay?" He asked. His thumb swiped at my cheek and wiped away the tears I didn't know I shed.

"What happened? What's going on?" I asked.

"I don't know. One minute you were fine and the next you were struggling against me. I tried to wake you up but nothing worked. You were crying and wouldn't wake up no matter how hard I shook you," Ethan said, his expression nervous.

"I had a dream," I said. I could tell him that I was dying in my dream but that wouldn't help anyone. If there had been something worth telling, I would have but since there wasn't, I decided to keep it to myself.

"What made you so sad?" Ethan asked.

"Just a bad dream."

We have so much going on right now, I don't want to burden him with the thought of me dying. There must not have been someone there. It was Ethan. That's the only thing that made sense.

"I'll get you some water," Ethan said. Sitting up, I grabbed my head. Great, a migraine. Leaning back against the bed frame, I watched as Ethan returned with water.

"Thanks, Love," I murmured as I grabbed the glass from his hand.

"I'm meeting with Darci today to gather the new warriors. I'd stay in bed with you all if I could."

"I know," I said. "But duty calls. It's okay. We've got responsibilities. I'm not going to stay in bed. After a bit of medicine, I'll be good as new."

"We've still got an hour until seven. I'll go get some medicine from the kitchen," Ethan said as he got to his feet.

I watched as he put on shorts and a body armor shirt. He was out of the door and I turned to the window. Looking outside, I thought about my dream. I still felt like the same person and this was the first time dream-me mentioned multiple names.

I tried not to worry about the fact that I recognized all the names. Everything was the same except I called Gabe by his full name. Just a few hours ago, Ethan and I had been talking about our plans for the future and children.

The dream showed me that I didn't get any of those things. It felt as if the Moon Goddess was taking them from me but I didn't know why. It was as if she was telling me I didn't deserve any of them.

What put this all into motion? Was it meeting Shane after my parents died? Was it meeting Ethan at the Crescent Moon Ball? Had there ever been a time when I could have stopped the wheels of time from churning?

My cheeks were stained again and I brushed the tears away. They kept coming up and for a moment, I let myself cry. Grabbing the bed sheet, I brought it up to my face, and let the tears flow.

Having these dreams telling me that shitty things were going to happen all the time made it harder and harder for me to stay positive. I didn't want to lose anyone, I didn't want to see anyone die.

Did I want to save everyone? Yes. Was I hopeful of the work Ethan was doing to ensure our pack was heavily guarded around the clock? Yes. Did I think we would win when I've already seen how it ended before? I don't know. What I did know was that I was hopeful but hopefully didn't mean we would win.

I've made progress, by beating Briana, I know I can defend myself. Have I ever gone up against an Alpha who wouldn't let me win? No, but maybe what I needed was to let myself get close to the Alpha who wanted to hurt my family.t

JEALOUS

Adea

After all, I have Alpha blood running through me too. I'm not used to thinking of myself as an Alpha's daughter. It has been so long, and after the way my life had panned out after their death, it never really crossed my mind. With what I have in mind, I need to remember who I am. If anyone can take Shane down, it is me. The wheels start turning and an idea begins to form.

From my dreams, I know how much I hate the Moon Goddess. I don't know how it started, or where the hate comes from, but when bad things happen, I blame her. Our kind worships and reveres her. She is the one who chooses our mates and blesses our bloodline. In this life, I can't think of a time when I blamed her for the things that have happened to me. Life just sucks sometimes. I don't think of her like a puppeteer pulling our strings.

What I do know is that fate is something we respect, but in my opinion, it isn't absolute. If you want to change something, you have to keep trying until you succeed. All I need to do is make the right choices.

With Olivia's death, it is confirmation that parts of fate can be changed. If I do something I didn't do before, it's possible to alter what is destined or intended to happen.

Thinking of the beautiful sky in my dream, I wonder if there is a way for me to save everyone else. Is there a way to save any one person? Would a future still be possible for me? If not, could I ensure my loved ones have a future? I will be happy if I can just keep them safe.

The doorknob turns and I bunch up the tear-stained sheets before pulling them over my chest. The door swings open ,and Ethan walks in with a tray of food. I smile at him when I notice someone behind him. Gabe follows close behind, holding a tray of drinks.

Gabe looks pretty banged up. He still has bedhead, his eyes are bloodshot, and he is still in pajamas. It seems I'm not the only one who didn't get any sleep last night.

It doesn't matter if Ethan is in the packhouse too, he has Leo guard me.

Gabe yawns as he draws closer. Stifling a laugh, I smile at my mate. He must have woken Gabe up on his way down to the kitchen. Because Gabe is my best friend, he woke him up early just for me. Perks of being my best friend.

Gabe doesn't say anything as he places his tray down on the table by the bed. His eyes search my face, and he gives me a knowing smile. Walking over, he presses a kiss to my hair and squeezes my arm.

He shoots me a look that says he loves me, but still isn't happy about being woken up early. Fighting to keep my expression neutral, I pretend I don't get the last half of what he says with his eyes. I thank my best friend before he turns around and makes his way to the door.

"I love you, Gabe," I call before he can walk out.

"I love you too, Ady." He gives me a weak smile.

"Since I'm up and already at my place of employment, I'll take over now," Gabe says, dismissing Leo. "You can go home."

"You sure? You can grab breakfast first if you want," Leo says. "A few more minutes won't kill me."

Gabe shakes his head."I prefer not to eat right when I wake up. I'll get something to eat when lunch rolls around."

"Suit yourself," Leo nods to us before heading to his room. Gabe winks at me before closing the door.

Returning my attention to Ethan, his lips are down turned as he brings the tray of food over to me. It takes me a minute to realize my mate is pouting. The big bad Alpha of The Desert Moon pack is pouting and I have an idea of why. He sits at the edge of the bed.

I lean over and poked the furrow in his forehead."Are you jealous of Gabe?" I ask.

"I don't know what you're talking about."

"You're not jealous of me telling Gabe I love him?" I tease.

"No, because I'm the only one you love," he says simply.

"I can't with you." I burst out in a fit of laughter. "You're jealous of Gabe!"

"I'm not," Ethan says indignantly, biting into an apple. Wiping my tears, I hold my belly as I laugh. When I look up, Ethan's eyes have softened.

"Thank you for preparing all of this," I whisper.

"No thanks needed," Ethan says.

Leaning in, my mate captures my lips ,and I kiss him back. I wrap my arms around his neck, and he growls as I deepen the kiss. The plates on the tray clatter as the bed dips. Ethan's hand grabs my side to stop me.

"I never thought I'd ever tell you no, but if we keep going, we're never going to leave this room. If I didn't have to get the forest guarded today, I would say fuck it," he says.

"I know," I lean in and kiss him again. "Plus, I don't remember telling you we were going to do anything."

His mouth opens and shuts. When he opens it again, I snatch his apple and push it into his mouth. He grabs it and bites a big chunk, the juice wetting his lips. He stares at me with narrowed eyes, a warning that I choose to ignore.

"I love you," I singsong, picking up my fork.

"I love you too," he says.

As soon as we are done eating, it is my turn to get ready. We take our trays down to the kitchen. The mood is light as the kitchen workers tell us they could have made something. Ethan tells them he wanted to make his mate breakfast in bed.

Alpha? Luna?

Yes, Beta?

Please meet me in the sitting room. I have news.

ATTACK

Adea

My mind races as we rush to the sitting room. Gabe followed us down, and shadowed us as we moved. Odis is already there, standing with Darci. Multiple different scenarios pass through my mind. Odis hardly mind-links both me and Alpha. I can't remember the last time he did this.

Are we under attack?

Is it about Shane?

Or Mavy?

Is there a problem?

"Sorry to disturb you first thing in the morning," Odis says to Darci. Gamma Darci bows her head to me and Ethan.

"You're no bother. I was already on my way here to meet Alpha," Darci says.

"It's nothing. What's wrong?" I ask.

"A meeting with the Alphas has been called," Odis announces. "Since there's a new Alpha, they have decided it is best if he is updated on the rules. He needs to be informed about the peace treaty Half Moon has with our packs."

"This is so soon. They just had an emergency meeting the other day," I say.

"What kind of meeting?" Ethan asks.

"A united meeting," Odis replies.

"What does that mean?" I ask, looking between them.

"A united meeting is where the Alpha, the Luna, the Beta, and the Gamma attend," Odis answers.

"Was it Alpha Rich who sent word?" Ethan asks.

"Yes, Alpha," Odis confirms.

"Was his seal used?"

"Yes, everything checks out," Odis says.

"I trust Alpha Rich. He wouldn't lead us into a trap," Ethan says before turning to me. "You don't need to worry. Before I leave, Darci and I will have the new warriors stationed. The pack will be safe. You will be safe."

"I know what we talked about the night you returned from the meeting, but now that we're faced with the issue, I'm not going to stay home. I'm going. I won't have us looking weak because of me."

"My Queen…" Ethan trails off.

I know what he's thinking. We agreed that I would stay out of the meetings for as long as possible, but now, a united meeting has been called. If it had been another emergency meeting, I might have skipped it, but this one requires my attendance.

I won't have Shane, or any of the other Alphas, thinking we fear him. I don't fear him. I fear what he can do to my family. After my dream last night, I'll do anything to help my pack. This way, when I see him, I can assess him and gauge his reaction.

"I'll be fine," I tell Ethan. "Everything will be fine. If Shane is crazy about me, he won't be able to hold himself back. If he does something today, we might be able to get him removed from the table. I don't know if we could take his pack from him, but we can at least disable any ties he could form with any of the Alphas in attendance, right?" I look to Ethan for a response, but he remains quiet. I turn to Odis and he nods.

"Yes, Darci and I will remain by your side, Luna. We'll keep you safe." Odis' reassurance helps.

"I'll also be there, Luna," Gabe says from behind me.

"I appreciate that. When is the meeting?" I ask.

"Tonight. I suggest we leave as soon as the warriors are stationed, so we can make it to Alpha Rich's pack on time," Odis says.

"Sounds good," Darci says. "We can get started right now. I already know which ones I want to station in the forest. I'm down a warrior, but we'll have a few extras after we're done. The sooner we get started, the sooner we get back."

"Agreed." Ethan finally breaks his silence.

"Sounds like a plan! I'll head upstairs with Gabe while you guys take care of that. I'm not dressed for an Alphas' meeting," I say, looking at my chosen outfit.. I am wearing jeans and a hoodie. "I'll go get ready."

"That's a good idea," Odis says.

As always, he is professionally dressed. Today, he is in a dark gray suit. Despite the way Gabe looked, Odis' hair has been swept back and his suit was crisp. The only indication that he might not be as perfect as he looks is his eyes. They are red, and he has bags under his eyes.

Ethan grabs my hand and pulls me until I am flush against his body. He kisses me like it is the last time he'll see me. My mind goes blank as his hand pushes through my hair and I kiss him back.

When we separate, we smile at each other. Remembering the others, my cheeks flush with embarrassment. I swear I see Odis cringe, and Darci wears a bored expression. Gabe sighs like he wishes he has someone.

"Well," Odis clears his throat.

"I'm ready when you are, Alpha," Darci says.

"Okay. I'll try to make it quick," Ethan says. He looks at Gabe and Gabe nods before bowing his head. "Let's head out."

With one final look, Ethan turns and heads out the door with Darci and Odis on his heel. On shaky knees, I head for the elevator with Leo on my tail. As if I'd conjured him out of thin air. He's by my side regardless of the fact that he's already off. I feel like I can't breathe. I just need a few moments alone. It isn't until the doors close that I collapse against the wall. Leo is by my side instantly.

"Are you okay?" He asks.

"Yes," I say. "There's no need to worry. A lot has happened in a short time. I have a lot on my mind and I'm tired. Aren't you off? " Leo gives me a doubtful look.

"I happened to be here. I think I can spare a few minutes," Leo murmured.

"I know you have to report everything to Ethan, but can you wait until after the meeting to tell him about this?" I ask.

When Leo doesn't respond I continue . "I don't want him to worry about me more than he already is. We need him to have a clear mind when we face the Alphas of the table so soon. We need to appear united and strong against Shane. I don't want him to be more distracted than necessary."

We walk in silence, and Leo supports me the entire way to the door of my room. I know he heard me, but it's up to him if he tells Ethan or not.

THE NEW ALPHA

Adea

By the time we make it downstairs, Ethan, Odis, and Darci are waiting in the sitting room. As we step off the elevator, their heads turn and I keep my eyes on Ethan.

His eyes widen in surprise before darkening with lust. I can't hide the blush that creeps up my neck and fills my cheeks. Ethan will always have this effect on me.

The things you do to me.

By the time we made it downstairs Ethan, Odis, and Darci were waiting in the sitting room. As we stepped off the elevator, their heads turned and I kept my eyes on Ethan.

His eyes widened in surprise before darkening with lust. I couldn't hide the blush that crept up my neck and filled my cheeks. Ethan would always have this effect on me.

The things you do to me.

Ethan's voice is downright sinful, and I nearly stumble as I make my way toward him. Odis and Darci dip their heads in greeting. Ethan steps forward, and his arm wraps around me, his hand resting on the small of my back. Goosebumps break out up my back, and my buds hardened at the possessive look in his eyes.

"You look good enough to eat," Ethan murmurs into my ear. His breath is warm on my sensitive flesh.

"Don't threaten me with a good time," I tease seductively. The corner of Ethan's lip curls at the challenge, and his eyes light up with mischief.

"The cars are ready," Odis interrupts.

Ethan's voice was dead right sinful and I nearly stumbled as I made my way toward him. Odis and Darci dipped their heads in greeting. Ethan stepped forward and his arm wrapped around me, his hand rested on the small of my back. Goosebumps broke out up my back and my buds hardened at the possessive look in his eyes.

"You look good enough to eat," Ethan murmured into my ear. His breath was warm on my sensitive flesh.

"Don't threaten me with a good time," I teased seductively. The corner of Ethan's lip curled at the challenge and his eyes lit up with mischief.

"The cars are ready," Odis interrupted.

Our Beta leads us to the front door and we follow him outside. Two cars are parked outside. Odis is headed to open the door for me when Ethan blocks his path.

"I'll get it."

My mate walks to the passenger's side and opens the door for me. I walked up to him and stopped an inch away. We are so close I can feel his body heat radiating off of him. His eyes are on my lips and as he leans in, but I duck into the car.

You tease.

Our Beta led us to the front door and we followed him outside. Two cars were parked outside. Odis was headed to open the door for me when Ethan blocked his path.

"I'll get it."

My mate walked to the passenger's side and opened the door for me. I walked up to him and stopped an inch away. We were so close I could feel his body heat radiating off of him. His eyes were on my lips and as he leaned in, I ducked into the car.

You tease.

Closing the door, I watched as Odis and Darci hopped in the car behind us. I wish Gabe could come with us to the meeting for emotional support but I can't trust him not to cause a scene. I wouldn't want to subject him to Shane's cruelty or presence, so I knew I made the right decision in not bringing him along.

The driver's side door opened and Ethan hopped in. He winked at me before checking the rearview mirror. His hand slid up on the exposed skin of my thigh. All thoughts of Gabe and Shane disappeared and I was thankful it was just the two of us in here.

"Ethan?" I asked.

"You're so fucking beautiful." My mate grabbed my hand and pulled it to his lips. My breathing hitched as he held eye contact while he kissed my hand. The temperature in the car had risen while Ethan reversed and sped out of the courtyard.

"Are we late?" I asked. Ethan shook his head.

"No, if we stayed any longer, we would not be on track to make it to the meeting on time. There's something about you in the color red that demands my attention and brings me to my knees,"

Ethan groaned.

"mm, we wouldn't want that now would we?" I murmured. "Of all things to be on our mind, it shouldn't be this." I couldn't help but smile. It felt like one of those teenagers you saw in public that couldn't keep their hands to themselves.

"It shouldn't but it is. I need to be focused on what's going to happen at the meeting. I should be linking Odis but all I can think about is bending you over the backseat and fucking you," Ethan said. His jaw was clenched and the muscle in his cheek tensed.

The slight blush in my cheeks had deepened. They were fully inflamed at this point and my breathing quickened. I squirmed in my seat and clenched my thighs together at the mental image he painted. Ethan pressed down on the accelerator and the car lurched forward.

"That is tempting," I breathed. I didn't even bother trying to hide my arousal. Ethan inhaled and turned his head over to look at me. His eyes flashed between black and yellow.

"Vixen," he breathed. His knuckles cracked and his hands tightened around the wheel. "It's more than tempting, My Queen. The sooner we get there, the sooner we get to leave, the sooner I get to forget the shitty meeting we're about to attend, and the sooner I get to bury myself in you."

Well.

Yes, please! While your mouth is hanging open, stuff it with his cock.

Korra!

Yes, Adea?

It's already hard enough to restrain myself from the mental images of different positions you're throwing at the front of my mind but-

Oh, come on, Adea. Why do we have to wait? We can have a little bit of fun on the way.

You can't seriously mean…

Oh, you know I do. I wasn't joking when I said stuff his cock-

Okay, okay. I get it.

I was as red as a tomato but I had to admit I didn't hate the idea Korra was suggesting. Ethan and I have had sex more times than I could count. I tasted him and he tasted me. I don't feel any shame in front of him but it wasn't often that I started things.

Blaming it on my confidence, I leaned to the left and stared out the window. Nonchalantly, I reached over and put my hand on Ethan's thigh. Ethan's muscles flexed under my touch but he didn't say anything. Sliding my hand up his thigh and over to the front of his pants.

"Adea," Ethan said cautiously.

I remained quiet, ignoring him, my fingers grazed over the hard bulge that demanded my attention. This only encouraged me more and without hesitation, I unbuttoned and unzipped his slacks.

I swallowed the lump in my throat when I found him commando underneath. My mouth watered and I gripped his hard length. I fumbled with the fabric of his pants as I pulled him out.

"What are you doing?" Ethan asked.

Ignoring him, I unbuckled my seat belt and turned my body towards him. I leaned forward until my ass was in the air and I could feel the fabric up against the back of my thigh.

BATTLE

Adea

The elevator ride is awkward the rest of the way up as Leo and I stare at each other. Leo doesn't say anything to my request, and I am starting to think he is going to mind-link Ethan. I wait in bated breath until he finally nods.

A blanket of relief washed over me knowing I wouldn't add more to Ethan's worries. I left Leo at the door as I went into my room to get dressed. With him locked out, I made my way deeper into the room. My breathing sped up with each step.

It wasn't until the bathroom door was locked behind me that the tears began to run down my cheeks. As soon as the shower was turned out, I gave myself over to panic and worry. In these few minutes, I let myself cry and scream. I felt cornered, I felt trapped knowing I had no choice but to face the boy that made my life more than difficult.

When I was done wallowing in my own self-pity, I hardened my jaw and pulled myself together. I would be facing Shane today but I wouldn't be doing it alone. I would have my family by my side. I needed to be stronger, not just physically but mentally. Not only did we need to show a united front but we needed to show that he wasn't even a spec on our radar. I needed to make sure he knew I wasn't scared of him anymore and he held no power over me.

I may have my weaknesses and I may need to work more on not being so negative but the weak orphaned Adea he knew was dead. The woman I was today was a strong fighter, a Luna, and loved. I had a family, a small one but a family all the same. The people I loved were alive and well and I would do everything in my power to keep them that way.

Turning off the shower, I wrapped my hair up in a towel before grabbing another and drying my body. When I was done, I stepped out with a towel wrapped tightly around my body. Steam billowed from the bathroom as I opened the door. Breathing in, Ethan's scent filled my senses and I was reminded that I was still at home, I was still safe.

I headed towards the closet as I tried to figure out what I would wear to the meeting. The other pack's Luna's would be in attendance and they would be dressed to the nines. Juggling between long and short, loose or fitted, I wasn't sure what I would wear. I needed something presentable but bold.

It was at times like these that I missed my friends and the simpler times the most. I missed Nikki's jokes, Mavy's constant scheming of how to get me dressed up, and Olivia's friendship. I missed having that girl bonding time, even if shopping and makeup wasn't my favorite thing to do.

A small voice in the back of my head whispered for me to cover myself, wear something long-sleeved, and hide in every way possible. There was a small part of me that wanted to cower and obey but that voice was drowned out by the woman I knew I was.

The Queen, the Luna in me, knew I was no longer the girl who bowed and offered her neck to him, to anyone. I wasn't a victim anymore and it was damn time I started acting like it. I wouldn't cower in front of Shane today, no, I would stand tall and wear my confidence proudly.

Thankfully, I didn't have to buy all of these dresses myself. I had a section of dresses prepared specifically for meetings or official outings. My fingers trembled as they grazed against the different fabrics. I wasn't paying attention to any of them until the soft silk underneath my fingers demanded my attention. Pulling out the hanger from the closet, I stared at the dress. It was confident and sexy and everything I needed at this moment.

The high neckline would cover my chest from wandering eyes, sleeveless, and the red silk would fall down my body but would do little to hide my curves. Flipping the dress around, an appreciative smile spread across my lips. The back of the dress was backless and dipped low. Holding the dress to my chest, it fell right above my knees.

There's nothing like pretty clothes to boost a woman's confidence. I didn't have to look any further, I found my outfit for tonight. I would pair it with black ankle strap heels with gold buckles. After laying the ensemble on the bed, I patted myself dry and lathered my body with cocoa butter lotion.

After I shimmied into my dress and stepped into my war shoes, I was almost ready. My hair was dry and I was no hairstylist, so I straightened it and let it hang. Staring at my reflection, my hair framed my face and all I needed to do was touch up my face. With a bit of mascara and bold red lipstick, I was ready for battle.

Leo heard my steps as I approached and the door swung open. With one foot after the other, I stepped over the threshold and out into the hall. Leo's gaze dropped to my legs and slowly trailed up, up, up. His eyebrows arched up as our eyes met.

"Damn son, you clean up nice," Leo said. I couldn't help the smile that pulled at the corners of my lips.

"Gasp, is that a compliment from the almighty Leo?" I asked in mock shock. A cock smirk spread across his features and instantly, I regretted saying the almighty bit.

"I dish out compliments where they are due," Leo crossed his arms and nodded his head as if he were some all-knowing guru. "I've got my sights set on a blonde."

"Oh, I know," I laughed.

THE NEW ALPHA

Adea

By the time we made it downstairs Ethan, Odis, and Darci were waiting in the sitting room. As we stepped off the elevator, their heads turned and I kept my eyes on Ethan.

His eyes widened in surprise before darkening with lust. I couldn't hide the blush that crept up my neck and filled my cheeks. Ethan would always have this effect on me.

The things you do to me.

Ethan's voice was dead right sinful and I nearly stumbled as I made my way toward him. Odis and Darci dipped their heads in greeting. Ethan stepped forward and his arm wrapped around me, his hand rested on the small of my back. Goosebumps broke out up my back and my buds hardened at the possessive look in his eyes.

"You look good enough to eat," Ethan murmured into my ear. His breath was warm on my sensitive flesh.

"Don't threaten me with a good time," I teased seductively.

The corner of Ethan's lip curled at the challenge and his eyes lit up with mischief.

"The cars are ready," Odis interrupted.

Our Beta led us to the front door and we followed him outside. Two cars were parked outside. Odis was headed to open the door for me when Ethan blocked his path.

"I'll get it."

My mate walked to the passenger's side and opened the door for me. I walked up to him and stopped an inch away. We were so close I could feel his body heat radiating off of him. His eyes were on my lips and as he leaned in, I ducked into the car.

You tease.

Closing the door, I watched as Odis and Darci hopped in the car behind us. I wish Gabe could come with us to the meeting for emotional support but I can't trust him not to cause a scene. I wouldn't want to subject him to Shane's cruelty or presence, so I knew I made the right decision in not bringing him along.

The driver's side door opened and Ethan hopped in. He winked at me before checking the rearview mirror. His hand slid up on the exposed skin of my thigh. All thoughts of Gabe and Shane disappeared and I was thankful it was just the two of us in here.

"Ethan?" I asked.

"You're so fucking beautiful." My mate grabbed my hand and pulled it to his lips. My breathing hitched as he held eye contact while he kissed my hand. The temperature in the car had risen while Ethan reversed and sped out of the courtyard.

"Are we late?" I asked. Ethan shook his head.

"No, if we stayed any longer, we would not be on track to make it to the meeting on time. There's something about you in the color red that demands my attention and brings me to my knees," Ethan groaned.

"mm, we wouldn't want that now would we?" I murmured. "Of all things to be on our mind, it shouldn't be this." I couldn't help but smile. It felt like one of those teenagers you saw in public that couldn't keep their hands to themselves.

"It shouldn't but it is. I need to be focused on what's going to happen at the meeting. I should be linking Odis but all I can think about is bending you over the backseat and fucking you," Ethan said. His jaw was clenched and the muscle in his cheek tensed.

The slight blush in my cheeks had deepened. They were fully inflamed at this point and my breathing quickened. I squirmed in my seat and clenched my thighs together at the mental image he painted. Ethan pressed down on the accelerator and the car lurched forward.

"That is tempting," I breathed. I didn't even bother trying to hide my arousal. Ethan inhaled and turned his head over to look at me. His eyes flashed between black and yellow.

"Vixen," he breathed. His knuckles cracked and his hands tightened around the wheel. "It's more than tempting, My Queen. The sooner we get there, the sooner we get to leave, the sooner I get to forget the shitty meeting we're about to attend, and the sooner I get to bury myself in you."

Well.

Yes, please! While your mouth is hanging open, stuff it with his cock.

Korra!

Yes, Adea?

It's already hard enough to restrain myself from the mental images of different positions you're throwing at the front of my mind but-

Oh, come on, Adea. Why do we have to wait? We can have a little bit of fun on the way.

You can't seriously mean…

Oh, you know I do. I wasn't joking when I said stuff his cock-

Okay, okay. I get it.

I was as red as a tomato but I had to admit I didn't hate the idea Korra was suggesting. Ethan and I have had sex more times than I could count. I tasted him and he tasted me. I don't feel any shame in front of him but it wasn't often that I started things.

Blaming it on my confidence, I leaned to the left and stared out the window. Nonchalantly, I reached over and put my hand on Ethan's thigh. Ethan's muscles flexed under my touch but he didn't say anything. Sliding my hand up his thigh and over to the front of his pants.

"Adea," Ethan said cautiously.

I remained quiet, ignoring him, my fingers grazed over the hard bulge that demanded my attention. This only encouraged me more and without hesitation, I unbuttoned and unzipped his slacks.

I swallowed the lump in my throat when I found him commando underneath. My mouth watered and I gripped his hard length. I fumbled with the fabric of his pants as I pulled him out.

"What are you doing?" Ethan asked.

Ignoring him, I unbuckled my seat belt and turned my body towards him. I leaned forward until my ass was in the air and I could feel the fabric up against the back of my thigh.

THE NEW ALPHA

Adea

By the time we make it downstairs, Ethan, Odis, and Darci are waiting in the sitting room. As we step off the elevator, their heads turn and I keep my eyes on Ethan.

His eyes widen in surprise before darkening with lust. I can't hide the blush that creeps up my neck and fills my cheeks. Ethan will always have this effect on me.

The things you do to me.

Ethan's voice is downright sinful, and I nearly stumble as I make my way toward him. Odis and Darci dip their heads in greeting. Ethan steps forward, and his arm wraps around me, his hand resting on the small of my back. Goosebumps break out up my back, and my buds hardened at the possessive look in his eyes.

"You look good enough to eat," Ethan murmurs into my ear. His breath is warm on my sensitive flesh.

"Don't threaten me with a good time," I tease seductively. The corner of Ethan's lip curls at the challenge, and his eyes light up with mischief.

"The cars are ready," Odis interrupts.

Our Beta leads us to the front door and we follow him outside. Two cars are parked outside. Odis is headed to open the door for me when Ethan blocks his path.

"I'll get it."

My mate walks to the passenger's side and opens the door for me. I walked up to him and stopped an inch away. We are so close I can feel his body heat radiating off of him. His eyes are on my lips and as he leans in, but I duck into the car.

You tease.

Closing the door, I watched as Odis and Darci hopped in the car behind us. I wish Gabe could come with us to the meeting for emotional support but I can't trust him not to cause a scene. I wouldn't want to subject him to Shane's cruelty or presence, so I knew I made the right decision in not bringing him along.

The driver's side door opened and Ethan hopped in. He winked at me before checking the rearview mirror. His hand slid up on the exposed skin of my thigh. All thoughts of Gabe and Shane disappeared and I was thankful it was just the two of us in here.

"Ethan?" I asked.

"You're so fucking beautiful." My mate grabbed my hand and pulled it to his lips. My breathing hitched as he held eye contact while he kissed my hand. The temperature in the car had risen while Ethan reversed and sped out of the courtyard.

"Are we late?" I asked. Ethan shook his head.

"No, if we stayed any longer, we would not be on track to make it to the meeting on time. There's something about you in the color red that demands my attention and brings me to my knees," Ethan groaned.

"mm, we wouldn't want that now would we?" I murmured. "Of all things to be on our mind, it shouldn't be this." I couldn't help but smile. It felt like one of those teenagers you saw in public that couldn't keep their hands to themselves.

"It shouldn't but it is. I need to be focused on what's going to happen at the meeting. I should be linking Odis but all I can think about is bending you over the backseat and fucking you," Ethan said. His jaw was clenched and the muscle in his cheek tensed.

The slight blush in my cheeks had deepened. They were fully inflamed at this point and my breathing quickened. I squirmed in my seat and clenched my thighs together at the mental image he painted. Ethan pressed down on the accelerator and the car lurched forward.

"That is tempting," I breathed. I didn't even bother trying to hide my arousal. Ethan inhaled and turned his head over to look at me. His eyes flashed between black and yellow.

"Vixen," he breathed. His knuckles cracked and his hands tightened around the wheel. "It's more than tempting, My Queen. The sooner we get there, the sooner we get to leave, the sooner I get to forget the shitty meeting we're about to attend, and the sooner I get to bury myself in you."

Well.

Yes, please! While your mouth is hanging open, stuff it with his cock.

Korra!

Yes, Adea?

It's already hard enough to restrain myself from the mental images of different positions you're throwing at the front of my mind but-

Oh, come on, Adea. Why do we have to wait? We can have a little bit of fun on the way.

You can't seriously mean…

Oh, you know I do. I wasn't joking when I said stuff his cock-

Okay, okay. I get it.

I was as red as a tomato but I had to admit I didn't hate the idea Korra was suggesting. Ethan and I have had sex more times than I could count. I tasted him and he tasted me. I don't feel any shame in front of him but it wasn't often that I started things.

Blaming it on my confidence, I leaned to the left and stared out the window. Nonchalantly, I reached over and put my hand on Ethan's thigh. Ethan's muscles flexed under my touch but he didn't say anything. Sliding my hand up his thigh and over to the front of his pants.

"Adea," Ethan said cautiously.

I remained quiet, ignoring him, my fingers grazed over the hard bulge that demanded my attention. This only encouraged me more and without hesitation, I unbuttoned and unzipped his slacks.

I swallowed the lump in my throat when I found him commando underneath. My mouth watered and I gripped his hard length. I fumbled with the fabric of his pants as I pulled him out.

"What are you doing?" Ethan asked.

Ignoring him, I unbuckled my seat belt and turned my body towards him. I leaned forward until my ass was in the air and I could feel the fabric up against the back of my thigh.

MY KING

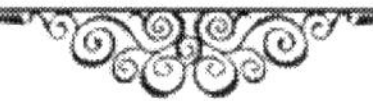

Adea

The thin fabric between my legs is the only friction I have. I put one of my hands on his thigh and wrap my other hand around the base of his cock. I try to wrap my hand around at least. There is an inch of space between my thumb and the rest of my fingers.

Ethan is not only long and hard, but he is wide too. I don't think I'll ever get used to his girth, but I have no complaints. He is really beautiful. Long, hard, and firm. There are a few veins that stick out as they run down the length of his cock.

His tip is a shade darker than his length, and moisture has already pooled at the top. Leaning forward, I dip lower, and run my tongue down the center of the slit. The salty taste coats the tip of my tongue, and I can't help the noise of pleasure that falls from my lips. There is dampness between my legs and the thin fabric beneath my dress is soaked.

"You taste amazing, My King," I groan.

The fabric is pulled up and over my backside. His strong hand slaps my right cheek, and I moan as I jerk forward. I can feel a puddle between my legs. I run my tongue up the underside of his hard shaft and Ethan curses.

"Two can play at this game."

Two fingers slide beneath the thin fabric and thrust deep into my aching core. His thigh tenses and his hips press forward with every lick. I am needy and aching as Ethan thrusts in and out of me. The squelching sounds from his fingers as they drove into me fills the car. It only pours gasoline on the fire in me. Saliva drips from my lips and slides down, coating his length. Wetness seeps between my fingers at his base.

"I'm trying to focus on the road, but it's hard when you're so wet and needy. It also doesn't help when the love of my life has her hand wrapped around my co-"

Before Ethan can finish his sentence, the hand around his base slides up and down his thick cock. I wrap my lips around his tip and bounce my head up and down on his length in circular motions.

"Oh, fuck! Oh fuck," Ethan grunts. "Yes, baby."

His fingers speed up as they thrust in and out of me. I don't want to go slow. No, today the two of us need it hard and fast. With each bob of my head, I take him deeper into my mouth while I jerk the lower half of his cock. Ethan matches my rhythm and I feel myself getting closer and closer to the edge.

I push my hips back against his fingers as much as I can. Ethan's fingers slam into me hard, and I cry out around his cock. His thumb presses into my clit, and electricity shoots up my body to my hardened peaks. I come hard and fast, but Ethan doesn't stop. He continues rubbing torturous circles on my clit as he fucks me hard with his fingers.

"Good girl."

Fuck, I lovedwhen he calls me that. My chest is against my hand on his thigh. His fingers pull out of me, and adjusts the fabric back between my legs. He squeezes my ass before flipping my dress back over my backside.

I lower my hand from his cock to his balls. My wet fingers smear the saliva that has dripped down. His hand grips the back of my head as I coat his balls with the cool liquid.

"Oh, shit," Ethan hisses.

I smile as I bob down on his length. His hand pushes me down as I go and I open myself up until his cock hits the back of my throat. He is hard and I can feel him stretching me. I swallow around him and Ethan groans.

"Fuck, Adea. That feels so good, baby."

I hum around his shaft, and his cock twitches. I slide up and down his length. I take him deeply each time, and keep up the circular movement as I lift my head and repeat it as I lower my head. I need to make him feel good. I loved making him feel the way I do. I feel powerful and in charge watching and hearing the way he reacts to what I do to him.

Ethan hardens and his hips thrust up every time I drop my head. I drag my tongue along his shaft and Ethan curses. I repeat the movement and force my head down hard on his shaft.

Ethan moans his release. It is low and sexy, and I feel triumphant as he comes. I stop moving as my lips press against his skin. I hold myself there as I gag. Ethan's grip tightens on the back of my head. I swallow and he groans. I bounce my head up and down his length while he comes down my throat.

When he is done, I lick him clean, and his hand drops from my head. I suck him while I sit up, and his cock falls from my lips with an audible pop. I think I like that noise more than I should. Sitting up, I lean in and press my lips to his before I sit back in my seat.

"Fuck me," Ethan says under his breath. "You can do that whenever you want." I cannot help but laugh. My mate grabs my hand and interlocks his fingers with mine. "You didn't have to do that."

"I wouldn't have done it if I didn't want to, and believe me, I wanted to."

"Well then. My Queen can have whatever she wants," Ethan says.

"I'm glad you know that now," I say.

Ethan laughs. Amusement fades from his face."We haven't had the opportunity to talk today. Are you ready?" Ethan asks.

"As ready as I'll ever be," I murmur. "With you by my side, I can face anything."

AMAZING

Adea

Ethan and I grow quiet as the pack territory pops up in the distance. Black walls over 20 feet tall surround Alpha Rich's pack lands, which was smart on his part. It isn't just a regular fence. What I am seeing is a fortress. Even as a wolf, we can't jump that high.

Desert Moon would be well protected if we had walls that high surrounding our territory. The material used looks sleek, and would be nearly impossible to climb.

As we drive closer, I notice a group of very large warriors standing guard outside. Slowing to a stop, Ethan lowers his window, and two of the warriors step up to confirm our identities and why we are here. I am not a criminal, but I had just been up to no good, and the guilt has me avoiding eye contact. When they signal the okay, I feel relieved.

They let us in, and as we drive into their territory, I take note of the various warrior check-in locations we pass on our way to the meeting hall. The warriors' facial expressions are stoic, and had Ethan not specifically told me he trusted Alpha Rich, I would wonder if they are friendly.

We also pass by large clusters of homes and large shops, but they are closed and the streets are empty. There isn't a soul in sight. We pull up to the meeting hall and it is packed. There are a ton of cars, too many to count. I wonder how we hadn't seen the meeting hall on the drive through the territory. The building looks to be as tall as the walls that surround the territory.

Ethan puts the car in park, and walks around to my door. Opening it for me, he offers me his arm, and I take it as I step out. My heels sink into the grass, and I put my weight onto the tips of my toes so I don't get stuck in the grass. Despite what I said, I am feeling a little jittery, but my mate's proximity calms my nerves.

"Have I told you how amazing you are today?" His breath fans my neck and causes me to shiver.

"Mm, let me think," I tease. "Yes, you have. Please, go on." Ethan's lips brush against my mark and I gasp. His fingers lift my chin and our lips meet in a sensual kiss.

"You're fucking amazing," he growls.

Even with my heels, on the tips of my toes, I can barely reach my mate's mouth. Thankfully, he is leaning down. My lipstick slightly smears on his lips and I dab it until it is gone.

"That's not the only place your lipstick smeared," Ethan whispers.

"Ethan!"

My face is inflamed, but before I can slap him, the sound of an engine cuts through the air. The two of us turn towards the noise, and Odis, Darci, and Leo pull up and parks beside us.

Remembering I owe him a slap, I slap his chest, and Ethan throws his head back and laughs. Goddess, I loved his laugh. The passenger's side back door opens and Leo practically flies out of it. In an instant, he is by my side.

Odis and Darci stride up to us, and everyone is accounted for. They nod to Ethan and he leads us in. The warriors stationed at the front doors pull the doors, and they creak as they swing open.

My heels clack against the marble floors, and I do a scan of the halls. There isn't a pack member in sight. Alpha Rich must have ordered his pack members to stay in their homes.

He can't do anything to hurt you. I won't let him.

I know. I'm safe.

Keep your chin up.

I will, my love. He's nothing.

That's my girl.

Ethan's words are soothing. As we near large double doors, I know we have arrived at the meeting room. On the other side of those doors are allies and foes.

For a second, I wonder about the other Lunas and what they think of the new addition. It would be great if the Lunas held meetings, just like the Alphas do. Four of Alpha Rich's warriors stand side-by-side outside the door. The two on the inside greet us and move to open the doors.

Ethan squeezes my hand before the doors swing open. The chatter comes to a standstill as the occupants turn to look at us. Several Alphas sit around the table, their Lunas on their right. The Betas and Gammas sit to their left. Most of the Lunas smile at me, and I smile back. I tell myself I won't look for him, but my eyes scan the table.

There are a few empty seats and I fight the urge to sigh in relief when I realize Shane isn't seated yet. My eyes drift to the snacks that are in front of everyone seated. I am reminded of earlier days when Mavy would share the snacks from Alpha Joshua. Had they still been alive, I would have eventually seen him and Luna Rose at these meetings.

There are only two sections to choose from. One section is directly in front of the door, and the other is on the opposite side by the wall. Ethan leads me to a seat on the opposite side of the room facing the doors we just walked through.

I swallow as we make our way through the room. I hold my chin high ,and nod as I make eye contact with a few people we pass by. Ethan pulls out my chair for me and I smile at him before I take my seat.

Leo follows closely and stands directly behind me. Ethan pulls his chair out and sits by my side. When he is seated, Darci sits two seats down from him. Odis remains standing, his hands on the back of his chair between Darci and Ethan.

ARRIVAL

Adea

Odis looks around the room and I do the same. This is a very large table; there are a lot of people that I am sure I would eventually get to know better. Darci looks forward. We haven't told her what Shane lookslike, but I'm sure Ethan or Odis has brought her up to speed. Ethan's hands are on his armrest, mine are in my lap.

"The Desert Moon pack has arrived, and everyone in our party is present, plus one," Odis says, nodding to Leo before taking his seat. Most of the people here don't seem to mind our 'plus one'. A handful of people turn their eyes on Leo standing directly behind me. There are four empty seats across the table. Shane will be seated directly in front of us when he arrives.

"Who is the plus one?" An alpha I don't recognize asks. He has light blonde hair, and even lighter skin. His nose is sharp, and his lips are thinned as he stares at Leo suspiciously.

"He is my Luna's guard, Alpha Jax," Ethan answers.

"Your Luna needs a guard?" The alpha asks. "You don't trust your second and third to keep her safe when needed?

"I'm more than capable of defending myself," I say.

"Why would you need a guard among friends?" Alpha Jax asks. He is looking at me now; his eyes are jade green. The way he says it isn't friendly and I want nothing more than to rip his throat out.

Woah, I don't know where that thought came from.

I don't know either, Adea but I agree.

We're at a UNITED meeting, starting a fight would be the opposite of what that stands for.

Don't snap at me. I wasn't the one who thought it.

"We've had friends turn their back on us. So it wouldn't be the first time I needed one among friends," I spit. I don't know why I am snapping at him. Olivia wasn't his fault, but there is something about his tone that is grinding my gears.

"My mate has had one since before our Ceremony. I have more enemies than I can count, and as you already know, the number of rogues has grown out of control. It's for my sanity, and I don't think we owe you an explanation," Ethan growls.

I am sure I don't imagine this guy's hostility towards us. I don't know who this Alpha Jax is, but he is being rude right off the bat. The last thing we needed was to start fighting. I need to calm Ethan down. Reaching over, I place my hand on his and squeeze. Someone clears his throat and everyone turns to it.

"Thank you for coming on such short notice," an older-looking Alpha says. He stands and smiles kindly at me. "Now that your pack is here, we're just waiting on one more to arrive."

"Of course, Alpha Rich," Ethan says.

My mate nods his head and sits back in his seat. So this was the

Alpha my mate respects and looks up to. His eyes crinkle at the ends as he smiles genuinely. By his side are his Luna, his Beta, his Gamma, and a fourth person I assume is his heir.

My body and soul belongs to Ethan, but I cannot deny how handsome this man is going to be. Long, dark brown, tousled hair hangs right above his shoulders. He has long eyelashes and brown eyes. His eyes land on me ,and I look away.

"This is the first time you're meeting her. I'm sorry for the late introduction. This my Luna, Adea," Ethan announces.

"It's an honor to meet you, Adea."

Alpha Rich introduces himself, his wife, and his heir. The heir will be taking over and we will be working with him soon. We are all talking when the creak and moan of the large doors opening announces a new arrival.

All heads turn in the direction of the door. My heart starts to beat a little faster, and I fight the urge to tighten my grip on Ethan. The doors are wide open, and a group of six people are led in by Shane.

I recognize Devin and Liam. I am not surprised to find them here, but I hadn't realized how it would make me feel. For a moment, I am transported back in time to when the three of them would show up outside my classroom.

If I had realized my dreams were from a past life, would I have been able to change things then? Could this all have been avoided? If given the chance, could we have been friends?

I shake my head; this is all pointless. Wondering about this now won't change anything. It can't change the atrocious acts Shane has done, or the crimes he's committed. It is too late.

Shane has changed since the last time I saw him at the trial.

From what I remember, he had been tall and muscular, but he still had his boyish features. The Shane that strides in isn't a boy, but a man, an Alpha. Confidence and arrogance surrounds him.

He's grown a few inches taller, his shoulders are broader, and his muscles have multiplied in size. He wears black slacks and a white button-down shirt that looks like it will pop open if he flexes. I don't miss the two piercings that press against the white fabric.

For someone who had just walked into a pack, fought, and took it over, he doesn't have a single bruise or cut on his face. I try not to think about how much stronger he has gotten since leaving Half Moon.

His chiseled jaw clenches., His lips are a healthy red, and his ears are pierced. A silver cross hangs from his right ear, and he has a diamond in the left. His Adam's apple bobs as he swallows.

His wavy black hair has grown longer, and falls below his shoulders. Even as a young teen his eyes had been cold, but there had been a slight warmth in them. Now, they are almost pitch black, and the look in his eyes are calculated and cold.

GAZE

Adea

As if on a mission, Shane scans the room like a hawk. I had hoped maybe he had given up on his obsession with me, but as he searches around the room, I know he hasn't. He is in search of someone, and I have a feeling that someone is me. I steady my breathing and ready myself for when he finds me. I will not show weakness here, or any sign of fear. Shane is like a predator and can smell fear.

His gaze freezes on each Luna with brown hair. The last time I saw Shane was during the trial ,and the time before that had been the night of the Crescent Moon Ball.

Without meaning to, images from that night spill into my mind: Shane's hand on my throat, the anger on his face, and his body pressed against mine. My breath hitches as I recall the way he'd forced himself on me, my lack of fight, and the fear that coursed through my body.

I remember the fear of being caught with Ethan, the

helplessness I felt under him, and the way he forced my submission. My mouth goes dry as I watch him. As if he can feel my thoughts, he meets my gaze, and our eyes lock.

A small smirk pulls at the corner of his mouth. He searches my gaze for the girl he remembers:. the girl who followed his every command, the girl who obeyed him, the girl who cooked his meals, cleaned his packhouse and slaved for his family. His eyes narrow as he waits for me to lower my eyes, to submit to him. I can feel it. I hold his gaze and refuse, making his eyes darken.

I will never admit it out loud, but I wasn't sure how I'd react when I saw him again. I know what I told myself, I know what I trained for, I know what I promised, but you never really know until you're faced with your abuser.

Shane dismisses my lack of submission, and his eyes trail down from my face to my neck. A growl emits from the back of his throat as his gaze freezes on my mark. Anger flashes in his eyes, and had I been the same person from before, I would have dropped to my knees, but I wasn't her anymore.

The last time we spoke, I had met Ethan for the first time. A day that should have been magical was overshadowed by Shane. He put his hands on me for talking to Ethan alone. He'd accused me of being easy. He had to have seen us during the ball; he had to have known he was my mate.

What did he think was going to happen? That we wouldn't be drawn to each other? We were going to go back to the packhouse, sleep in separate bedrooms, and only hold hands? I scoff. I think the fuck not.

His gaze trails lower, and there are yellow flecks in his eyes. Max is pushing forward. Would he cause a scene? Or did he have a better grip on his wolf now than he did in the past? Worrying about Shane's movements hasn't been a concern in a very long time, and I am not going to pick that nasty habit back up.

I feel Ethan tense beneath my hand, and I remember to keep breathing. The room has grown silent, and I was beginning to wonder when someone is going to say something. No one says a word, ormoves until Alpha Rich stands up.

"Welcome, Alpha Shane. Please, come in and have a seat," Alpha Rich's voice carries as he gestures toward the only available seats.

In a flash of movement, Shane is standing behind his chair, his hands gripping the back of the seat directly across from me. Ethan hasn't moved, but Leo has gone into defensive mode behind me. Shane doesn't pay him any mind. His scent is radiating off of him, and the familiar smell tickles my nose.

"Welcome, Alpha Shane," Alpha Jax says.

Ethan's eyes dart to Alpha Jax, and I can tell by the look on Odis' face he wants to scoff. Alpha Jax is clearly a suck-up, and wants to get on Shane's good side. If there even is such a thing. When Odis sees me looking, he shoots me a smile before quickly returning his mask of professional indifference. I don't return the smile; he was still on my shit list.

Shane's gaze remains on me while he pulls out his chair and takes a seat. I don't recognize the other three men that came with him. They make themselves comfortable by the door. Despite their laid-back appearance, their eyes are constantly scanning the room. Devin and Liam sit on both sides of Shane; one seat remains open. I assume it is designated for his Luna had he brought one.

"Now that everyone is present and seated, the United Meeting begins now. Since we have a new Alpha in command of Half Moon, one is necessary. I would like to start off by welcoming Alpha Shane to the Alphas' Table."

A collection of welcomes pass around the table, none of which come from anyone in my party. Alpha Suck-Up and the members of his party, along with at least two other packs, actually clap.

Shane doesn't bat an eye at Alpha Rich's words. He doesn't utter a thank you, and not once does he look away from me. His eyes are glued to my face. I am not the only one who noticed this. Everyone around the table stares back and forth between Shane and I. By my side, Ethan's gaze is locked on Shane, and I can feel his irritation.

Sensing the thickening tension, Alpha Rich clears his throat, and I turn my gaze to him. So do the rest of the wolves in attendance. I won't give Shane any more of my attention. We may be here because of him, but he doesn't deserve any of my time.

HYPOTHETICALLY

Adea

"Everyone present had an alliance with the previous Alpha of Half Moon," Alpha Rich says. "Your attendance shows you would like to take his spot here at the Alphas' Table and continue said alliance." When Shane doesn't speak, he continues. "Does anyone have any questions?"

When no one answers, Alpha Rich nods his head. "There is also a peace treaty."

"Explain the details of the peace treaty, would you?" Shane asks, his voice a low rumble.

"It's a simple one. The peace treaty stands for every Alpha and his pack present," Alpha Rich looks around the table. "By coming to The Table, you swear there will be no wars waged against any other pack here."

"What happens if the Peace Treaty is broken?" Shane asks.

He said it as if he were talking about a simple matter, like the weather, or what he ate for lunch. I forget that I am ignoring

Shane, and I just about break my neck as I turn my focus onto him.

He is blatantly speaking about the elephant in the room. Shane's arrogant smirk pulls at his lips again. It feels like a game, and I have just lost.

His question is a clear threat. It wasn't targeted at any other pack in this room but Desert Moon. I can feel Ethan's anger rolling off of him, and I gently squeeze his hand.

The room is quiet, so quiet, that I could hear a pin drop. I am not the only one who holds their breath at that question. Alpha Rich blinks and his brow furrows as he tries to figure out if he had heard Shane right. When he realizes Shane has indeed said what he said, and is also dead serious, Alpha Rich speaks.

"Hypothetically... the terms of the Peace Treaty state that if a pack breaks the treaty, the rest of the Alphas from The Table will come to the attacked Alpha's pack's aid. The Peace Treaty demands our commitment, and ensures a peaceful coexistence."

Shane leans forward, his elbows on the table, and his hands clasp in front of him. The veins in his hands are popping out, and his knuckles crack as he squeezes his hands together.

Shane smiles at me as he mulls Alpha Rich's words around, his dimples popping out as his smile deepens. His eyes light up as he holds my attention.

To his right, Devin is sitting up straight in his seat and hasn't commented since sitting down. He's finally gotten his seat as Beta, and I wonder if it is as cracked up as he'd hoped it would be. The expression on Liam's face is one of a doomed man, but I have no pity for him.

"I'll keep that in mind," Shane answers mysteriously. Shane leans back in his seat, way too comfortably, as if he is watching a football game.

"Excellent." Alpha Rich's reply is unsure. "We are here to bear witness to you swearing allegiance to the Alphas gathered here today."

"Other than the times I've met you, when I came with my father, this is practically my first time speaking to anyone here. Why should I swear my allegiance to men I do not know?" Shane asks.

"All new Alphas don't know anyone at The Table," Alpha Rich said, treading carefully. "But as time goes on, our bond deepens as we get to know each other. The benefits of having a seat at The Table outweigh not having one."

"It was simply a question," Shane says nonchalantly.

"Would you like a seat at the table, Alpha Shane?" Alpha Rich asks. Shane gives a curt nod.

"Please stand."

Shane's eyebrows rise at Alpha Rich's command. Without a word, he gets to his feet. His Beta and Gamma do the same.

"Do you swear to uphold the Alliance and the Peace Treaty signed by your predecessor?" Alpha Rich asks.

"I do," Shane answers. His men repeat his response.

"You may be seated," Alpha Rich says.

The three men take their seats, and Alpha Rich smiles looking around the room.

"It's official. Alpha Shane and The Half Moon pack are a part of The Alphas' Table."

The rest of the meeting consists of Alpha Rich going over the laws The Alphas' Table abides by, the usual meeting times, and emergency procedures. Following this, each Alpha introduces themselves. When it comes to Ethan's turn to introduce himself, he stands up and does so. The tension between the two of them is so thick you could cut it with a knife. Now that Shane has been sworn in, and introductions were over with, I am ready to go.

"You still need to give due notice before crossing anyone's territory," Alpha Rich says. The meeting is nearing an end. "Until you are on close terms with the Alpha, notice before arrival is expected."

"Noted," Shane says.

"I believe we've covered everything of importance today," Alpha Rich says. "If you have any more questions when you go back home, feel free to reach out to me."

"Thank you, we will," Beta Devin says with a nod to Alpha Rich. Getting to his feet, he dips his chin respectfully. "If Alpha Shane needs anything, I will be the one you will speak to or see. I'm Beta Devin," Devin says.

"I look forward to working with you in the future, Beta Devin."

"As do I," Devin says as he takes his seat.

"I am happy to announce that the United Meeting has ended. I want to thank everyone for showing up. I know the meeting was called last minute, but I appreciate all of you putting in the effort, and being here today. Unless there is an emergency, I will see all of you at the next scheduled meeting," Alpha Rich concludes. He sighs and with a kind smile on his face, he looks around the room.

The room erupted in applause as Alpha Rich takes his seat. His Luna hasn't said a single thing the entire time, but she smiles warmly.

DARKNESS

Adea

Finally.

I'm as ready as you are, Adea to leave this room.

Seriously. Let's hope we can dip out of here before anyone attempts to spark up a conversation, Kor.

As long as we don't have to talk to him, I'm fine. I know.

I'm sure Ethan will stand up soon. We can't appear anxious.

But we are anxious.

Are you whining like a pup?

Maybe.

Korra's whining lightens the mood, and I have to fight a smile from spreading across my face. Since Alpha Rich has ended the meeting, it has grown loud with conversation.

Most of the members are still seated, but a few had gotten up to chat with others. Alpha Jax is approaching Shane and I am thankful Shane will be distracted.

I wait, not so patiently, for Ethan to stand up first. If we are going to get out of here, now is the time. The last thing I want is for *someone* to make their way over to us.

I just about cry for joy when my mate gets to his feet. Instead, I get to mine. Leo pulls the chair out from behind me, and I follow after Ethan. He waits for me to catch up, and continues when I am by his side. Odis and Darci follow close behind.

Alpha Jax is talking enthusiastically to Shane. Shane isn't paying attention. His eyes are on me, and I feel my heart rate speed up. We are about halfway to the door. We are close, so close.

Without a second glance at Alpha Jax, Shane stands and strides to the left of the table, effectively blocking the exit. All too quickly, his Beta, Gamma, and the three men that had been by the door are by his side.

Damn it, we had been so close!

I know, Kor. Shh. I need to focus.

Now that I am standing, I realize how tall Shane has gotten. He stands two feet away from us, and he is about the same height as Ethan. Even with my heels on, I have to crane my neck to look up at him.

"Watch yourself," Ethan warns.

Shane doesn't look at my mate; he doesn't say a word as he stands across from me. He doesn't need to. His eyes trail down the rest of my body and lock on my legs. Remembering the night of the ball, his opinion on my dress flashes through my mind. The one I have on today is shorter. When his eyes return to my face, I know he is angry, but that isn't my concern. I am dressed to impress *my mate*, and I won't apologize or cower under his eye.

"See anything you like?" Ethan says quietly. It doesn't matter how quiet he speaks, even with the loud noise, everyone in this room can hear him. Shane doesn't speak or look at him, but he growls in response. A low threatening sound.

"My mate is beautiful, isn't she?" Ethan taunts.

Ethan's hand wraps around my waist, and my eyes almost pop out of my head. At no point in time, have I ever seen Ethan jealous. Other than with Gabe, but that was playful. This… this… is something else entirely.

The muscles in Shane's jaws tick violently, his nostrils flare, and the yellow flecks in his eyes grow bright. His eyes darted between my eyes and the mark on my neck. I'm not going to encourage a fight here, but I'm also not going to push my mate away. I stand tall, my chin firm, and my eyes on Shane.

"Hey, Ad-y," Devin calls from beside Shane.

He calls me by Gabe's nickname. The same nickname Shane liked to use while teasing me. What is this? High School? Is he really trying to make me feel small? Here, of all places?

"Devin," I say, keeping my facial expression stoic. I am not about to give him the satisfaction of seeing my annoyance.

"Hey, Adea," Liam says.

"Hi, Liam."

The Liam I remember used to smile a lot, but the man in front of me now is a shell of the boy I knew. There isn't a smile anywhere to be seen, and I wonder what he could have been through, or done, since being under Shane's command to make him this way.

Wait, no, that's not right. That would have been the right way of thinking had we still been children but we aren't. All of us are adults and can make our own decisions.

Liam is a full-grown adult now, and can choose to stop

following Shane's every command and whim. Whatever choices he's made or crimes he's committed are his own. If Liam is here, especially as Shane's Gamma, it is because he wants to be.

"Are you not going to say hi to me?" Shane asks.

I looked at him. Shane's appearance and position may have changed, but his jealousy and temperament are still the same.

"I have nothing to say to you, Shane."

His eyes darken and he shivers. I hate knowing that his name on my tongue turns him on. He is so close now, his scent is overpowering. My natural instincts are telling me to run, but I don't back down.

"Come on, Ady," Devin says. "You don't know what he's done to get here."

I cannot believe what I am hearing. Is he actually defending Shane right now? I can barely stomach it as Olivia pops into my mind. The things he did to her.

If I hadn't had Ethan by my side, I might have emptied out my stomach. Not only did my pack lose a Gamma, but we also lost a warrior and a true friend. My best friend lost the woman the Moon Goddess made for him, his life partner.

"Oh, I think I do," I spit. "And I don't give a flying fuck." The words spill from my mouth without thought. I clench my jaw and glare at Devin as I try to calm myself.

DISGUST

Adea

No matter how hard I try, I can't calm down. So, I work on relaxing my face, calming my breathing, and the bite in my tone. I know this isn't the time or place for this conversation. I don't even want to have this conversation. The only thing I want to do is rip Shane's heart out. This alliance, this peace treaty, and this meeting are the only things stopping me from doing it right here, right now. The moment I lunge at him, the treaty would be null. Desert Moon would be out, and Ethan would lose his seat at The Alphas' Table. Even if we had every reason to want his blood, to demand his life, we can't have it. Not right now at least. Not in this room.

When I had my mind and temper under control, I focus my attention back on Shane. I hate the way he still looks at me like I am his. I hate the warmth in his eyes he gets when he looks at me, and I hate that he hurt people in the name of this twisted idea of love he has for me. I hate being the reason for their death, pain, and suffering.

I hate being the reason.

Seeing him standing here with that look on his face is the straw that breaks my resistance. I know where I am, I know who sits around us, and I know this is the man that abused me. Does that stop the word vomit from coming out? No. It doesn't, can't stop the long-overdue words from spilling from my mouth.

"If it weren't for my required attendance, Beta," I say through clenched teeth. "I would not be here. I wouldn't have come if someone promised me all the riches in the world. The number of atrocious acts you have committed since I've known you are far too many to count. Not just to me and my family, but to yours as well. You have not only cost me part of my family, but you've also hurt those I'd give my life for.

"So no, Devin, I don't care about Shane's feelings. I don't care about what you want, Shane. I don't care about your reason for doing the shit you've done, and I hate the thought of being the motivation behind those acts. It hasn't even crossed my mind to care. I'm mated to Ethan; he is made for me, and I for him. Everyone in this room already knows I'm loyal. You're the only one who doesn't seem to know that. I shouldn't have or need to explain myself to you. There is *nothing* you have that I could want. There's nothing you could offer me, that would make me want you. I have hated every single minute that I've had to sit across from you and see your face. I can't stand the fact that I've had to breathe the same air as you. You *disgust* me."

I feel a sense of relief wash over me after the words spill from my mouth. I take a step closer during my speech, and I feel amazing standing up to him. This has been a long time coming, and I feel drunk on power as I almost stand toe to toe with the asshole who's made my life so fucking difficult.

Shane searched my face for something. For what? I don't know, and I didn't care. All I want is to hurt him. I want to see the look on his face when he realizes I mean every word. He stares at me with a look that says he isn't affected. There isn't any shock or anger on his face. It makes me want to punch him. My fingers twitch. Goddess, I want to hurt him. Not only mentally, but physically.

I fight back the smile that wants to pull at my lips. I've forgotten Ethan is by my side. I've forgotten we are in a room full of people that could hear our every word. My focus is on the man in front of me, the worthless piece of shit in front of me. A wave of overwhelming anger fills me and I don't know how to bottle it. Hell, I am not sure that I want to. I've finally said the things I needed to say, and I don't regret it. I've been scared of him for far too long.

My chest rises and falls as I glare up at him. The only things I want right now are to hurt him, and for him to get the hell out of my way. Shane takes a step closer to me, and I blink as I am brought back to reality.

"Did you miss me?" Shane asks.

His voice is quiet, and had I not been a wolf, I wouldn't have heard him. Did he just ignore everything ? Did he not hear what I just said? He holds my eye contact and I refuse to look away. For the first time in a long time, he has a look in his eye that I remember. One that stared down at me after I'd hugged him as a young boy. Had he not done any of the things he'd done in the past year, I might have hesitated.

"No."

The small flicker of the boy I remembered is gone and replaced by darkness. Leo reacts, and so do Shane's men. Leo puts his hand between the two of us. Shane's men are on Leo as they anticipate his next move. My heart stops beating as Shane ignores everyone else but me, and inhales deeply.

"Let's not pretend that we both don't know how this all ends," Shane whispers.

I look up at him, my eyebrows furrowed, my nose wrinkled, and my lips turned down as I search his face for answers. What does he mean? What can he mean? He can't know about us? About before? No, that's impossible.

"My family and I want to leave. Please get out of the way," I say. I try and fail to keep the tremor out of my voice. Shane stares down at me menacingly before taking a step back. I don't miss the possessive look in his eyes.

"I'll be seeing you again soon, Ady."

BALLS

Adea

Wow.
I know…
I can't believe you just did that.
I honestly can't believe I just did either.
It's about damn time, Adea!
I knoooow.
How do you feel?
Jittery.
I bet. Well done.
Thank you, Kor.

Suspicion mixes in with the excitement coursing through my veins from telling Shane off. I've never felt so free in my life. Even though his words have my mind churning, trying to find the meaning behind them, I feel as if a burden has been lifted from my shoulders.

The way he responded sounds as if he didn't he didn't hear a word that left my mouth. I feel a sense of irritation at this, but not enough to bring me down from the mental pedestal I currently stand on.

My heart is beating out of my chest, and my fingers shake. I know I am the only person who has spoken to him that way and lived. I feel downright giddy and cannot help the smile that spreads across my lips.

I step past Shane and keep my eyes trained ahead of me. Ignoring the men that have surrounded us, I make my way to the doors. The room has gone deathly silent, but I force myself to keep going. As we near the exit, the warriors open the door. With my head held high, I walk out with my mate by my side.

Oh shit, my mate. I won't say I forgot about him during the conversation with Shane, but I had been so focused on Shane and ripping him a new one, that I kind of forgot my mate was present. What had I said?

As soon as the doors close behind us, I look up at Ethan. His jaw is clenched tight and I sigh as I stare at the beautiful man I get to call mine. It must have been just as hard for him to sit across from Shane as it had been for me.

I feel an overwhelming sense of love and gratitude for my mate. Not only did he support me in there, but he didn't try and step in to fight my battles for me. He was already my knight in shining armor, and I know he has my back. Even so, I love that he stood aside and let me do what I needed to.

The door may be closed, but we were still too close to everyone to have a conversation. The sound of my heels clacking against the floor fills the silent halls. The warriors at the entrance of the meeting hall open the final doors we have to walk through, here at Alpha Rich's meeting hall. Ethan is my rock as we descend the stairs.

The sun has long since set, and if not for the street lights, we would have been surrounded by darkness. We stop by the passenger's door to our car and Ethan looks at Darci, Odis, and Leo. Darci hasn't been with us for long, but the look on her face is one of what I would call pride. Odis beams at me.

"Amazing job, Luna. I know that couldn't have been easy," Odis says.

"It was a lot easier than I thought it would be!" I laugh.

"I'll say," Leo says. "You went offfff. I know of a little blonde-haired man who'll be proud."

Thinking of my best friend, I can't help but smile. Leo usually regards me with indifference unless Gabe was concerned. Right now, he smiles at me sheepishly. If Ethan wasn't here, I feel like he might have clapped.

"I don't know much about him, but he must have deserved what he got," Leo says. His eyes dart to Ethan and he adds, "Luna."

"He definitely did. You were pretty fast back there, Leo," I say. It isn't often that I gave Leo compliments, so they are a bit rusty coming out.

"I'm Speedy Gonzalez," Leo says, puffing out his chest.

"Mm-hmm," I roll my eyes. "Anyway, I want to thank you guys for having my back in there."

"Any time," Odis says.

"It's kind of my job," Leo shrugs and Darci nods.

Ethan reaches for the handle, and opens the door for me. When I am seated, he closes the door and turns back to Odis, Darci, and Leo.

"Follow close behind," Ethan orders.

"Yes, Alpha," Darci and Odis reply.

I have so many things on my mind. Doors slam, engines rev, and we are off. The drive through the territory is quiet, and I am not sure of what to say. Is he angry? I can't see why. I can see Odis' car in the mirror as we drive. It isn't until we leave the gates of Alpha Rich's pack, that Ethan relaxes in his seat. The stars are out tonight and they light up the sky.

"How do you feel?" Ethan's question has me turning from the view and looking at him.

"I feel great. I was late, but those words needed to be said. Are you angry? Did I do something wrong?"

"Why would you ask that?" Ethan's expression is bewildered as he stares at me.

"Well, the car ride has been awkwardly quiet, and you haven't said a word to me. Hell, Ethan, I don't know if you've even looked at me since we left the meeting." Ethan grabs my hand and intertwines his fingers with mine.

"It's baby."

"What?" I ask.

"It's not Ethan, it's baby."

"Of all the…" I burst into laughter.

"I'm sorry," Ethan murmurs.

"Mm?"

"I have a lot on my mind, and I am beating myself up about it. I wish I could have done more for you. It was eating me alive, not being able to do something. I'm an asshole." He checks the road, and looks back at me, our eyes locking.

"Let's start over. Not only are you amazing, beautiful, and strong," his eyes twinkle as they stare at me. "But you were breathtaking, My Queen. You have more balls than some of the Alphas at the Alphas' Table tonight. I'm so proud of you." Tears prick my eyes as he squeezes my hand.

PUPS

Adea

Ethan kicks open the door, and the minute the door closes, his hands are all over me. I feel his firm grip on my hips, and when they are on my back, I arch into him. One hand wraps around the back of my neck and pulls me closer, while the other grabs my ass. His lips smash against mine, and I sigh as my soft body molds against his hard one. Our tongues dance, and we kiss as if our lives depend on it.

We separate and I am about to protest, when Ethan drops to his knees. The words die on my lips. His chin is lifted, and his eyes are on mine as his fingers lift my dress up, revealing the thin material separating my lips from his.

Ethan leans forward and nips the material between his teeth. His breath on my skin has my hips bucking forward. Slowly he pulls down the material and pushes it down with his hand the rest of the way.

Slowly, his fingers slide up my thigh and spread my lips apart.

Leaning forward, he exhales. His breath on my wet core has my clit hardening. He hasn't even done anything yet, and I am panting.

"Ethan, please."

My mate doesn't listen to me; he doesn't even bat an eye, as he stares up at me. His lips are so close, and yet, so far. I push my hips forward, and his hand on my belly holds me firm.

Ethan's lips part, and his wet, pink tongue slides out. He inches closer, and his tongue runs up my aching clit. I grab the back of his head with both hands, and throw my head back. Ethan's tongue slides up and down my hard nub. My hips jolt back with each slow slick of his tongue.

"Your mouth, now," I demand.

He only laughs, his head moving, as he licks up my sensitive mound. I widen my legs, my lips separating. The speed of his tongue increases and I am nearing an orgasm. I grip his hair and pull him closer.

"That's right, baby. Come for me."

"Oh, Ethan!" I scream.

He's only just begun, but with one final flick of his tongue, I am coming hard. His tongue flicks up and down my clit. Leaning back, his head moves up and down as he licks up my juices.

"You like coming on my tongue?" Ethan asks.

My eyes are closed as my legs and hips jerk. I am too busy catching my breath to answer. I cry out as Ethan's teeth bite down on my clit. My eyes fly open and I look down to find my clit between Ethan's teeth.

"Yes, I do," I half moaned, half cried. "Now stop biting me." His teeth bit down a little harder and my hips bucked against his face.

"Say please," Ethan says.

"Mmm, Queen's don't beg."

"You're absolutely right, but that doesn't count when it comes to us. No, Queens beg their Kings, and only their Kings. I'd very much like to see you beg," Ethan says mischievously.

"Please."

"See? That wasn't so hard," Ethan says smugly. He releases my sensitive nub and gets to his feet. He smiles at me with an accomplished smirk.

"But it was," I laugh.

Ethan unbuttons and pushes down his slacks. I help him with his shirt. When he is naked in front of me, my eyes ravage his body hungrily. His massive cock is erect and my mouth waters at the sight.

I grab the hem of my dress, and was about to pull it off when Ethan speaks. I take a step closer, and my hands slide up his taut, muscular torso before I press my lips to his chest.

"Keep it on. I've been wanting to fuck you in that dress since you put it on," Ethan growls.

His hands wrap tightly around my waist, and I am hoisted into the air. Instinctively, I wrap my legs around his muscled torso and my arms around his neck. I can feel his hardness pressing against my cheeks.

I wiggle my behind, and cry out when a firm hand slaps the bottom of my ass. The sensation causes me to jump upwards, my chest rubbed against my mate's chest and wetness pools between my legs. My mate smiles seductively at me, his eyes dark and heavy with lust.

"I'm going to fuck you. All you have to do is hold on."

"Okay," I breathe.

Ethan lifts me up, and I feel his head at my entrance. My legs are wrapped around him, and my lips are ready. I am expecting him to impale me on his hard cock, but that's not what he does.

His tip slides into my wetness, and I tighten my hold around his neck. Slowly, my mate lowers me. He fills me inch by inch, and my jaw goes slack as he fills me. My eyes roll back in my head as he continues to lower me onto his hardness. I feel as if I will break as he pushes deeper and deeper. I groan when he fills me and his balls pressed against my backside.

"Ethan." His name is a whispered prayer on my lips.

"Yes, My Queen?"

"Fuck me, please."

I gasp as he pulls out of me before he impales me on his fat cock. I cry out and press against him. His hands leave my waist and squeeze my cheeks. I can feel my wetness dripping down onto him.

"Goddess," he groans, lifting me up again, "you are," I am slammed back down hard on his cock, "SO. FUCKING. PERFECT." The wet sounds of him thrusting in and out of me are erotic, and turn me on even more.

"Oh, yes! Ethan, please!"

My mate thrusts into me, and I groan as he hits that sweet spot over and over again. My orgasm rips through me as I come on his cock. Ethan curses as my pussy squeezes tightly around him.

"Shit, Adea."

I throw my head back as he bounces me hard on his hard length.

"Fuck, yes. You're squeezing my cock, I'm going to," Ethan groans, "fuck baby, I'm coming."

I cry out as he fills me. "I'm coming, fuck, just like that baby." I slump against my mate. My body twitches from the aftershock of my orgasm.

"Goddess, bless us with pups."

SOON

Adea

I'm sorry, what?

What is it, Adea?

I ignore my wolf. I am too stunned to speak. My heart drops out of my chest, and the happiness I'd been feeling is gone. My body freezes, and I stop breathing. I can't have heard him right. Did he just…?

I'm failing to understand what's going on, Adea. Ethan's our mate. It's natural for us to have pups. What's not natural, is your reaction.

I am not sure what to think or how to feel. I knew when I found my mate, pups would eventually come. There may have been a time that pups crossed my mind, but that was before.

Had I not had the dream where I felt my despair so clearly, this wouldn't have bothered me. If I don't have a pup, I won't have to worry about losing it with what's to come.

Had I not been reminded of the miscarriage in my last life, I might not have minded. No, I *know* I wouldn't have minded. I want the future all mated wolves have.

When you find out you are having pups with the love of your life, it's a happy time. I would have been happy, should have been happy. So why do I freeze? Do I not want a child with Ethan? No, I definitely do. I know that with my heart and soul.

Having pups is a part of life, a part I want with my mate, eventually. It is the next step for us, and will be *when we are safe*. Under different circumstances, I would have cried and been emotional about Ethan wanting to start a family right now. I am emotional, but I am also well aware of the dangers we face with Shane.

In my previous life, he hadn't known about the child. What would he have done if he knew beforehand? I try not to think of the possibilities, but I know my child never would have lived to breathe his or her first breath.

What I fear is losing it. What I dread is having to live my past life again, without my loved ones in this world anymore. Tears fill my eyes and blur my vision. There is nothing I wanted more than to live happily with Ethan and a pup... no, with *pups* that look like him.

I want that, desperately, I do, but I can't. We can't start a family and bring pups into this world. Not yet. Who knows how long we have before Shane tries to strike us down? How long do we have?

No, we can't bring defenseless pups into the world while he is free to do whatever he pleases and moves without punishment. It isn't a good idea. Not until Shane is out of our lives for good. We won't be safe; our kids, our family, and our pack won't be safe with him still breathing. We need him dead. Shane has to go. That is the only way.

Let's not pretend that we both don't know how this all ends.

His insidious words start playing on repeat in my mind. What did he mean? *Let's not pretend…* Goddess. Does he know? COULD he know? Is that even possible? Maybe someone told him. No… there aren't many who knew of my dreams. Even then, they don't know the entirety of them, and those who do know were a part of my inner circle.

If no one told him… does that mean he had the dreams too? What would that mean for me if he knew? Goddess, I hope he doesn't have the dreams. Is that what this is riding on now? Hope? Do I have to leave it up to hope to ensure my family's future?

Would I let it stop me from doing everything in my power to stop it from repeating, to stop Shane? Maybe this was what I can do. Maybe I can change fate if I…

"Adea?"

The concern in Ethan's voice cuts through my thoughts like a knife. I try and fail to calm my rapidly beating heart. Blinking, I focus on my mate. His eyes are searching, his forehead wrinkling as he watches me.

"Are you okay? What happened?" Ethan asks.

"I… I spaced out."

"I know. You've been out of it for a few minutes. I carried you to the bed," Ethan says carefully.

I'll be seeing you again soon, Ady.

Shane's voice is in my head. No, I can't. I can't let him come to me. I have to do something about it. If I'm going to, it has to be now. I'm going to do something about it.

When the faucet turns on, the thoughts flood in again like

water breaking through a dam. We're sitting ducks if I don't do something. If I stay, we're just waiting for Shane to make the first move and I've seen how that plays out.

I know how that ends, and I can't, no, I won't, let that happen again. I've been racking my brain trying to figure out what to do to prevent history from repeating, when maybe all I need to do is make a decision I haven't made before. If I do something different, I can change things. I know I can. Shane can't come here and hurt those I love if I go to him first.

Adea.

No. I will not have Kor trying to change my mind. For the first time, in probably the entirety of my life, I am finally thinking straight. I have an actual answer to my problem.

This is not thinking straight, Adea. Say you go to him. What then? What do you do when Shane has you?

I'll kill him.

I push Korra to the farthest parts of my mind and lock her there. I have made the choice to kill him, and I know I can do it. I've done it before. I've seen it, so I know. I've even seen the weapon I use. The sword, Alpha Joshua's sword. He used to keep it in his office.

My stomach is in my throat as I contemplate murder and treason, but if that's what it takes to keep my family safe, I'll do it. I'll do anything.

My heart was starting to break. I'll do everything in my power to come back. I may not be able to have a future with Ethan… but if I can keep him, Gabe, and the rest of our pack safe… I'll do it..

MY LIGHT

Adea

The running water shuts off and Ethan reappears in the doorway. His I-just-had-sex hair only makes him hotter. My eyes take in his strong muscular shoulders, before dropping to his flexed biceps, and chiseled torso. I am the luckiest woman alive. No matter what happens, I've been blessed with the time I've had with Ethan.

His expression is one of clear unease. He makes his way toward me on the bed with a cloth in hand. My heart warms at the sight of my mate coming to take care of me like he does every morning. I was blessed with a mate who not only loves me, but one who is consistent in expressing that love. Even though he doesn't need to, Ethan takes care of me as no one else has since the beginning.

There is one problem with my plan. The only problem with the plan I've been cooking up in my head is Ethan. I do not account for my overprotective mate. I don't have to ask him to know what he would think of my plan. He would do everything in his power to keep me here, to keep me safe, and I love him for that, but this is something I am going to do. I've made up my mind; now, I have to figure out a way to either keep him here, or sneak out. I'm not going to fool myself into believing he will just let me go.

My heart breaks at the idea, but I think of one way. If I start a fight, a terrible one, I could move into another room. The plan is stupid. Not only would he never allow me to leave things unsaid, but he would also do everything he could to make sure we resolve our fight.

The only other option would be to leave while he's sleeping. He will try and come after me, but if I say I need space, maybe I can delay him. He just might give me some, but I will also have to get past Leo.

My over-alert guard is right outside the door. It will be impossible to get away from him during the day. The only way sneaking out is possible, is if I sneak out at night while Leo takes a bathroom break.

I'll be damned if I sit here and wait for Shane to take me. I refuse to make it easy for him, and fate is obviously on his side. I gasp as snippets of my dreams rush to the forefront of my mind. My mouth goes dry. No. I won't let that happen, not again.

I'll fight with Ethan. It will hurt, but maybe I can make him think I just need time to cool off. I'll tell him that before I leave the territory. If I don't do this, Shane will come for me.

Whereas if I do this, let him take me, I'll lure him into this false sense of victory. I will have the upper hand. He will be out of the way, and my pack will be safe. I can avoid unnecessary bloodshed.

The image of Gabe's detached head in my hands causes my body to freeze. I see my mate's heart ripped from his chest while blood drips from Shane's hand. I feel the all too strong feeling of our mate blond snapping. My body wegoesnt into panic mode as these images flash, but it is the reminder and the confirmation that I need.

The past month of training, the ceremony and the happiness I have been able to experience would all be gone. If I can only stop him from taking me, maybe I can stop or delay what is already set into motion. To do that, I will need to convince Shane of my decision.

My mate is on his knees in front of me, his eyes downcast while he cleans me up. My heart is breaking with the thought of what I am about to do. My chest aches as I take a deep breath and steel my resolve.

"I don't want pups."

The hand that has been dabbing at the evidence of our lovemaking freezes, and slowly, Ethan lifts his chin. Shock followed by sadness sets in as he looks for an answer in my eyes. His brows furrow and his lips are sealed tight. Putting down the towel, Ethan squeezes my hands before lowering his head and kisses the back of my hand. The act is so loving, despite the hurt he must be feeling from what I said. His breathing shutters as he tries to find the words to say what he's thinking.

"I know what I said was unexpected," Ethan says slowly, carefully thinking out his words. "Maybe it wasn't the right time to say that. I wasn't thinking. I.... the thought of seeing you with a baby crossed my mind, and it just came out. I want nothing more than to live happily by your side. This week has been nothing but stressful with Shane taking over Half Moon, and seeing him tonight... I know the time isn't ideal. Things don't look good right now, but I hope my efforts have helped to soothe your worries."

"Ethan, I—"

"Please, just let me finish," Ethan interrupts.. Goddess, I need to stop him. His words are making this harder than it already is. Biting my lip, I nod, and Ethan continues.

"I know I screwed up by not killing him when I had the chance to at the trial. It eats at me every day, knowing I let him get away, but I'm doing everything I can to keep you and our family safe. I know this is all my fault, but I hope I can give you even a little bit of ease during these difficult times. You're my light in the dark times, Adea. Even when our nightmares become reality, I will continue to choose to live happily. I choose you, and the life we have. I choose not to let all of the negative shit that happens taint the happiness I have with you."

EXPLAIN

Adea

Is it possible to be happy and sad at the same time? My chin trembles and I clench my jaw to stop it. Tears blur my vision and I blink hard and fast as I curse the tears and fight to keep them from overflowing. I love this man so damn much. What did I do to deserve him? His words are comforting and reassuring.

"This has nothing to do with Shane."My voice is low, and I've done my best to rid it of all emotion.

Confusion flashes across his face as he hears the difference in my tone. I feel like such a bitch for ignoring everything he just said. My stomach drops. With one sentence about Shane, I've totally disregarded his heartfelt words. Even with that, my mate doesn't look hurt. He is still kneeling while he stares up at me as he tries to be understanding.

"Tell me. What does it have to do with, My Queen?" Ethan asks.

"It's as I said. I don't want to have pups. Not now, not ever."

"We've talked about pups before. You were ok—"

"I don't want something that will take over my life. Pups would do that, and it would change us. It would strain our relationship. I have things I want to do, places I want to see. How can I do any of that with a pup?"

"I… I don't know where this is coming from. Pups aren't the easiest to deal with, but… nothing in life worth having is easy. As for the things you want to do, I wholly support you. We can, and will, do all of it, everything. Even with pups. Can't we do all of it together? As a family?" Ethan asks.

"You say that now, but would you still say it when we've had more sleepless nights than we can count? Traveling with pups will be difficult: the screaming, the crying," I shake my head. "A family will only complicate things. Pups will demand our full attention and we will have less time together."

"Can we talk about this? Please?" Ethan asks..

"You are enough for me. Am I not enough for you?"

"You are, baby, you are more than enough," Ethan says, pulling my hands to his chest.

"A child will only bring death to our loved ones. I've seen it."

At this, a look of confusion spreads across my mate's features. He leans back and searches my expression, looking for the punchline. When he doesn't find it, my hands drop to my lap as he gets to his feet.

"Is this true?" He asked.

I nod.

"When?" When I don't respond, his eyes drop to the floor as he thinks. "Is this what the nightmare was about? The one I had to shake you to wake you from?"

"Yes."

Lies. All lies.

My mate thinks for a second. I am expecting anger or for him to be upset.

"Why didn't you tell me?" He asks, his voice was quiet. I'm caught off guard for a second, and I struggle to find the right words. "It could be wrong, all of it could be wrong."

"Everything? From the very beginning?" I shake my head. "My dreams aren't just dreams, Ethan. We both know this. I won't pretend that everything is a coincidence. This isn't our first life together. This isn't the first time we've faced off against Shane. He will stop at nothing to get what he wants."

"You," Ethan says. I know the bite is meant for Shane, and isn't directed towards me.

"He is what we should be focused on."

"We've focused on him long enough. It's more than what he deserves. Longer even than necessary." My mate is trying to remain calm, but I can see this is bothering him. He turns away from me and starts pacing in front of the bed.

"When I saw him yesterday, I..." I trail off. I don't know what to say. Ethan stops in his tracks. I can't even hear him breathing. He's misunderstood, I can feel it. Instead of making it better, I don't.

"You what?"Ethan's voice is low and quiet. He turns around, and I can see the storm brewing just below the surface. My mate has never spoken about any insecurities, but now, as he faces me, I can see it clear as day. He thinks I might feel something for Shane.

When I don't say anything, he stalks back to me. Ethan stops a little more than a foot away. His chest rises and falls with each angry breath he takes. While I'm doing the exact opposite, my breath catches as I crane my neck to stare up at my mate.

The look on his face almost shatters my resolve, but I remind myself this anger he's feeling is proof he's alive. I would rather have him hate me than to be selfish, keep him by my side, and no longer have him living in this world.

"Is there something I need to know? I'm trying hard not to doubt you. I've never pushed you about it because it's none of my business, and I didn't want to push you to talk about the abuse. You're making it hard not to second guess everything that I know to be true.

"The night we met, you told me you were seeing someone. You told me you weren't dating him, but you guys had done things together. When I found him on you, my wolf and I moved at the same time. All we saw was someone dared to touch what was ours. I knew from the trial that Shane had been abusing you for some time. I never wondered if you wanted it. If you loved him. Was it, or was it not, abuse? Was there something there? Was there more to your relationship than you let on?"

When I didn't answer, Ethan speaks again. "Explain! You what, Adea?"

CAN'T

Adea

I am too stunned to speak. Ethan has never yelled at me, but when he demands I explain, his voice was loud enough to carry outside. No one is perfect, but I am shocked to hear that Ethan thinks this way. Was this all brought on because we saw Shane again? The last time the three of us were in the same room together had been the day of the trial.

"Fucking say something, please!"

"I don't know, Ethan. I… "

Goddess, what do I say? I don't know if I can say that I love Shane and have him believe me. Passing it off as the truth is something else entirely. From the way Ethan's looking at me, I don't think I'll have to do much to convince him. He will believe whatever I say.

"I don't know if you know what the meeting did to me. Seeing the two of you across from each other. He couldn't take his eyes off of you, and it looked like you couldn't stop either. I wanted to rip his eyes from his sockets and stuff them down his throat. It wasn't just the fact that he stared at you, but the way he looked at you. Yes, he's obsessed. Yes he's toxic as fuck, but fucking hell, Adea, he loves you!"

"I can't control anyone's actions, but my own!" I raise my voice.

"A man doesn't love someone without having had a reason to. Did you give him one? Before you became mine, did you give him a reason for him to hold on like this?"

"You already know we were together before. That was before he did the things that he did to Olivia and before he killed his parents. That was before you. Shane is obsessed."

"Did you love him?" Ethan asks.

"I did nothing but obey my alpha," I say. "At the time, that was all I could do."

"Did you love him?" Ethan repeats. "Did you let him do those things to you? Did you want it?"

I don't know how many times I've asked myself these same questions. The way my heart thumped when I was in front of Shane before I came to Desert Moon. The way my body reacted to him. I never found an answer. I hate myself for the way I reacted. It had felt like a betrayal. I had feared Shane, but did I ever hate him? It feels like a lifetime ago.

"It isn't that easy, Ethan." This is the truth. It was never that simple. Nothing was when it came to being a slave under Shane. "Yes, I had feelings, but they were a jumble of feelings, and the lines had blurred between the two of us." He was supposed to be like family, but he never treated me like it. He always held me at arms length. I've long since put that behind me. I love Ethan now, and only him.

"So, you did have feelings for him."

"At one time, yes, I had feelings for him," I say.

"You said when you saw him, you felt more," Ethan's voice was hoarse. His shoulders were tense and the look on his face was one of defeat.

"It's been a long day and I think we need to end it here."

I couldn't bear to keep looking into his eyes while I lied and hurt him. It cut me deep. I turned from him, rolled on my side, and pulled the blanket up over my body. Tears filled my eyes. The bed dipped, and I rolled back an inch as the sheet was pulled off of me.

Ethan was on top of me, he leaned down and he had a hand on both sides of my head.

"No, we're not going to end it here. What did you mean you felt more?" I had no choice but to turn on my back. The tears stream down my cheeks as I look up at my mate.

"When I saw him again, I did wonder if things could have been different."

I didn't say anything else. I left it open for interpretation. Ethan flinched at my words. His brows furrowed with hurt, his eyes widened, and he looked as if I'd slapped him. His lips parted but nothing came out, the words died on his lips.

Ethan threw his head back and a painful roar filled the air. It was my turn to flinch as he leaned forward and pressed his forehead against the bed. His breath was hot against my neck. It felt as if we were frozen in time. In one swoop, Ethan was above me again.

"You asked me if you were enough and I told you you were.

Now, I want to ask you the same thing. Am I enough for you?" Ethan asked.

I turn my head to the side and squeeze my eyes shut. How can he even ask that? Does he really doubt me that much? Goddess. I know this is good but it hurts. It hurts so much.

His hand is on my chin and I'm forced to look at him. The metallic taste of blood fills my mouth and I realized I bit my lip hard. My mate crushes his lips to mine and I can't help the sob that escapes. He swallows it and kisses me fiercely. I lift my hands and push against his chest. It's nothing as they bounce off his chest. He grabs my hands and holds them above my head. I'm defenseless under him but I have no fear. Ethan would never hurt me. It doesn't matter how angry he is. I know him. He bites my lip and I cry out. I'm not even angry. I'm hurting him.

"I can do everything for you, Adea. Ask me for anything and I'll give it to you but this, not this." Ethan growls. He kisses me before pulling back. "The Moon Goddess made you for me, she blessed me with you. That's my mark on your neck, it's my bed you sleep in, it's my pups you'll have. I'm sorry. I love you too much to let you go. I won't let him have you. I can't."

Criminal

Adea

"I don't believe this sorry excuse you're giving me about not wanting pups. You do want pups but after seeing Shane, you don't want pups with me. You want him and it fucking hurts. Has he made you waiver? Fuck! I never said I was a good man but I've done everything I can to be good to you." His voice was filled with pain. "He can't have you."

"Let go of me, Ethan."

I didn't fear him, I knew with every fiber of my being that he wouldn't hurt me. I widened my eyes and I swallowed nervously as I stared up at him.

"I'd never hurt you, Adea," Ethan said. "I just… I don't… you can't…"

"Please."

He released me instantly. I brought my hands down and wrapped them around myself. He let out a ragged breath and rolled off of me. My mate sat up in bed, his back was hunched over, and his head was in his hands. I wanted to reach out and touch him but I didn't, I held back.

I set out to start a fight and I did. I needed to hurt him and I did. My shoulders shook as the tears flowed freely. My breathing quickened until I couldn't control it and I was gasping for air.

The bed creaked and dipped as he lay down next to me. I felt his hand, it was so close, the warmth radiated from it, and I could feel it on my shoulder. He was almost touching me. How much I craved his touch after that terrible fight.

I resisted the need to lean back into it, to lean back into him, to feel his touch. I held back the urge to kiss him, touch him, and make it better. I forced down the words that would reassure him of my love, reassure him of our bond, reassure him of how it was him and only him. The warmth was gone and I could only assume that he pulled his hand back.

"I love you, Adea. It's you and will only ever be you for me," Ethan murmured.

I didn't respond. I squeezed my eyes shut and didn't move. I pretended to sleep and waited for his breath to even out. Now that we had fought, I needed to listen out for Leo. As soon as he stepped away, I would leave. I'd grab one of the keys to one of the cars out front and drive.

I'd get as far away from the packhouse as I could before he woke up. I needed him to think I was still on the pack lands. As soon as he realized I was gone, he'd search for me. That's if Leo doesn't notice I'm gone, and he shouldn't. Not if I can pull this last minute, not well-thought-out plan. When he comes back from his break, he won't open our door while Ethan's here. He will assume we're still sleeping and won't think anything is out of place. He will then stand guard outside the door like every other night until Gabe comes to switch shifts or when Ethan realizes I'm gone.

I was positive he would link me as soon as he woke. When that happens I need to be as far away as possible while still being within mind-linking distance. He would try and get me to come back and by then I would need an excuse.

My mind was racing with the steps to my plan. I would need to convince Ethan that I'm within the pack, staying within the pack and that I need to be alone because of the fight. If he thought I was leaving the pack territory, I'm not sure what he would do. Based on how he reacted tonight, I can't assume he wouldn't come after me.

I could only hope my mate would give me space. If he didn't and demanded to know where I was, I would go as far as telling him I couldn't be with him. I was sure it wouldn't come to that and he would agree to give me the space I asked for.

I would do whatever I needed to do to convince him that I was safe and not to look for me. Sounds easy enough, right? I sighed. My thoughts were interrupted when I heard the floor outside the door creak notifying me of Leo's departure.

That was so quick. How long have I been waiting? I looked outside the window, the moon was starting to dip under the horizon. Goddess, I didn't have much time.

I froze and tuned into Ethan's breathing and confirmed he was asleep. This was it, this was my chance. If I didn't go now. I'd never leave. I wouldn't be able to.

I slipped out of bed and made my way over to the wardrobe as quietly as possible. I pulled on jeans and a hoodie and looked at

Ethan for the last time. I wanted to touch him before I left but I didn't want to risk waking him.

The door shut in the hallway and I knew Leo was gone. I opened the door slowly and slipped out into the hall. It felt as if someone had started a stopwatch and I was fighting against time. I made my way down to the elevator as quickly and quietly as possible. It opened and closed before Leo came back out.

My heart was racing by the time the elevator stopped on the ground floor. I ran behind the counter and grabbed the keys to the jeep. From there, I sprinted like a criminal on the run. I pushed the doors open and the crisp cold early morning air hit me.

My cheeks cooled and my nose started to run as I made my way to the jeep parked across the parking lot. I shoved the key into the ignition, didn't bother warming the car, and reversed.

With the packhouse behind me and the winding road in front of me, I stepped on the gas. The sun was starting to rise. I needed to get as far away as possible.

LEFT

Ethan

Bright rays caressed my skin and just like that, I was awake. My first conscious thought was always her. Normally when I woke up in the morning, my mate was fast asleep in my arms or on top of me, and I would watch her sleep for a few minutes. It was at that moment that life stood still and everything was right in the world, it was just us. If not for the headache that threatened to split my head open, that's what I would be doing. Our bodies were not pressed together and I couldn't feel her warmth.

Fuck, I felt sick to my stomach. My head felt heavy as I rolled over on my side. As I reached out for my mate, the memory of last night replayed through my mind. It wasn't like I needed the reminder, I remembered it plain as day. It didn't stop me from seeking her out when I first opened my eyes.

I had gone to bed feeling as if I'd been punched in the gut but I told myself to stop hovering, that she would come when she was ready. I told her that I loved her but she didn't respond. She was angry and I didn't want to push her.

I didn't believe she didn't want me, not for a second. It was the hesitation I saw on her face whenever Shane was involved that scared the living shit out of me. Was it because she feared him or was it because she still felt something for him?

The change in her face added gasoline to the small fire of insecurity I felt when it came to him. The looks, the way her heartbeat sped up as she looked at him only made the insecurity fester into something ugly. The warning signs screamed that she wanted him. I knew it was all in my head but that small dark part of me told me it was there.

I was the biggest asshole in the world for unloading on her. She didn't need that and it didn't make the situation any better but when it came to him, common sense flew out the window.

Last night, I went off on her when I should have kept my feelings in check. When it comes to Adea all I do is feel. She's not just my mate but my person. It wasn't her fault, none of this was her fault. I know the right thing to do was to give her space, so I gave her that last night but Goddess it was hard. Elijah demanded that I pull her into my arms and held her. Goddess, I wanted to but I just wanted to make it better and I didn't know how.

It was a struggle keeping away from her. The Alpha in me demanded that I make her fall to her knees and submit to me but the man in me that loved her more than life itself didn't want to force her to do anything. She's My Queen and if I was the one responsible for hurting her, I would try my damn hardest to give her space to breathe.

I love her and she loves me but it was hard to ignore that negative voice in my head. The one that told me she was going to leave me if I kept pressing her. I hated to admit it but it was part of the reason why I didn't touch her last night. She'd looked so broken, so hurt, so quiet.

I knew my mate would never leave me, deep down I knew but that damned voice was loud, louder than my ability to think straight. It's why I didn't force her to look at me, why I didn't hold her down and kiss her until she was breathless. As much as I wanted to make her tell me she didn't mean any of it, I held back.

My hand landed on cool sheets. I swiped my hand left and right as I searched for her, as I sought her warmth. When I came up empty I froze. My ears strained as I listened, I realized it was quiet, too quiet. I couldn't hear her slow breathing or the sound of her heart beating. The silence was deafening.

My eyes flew open, the first thing I saw was an empty bed. I was alone and my mate was gone. The sheets pooled around my waist as I sat up in bed. The room was spinning but I focused on the bathroom door. It was wide open, the light was off, and it was empty. She wasn't there.

Jumping to my feet, I throw on shorts and groan as I run for the door. My mind went to the worst possible thing but my heart assured me she was fine. I just needed to see if Leo was outside. If her guard was gone then I would know he escorted her either down to breakfast or wherever she went.

My heart rate sped up as a sinking feeling started snaking its way through my chest. When I wrap my hand around the door handle, I throw it open and find Leo standing guard. My suspicions are confirmed and my heart drops.

Leo turns to me and bows his head but I ignore him as I look down the hallway. I know she won't be there but can't help but scan it hopefully. Her guard is speaking to me but every word is muffled. My mind was going to that dark place I'd locked up since she walked into my life.

The one that made me strong enough to get to where I am. The one that made me want to tear everything apart just to find her despite the hole she'd left in the middle of my chest. If not here, where would she be? How would she have left?

She left me.

She left me.

She left me.

She left me.

ABOUT THE AUTHOR

Jp Sina is a Samoan-born American writer of all things dark and paranormal. She is a book obsessed reader turned author. She started writing on GoodNovel in 2021 and published her first book the same year. She currently resides in Auburn, Washington.

Her days are spent chasing her kids around the house, making sure her young-at-heart cat Yuri eats, and reads in the dead of night. She writes when she isn't reading and reads when she isn't writing. Dark Alpha's and coffee are her happily ever after, although you aren't promised one in her stories.

Also by Jp

The Forbidden Series:

The Forbidden Alpha	*December 2021*
The Forbidden Luna	*March 2022*
The Forbidden Beta	*June 2022*
The Forbidden Choice	*July 2022*
The Forbidden Mate	*August 2022*

The Forbidden Novellas:

Alpha Shane	*Coming Soon*
Gabriel	*Coming Soon*

Kacie's story:

My Alpha's Mark	*Exclusively on GoodNovel*

Made in the USA
Columbia, SC
16 July 2022